John Parker is a qualified metallurgist and former Fellow of the Institute of Corrosion who spent most of his working life in the power industry. He was Chairman of the British Standards Institute Corrosion Committee and UK Representative on both the International Standards Organisation and European Federation of Marine Corrosion, Committees.

His hobbies include Family, Literature, Genealogy, Orienteering and Road Running. John is married with three children and lives in Wiltshire. He may often be found amongst his fellow stragglers near the back of the field in the Saturday morning Swindon Park Run.

THE WEST WINFORD INCIDENT

THE WEST WINFORD INCIDENT

JOHN PARKER

Matador
9 Priory Business Park
Wistow Road
Kibworth Beauchamp
Leicester LE8 0RX, UK
Tel: (+44) 116 279 2299
Fax: (+44) 116 279 2277
Email: books@troubador.co.uk
Web: www.troubador.co.uk/matador

ISBN 978 1784621 070

British Library Cataloguing in Publication Data.
A catalogue record for this book is available from the British Library.

Typeset by Troubador Publishing Ltd, Leicester, UK
Printed and bound in the UK by TJ International, Padstow, Cornwall

Matador is an imprint of Troubador Publishing Ltd

To the family – the fundamental unit.

Ah, but a man's reach should exceed his grasp,
Or what's a heaven for?

Robert Browning

1

1969

The noise was deafening as the steel turbine disc burst, flinging fragments from the spinning rotor; huge chunks of high energy shrapnel released, some burying themselves deeply into the concrete walls of the test pit.

Several seconds elapsed.

"Bloody hell, what a show. That's just about wrecked the bloody test rig."

"Yeah! Spectacular wasn't it? Still below normal overspeed test level. They'll never believe it."

Despite their apparent nonchalance, it was clear that both technicians were deeply shocked. The relative ease and the catastrophic nature of the failure of this turbine disc was as spectacular as it was unexpected.

Fortunately, the automatic trip cut off the power.

★

"Oh! look what you've done now," cried Katy. "It's smashed to pieces."

"Wasn't my fault, you shouldn't have rushed in like that," retorted her elder sister, "I was just about to wrap it up."

"What's all the noise about? Can't you two do anything quietly?"

"Jo's broken my French pot, the one I brought back last year."

"Didn't do it on purpose, did I? Anyway it was cheap and nasty."

"Was not. Mum, tell her to do her own packing and leave my things alone."

"It might be as well if you did do that, Jo."

"Side with her, as usual. It was an accident. I thought I was helping her. Let her do her own stupid packing, I don't care."

"Well, let's have a rest shall we? Daddy should be home soon."

After some half-hearted pushing and pulling, the girls followed their mother downstairs. Normal sibling hostilities had been heightened over the past few weeks as the time for the house move approached. The girls' apprehension was natural as they had lived in the house all their lives. It was the first family home into which their parents had moved twelve months after their marriage, following the birth of their daughter Josephine.

Almost fourteen years, no wonder that so much stuff had accumulated. Sue knew she would have to be resolute. Some things just had to be ditched. Her reluctance to be too severe on the girls stemmed from their hostility to the move, especially Jo's. The thought of leaving Birmingham and all their friends was not one either girl relished, though young Katy seemed partially won over, the promise of a new bicycle having helped. Jo, however, was not to be bribed. There was no way that she would willingly accept her life being ruined. She was a one city girl and the fact that they were to be dumped out in the middle of bloody nowhere was totally unacceptable. Where the hell was Wiltshire anyway?

Sue was thoroughly excited at the prospect of a change of scene, complete change of life really. She had provided the impetus and encouraged Dave to apply for the job. For some time she had felt that her husband had far more talent than that required by Fisher's Tubes. Even if he was to become Chief Metallurgist at such a small company it would not be such a great advance and they could certainly use the higher salary that this new job offered. Not that it was just a case of more money. She believed that Dave would relish the opportunity to flourish in his new surroundings. The girls would settle and soon adapt to country life. The new house, more money, Dave fulfilled, and she with all her plans. Yes, it was going to be a marvellous adventure.

"Anyone home?"

"Daddy, Jo's broken my pot," greeted Katy, rushing into the hall.

"Well, I'm sure she didn't mean to. We'll soon get you another one," soothed her father, dropping his car keys into the dish on the hall stand.

"No, it was my French one and we won't be going back there for ages."

"Well, let me get into the house anyway. How is everybody? Had a good week?"

"Oh! Sure." The sarcasm evident in Jo's response, as she rose from her seat, left little doubt regarding her feelings at the prospect of being a week closer to her descent into social obscurity.

"No change there I see," grimaced Dave.

"Don't fret love." Sue kissed her husband. "Mmm, that's nice. Jo will be OK once we've settled in, it's only to be expected that she's apprehensive. Actually she has been quite a help today with the packing. I couldn't believe it. She'll come around, I'm sure."

Dave decided he had time for a run before the evening meal. As he went upstairs to change he tapped on Jo's door.

"You OK, Jo? Got all your stuff packed yet?"

"Huh!" was the succinct reply.

Making a mental note to have a chat with her later, Dave set off on his run. He started slowly easing the stiffness from his legs following the drive back from Wiltshire. He was encouraged as this would be the last time; he wasn't due back at work until after the house move. As he ran along his well-worn route across the local common he reflected upon his new job with the Strategic Supplies Authority. The first two weeks had gone well and he felt encouraged that once the house move had been completed he would be able to settle into this new challenge.

He finished his run with a short burst of speed as far as the corner then, as he warmed down with a slow jog along his street, he thought how modest the row of small semis all looked. How differently he had viewed them when they had moved in, so full of optimism, all those years ago.

★

The impressive house was set well back from the tree-lined pavement. It was difficult to believe that it was only a hundred yards from the busy Warwick Road. Living out here in Solihull was the pinnacle of the aspirations of many Birmingham folk; an irrefutable sign that you had made it, which clearly Sue's brother Barry had.

"Oh! Barry's been out with the lawn mower," observed Sue as they approached her brother's house.

"What did you think?" Dave turned the car into the drive. "You wouldn't expect anything less. I'm surprised that grass dares to grow above regulation height around these parts."

"Come on love, you have to admit it is a beautiful place and they keep it so nice."

Dave grunted by way of a reply. Sue was right, of course. She and her sister were unashamedly envious of their brother's house and he could see why. As for himself though, even if he had Barry's resources, he would not feel comfortable living in a place filled with the sort of furniture and fittings that demanded constant respect. He preferred a home to live in rather than one that barely tolerated his intrusion. Despite that, he had to accept that this was the only family venue that could host such a farewell get-together and even then the elegant dining table would need to be augmented with its poor relation from the kitchen to enable them all to be seated at the same time.

Dave parked next to Pete's car. The others had already arrived. The front door opened and they were surrounded by a posse of excitable cousins. It never failed to surprise Dave that, although all the kids saw each other often, their pleasure at meeting never seemed to diminish. Today the greeting was more animated than usual, which reflected the fact that no Turner family member had moved away from their home town in living memory – a momentous day indeed.

The pitch of the children's greeting was mirrored by the grown-ups, endorsing the unprecedented nature of the occasion; its significance spanning the generations. The cousins swirled around forming an excited vortex, which hovered briefly in the spacious hallway before gaining energy and swooping upstairs, accompanied by squeals and giggles.

The adults fell into a mixture of kissing, cuddling and handshakes, which, though not matching the youngsters' vitality, manifested the extent of the genuine good feeling between them all.

"Right, first things first. Let's get the drinks sorted." Barry was a good host. "Usual selection for the ladies – Babycham, lager, gin even, plus the soft stuff and a treat for the gents – a keg of Watney's Red Barrel to be got through, and your usual brown ale, Dad."

Sue and her sister, Jenny, went off into the kitchen to help Velma and catch up on the latest news. Dave shook his head in bewilderment. It must have been at least four days since the sisters had last been together, not to mention the statutory telephone calls since then. What a family. Dave had a sister, living in Stoke, and though both of his parents were still alive and living in Birmingham, his family only met occasionally with the odd phone call to keep in touch. Certainly nothing like the Turners.

Dave and the men-folk gathered in the lounge where they found Sue's parents settled on the sofa.

"Not wanted any longer," announced Mrs Turner (Senior), with a sniff. "My offer to help in the kitchen was refused. I expect that you'll be disappointed David, I know how much you like my milk puddings."

Dave made appropriate noises of assent. Lunch was served and the cousins were persuaded to give up their secret activities and join the oldies at the table.

"I guess that you are getting excited about the move, Dave," said Jenny's husband, Pete.

"Yes. Even though I've only travelled up and down to Wiltshire a few times I shall be glad when we're settled."

"Is the job what you expected?" asked Barry, circulating around the table topping up drinks.

"Thanks. Well, it's early days, but so far, so good."

"What's this new organisation all about?" asked Pete. "Jenny gave me a rather garbled account, but you know as well as I do that the Turner sisters," he paused here to nod meaningfully across the table in the direction of the said sisters, "are not very technical at the best of times."

Dave briefly outlined his understanding of the idea behind the recently formed Strategic Supplies Authority, which the government had set up to ensure the integrity of some of the country's main essential services. A small proportion of certain assets from existing utilities, electricity, water, gas and so on, had been transferred to the Authority. The idea was to integrate the organisation of these under the SSA, with the intention of ensuring a reliable, coordinated, network of independent supplies to vital services in the event of major emergency.

"So you're now a civil servant."

"Typical Labour ruse," broke in Barry, "extend public ownership. More inefficiency."

"I think it's a sound idea for essential services at least," countered Dave.

"But where will it end?" persisted Barry. "What about fuel supplies, food even? No, it's just another of Harold Wilson's half-baked ideas. Completely illogical."

"I'm inclined to agree with Dave, at least in principle," said Pete. "It is a little odd though, when you think about it that the most likely threat to essential services, in the short term at least, would seem to come from the unions, Labour's main supporters."

"I thought that this was supposed to be a party, so leave all your political arguments for another time," burst in Jenny, conscious of where this conversation would lead if left unchecked.

"It's a deal as long, as we don't get drawn into the merits of some new-fangled kitchen accessory or whatever, from you lot," replied Barry. "Any more drinks for anyone?"

"Please," called Sue, waving her glass unnecessarily high. "Just another Babysham, brother dear."

As soon as lunch was over the cousins rushed away from the table to continue their important business. The men agreed to wash up, by which time the mood had changed and so Dave was spared the necessity of explaining further, the role of the new organisation and his place in it. One thing that Barry and Pete were in complete agreement about, was in offering their commiserations to Dave, who would now be deprived of decent football down in the sticks. They even went so far as suggesting that his new local club, Swindon Town, might not offer very much more by way of footballing skill than the Villa, a sad indictment indeed. Dave readily admitted that this was certainly one of the crosses he'd just have to bear.

The rest of the afternoon passed pleasantly, aided by Barry's cigar selection and his determination to finish off the Watney's. Dave reflected as they drove home, that there were advantages to being associated with such a closely-knit family. Sue was quiet. The move was a major step and although the prospect excited her, an element of sadness was only to be expected.

On the plus side, she was pleased that they had found a buyer for the house so quickly and at the asking price too. This would mean that there would be some cash left over after the move which, together with the rise in Dave's salary, should make things much more comfortable.

But what of her own plans? As soon as they had all settled in, she intended to look around for something just for herself. She had been devoted to motherhood and homemaking for long enough.

★

Dave had been impressed when he had visited the Scientific Services Departmental Laboratories for his interviews. They were modern and well equipped. He had been appointed to join the Materials Section. Although his previous job, at Fisher's Tubes, had also been in the Materials Section, that was, he imagined, where the similarity ended. The main difference would be the wider variety of the work here, as everything was on a much larger scale. The Strategic Supplies Authority was, after all, responsible for numerous operating units around the country – power stations, water works, gas installations and so on. He could be involved with any of these.

Though the increased salary would be welcome, it was not the main reason for his delight at landing this job. He was looking at the bigger picture, his long term career. He was moving away from general metallurgy and taking up a specialty – he had been appointed leader of the recently formed Corrosion Group – which he felt offered a better opportunity to make his mark; small pond syndrome. In addition, the emphasis would be on applied research. This had always been his ambition.

Was his interpretation of the new job accurate? He'd soon find out.

He had been lucky to find accommodation in Devizes for the couple of weeks before the house move.

"Hello David, nice to see you again," greeted Tony Richards, with a warm handshake. Dr Richards was head of the Materials Section.

"Good trip down?"

"Only from Devizes this morning. I came down last night."

They settled comfortably and Tony gave an outline of the Section's organisation and work. Dave had learned at his interviews that the Strategic Supplies Authority, which had been set up in January 1967, had its headquarters in London. In addition to all the working units around the country, there was a Central

Laboratory for Pure Research at Slough and themselves, the Scientific Services Department, in Wiltshire. The Scientific Services Department was divided into sections including the Materials Section.

Tony explained that the work with which they were involved at the moment was mainly concerned with the power stations now under the Authority's control, whilst that from other sources was sporadic. He thought it would be best if David familiarised himself with the routine work and later they would discuss a longer term project, which he was hoping David would take on.

"Right, let's go and meet the inmates." The usual flurry of handshakes and confusion of names, which would only become fixed in Dave's mind during the next week or so.

During his second week he was pleased to receive an invitation to join some of his colleagues for a few drinks at The Bear in Devizes. This was enjoyable, as was the local, Wadworth's 6X, brew. It was also useful in getting at least some of those names memorised. Of all the groups within the Materials Section, Dave thought that his was the most interesting, based upon what he learned about the others that evening, with the possible exception of the Fracture Group whose work sounded fascinating. The fact that they made extensive use of the Scanning Electron Microscope (the new toy) added to its appeal.

★

This is rapidly losing its appeal, thought Sue. Exciting though the prospect of moving was, packing was becoming a chore. Would they need these stair rods? Would those curtains fit? The removal men would be here any minute and Dave should be back by now. Just going for petrol, he had said, but she supposed that he had thought of a final chum to see. She was anxious to check what would fit into the boot of their Morris 1100, as she hoped that they could take some of the more fragile items with them. They boasted 'Fowler's Removals – Safe in Our Hands', but who was to know until it was too late?

The van arrived. It was actually happening. Sue was pleased to see Dave following. During the next three or four hours, beds, tables, chairs, wardrobes, books and the rest of the paraphernalia that made up late 1960s family life, were hustled into the van's interior, packed and arranged with the deft skill of a dry stone waller. So much stuff into such a small volume.

"See you down there missus." And off they went crawling down the street.

Following the last hugs and waves from the neighbours and accompanied by the girls' sniffs and tears, they drove away to their new life.

On their arrival the girls made straight for their respective rooms, armed with posters and Sellotape. This was a civilised invasion as the quarrels over the allocation of rooms had been fought and settled following an earlier visit the previous month.

Dave and Sue had three days for combined activity before Dave was due back at work. Sue had devised a plan to maximise her husband's usefulness during this period. The main items on her agenda included assembling the beds, followed by fitting curtain rails and light shades. There were extra shelves needed here and there and that bathroom cabinet had to go. As for the boxes containing Dave's books, college stuff and the – 'goodness knows what you want to keep those for' – keepsakes, they were at the back of the queue. A 1947 Football Annual? – I ask you.

So, Sunday night already.

"Let's leave it at that," suggested Dave, "I don't want to miss the moon landing, it will be on TV shortly."

Sue and Dave settled with their daughters to witness this astonishing event. At last, Neil Armstrong descended the steps and his fuzzy black and white image could be discerned. After a brief comment upon the powdery surface, he announced "That's one small step for man; one giant leap for mankind."

"Well," said Dave, "I guess we beat him to it with a sizeable leap of our own."

It was gripping television. They remained to watch Buzz Aldrin join his colleague before going to bed.

2

During the following weeks life settled down into some sort of routine for Dave, both at work and at home. He had successfully assimilated most of his colleagues' names and learned something about them. He had discovered that he had much in common with most, being of similar age and being imported from outside Wiltshire. This made for a greater willingness to socialise than perhaps would have been the case had they all been locals. He had formed a particularly easy relationship with Harry Slack, known as Gritty, who, though employed as a scientific assistant, was mature both in years and certainly in common sense.

The work in his group was going well and he'd been pleased to find that he had a lot of contact with other groups, as investigations often overlapped into more than one area of expertise. This had been particularly true in the case of the Fracture Group, where Mike Pearson, the leader, had been especially cooperative. He had given Dave an insight into the basic principles of electricity generation as this was the main source of their work.

A few days later Dave was called into his Section Head's office to discuss the proposed long term research project. This would entail the design, setting up and running of a corrosion test facility at Thornton Power Station. The plan was to use this facility to evaluate the suitability of some of the recently developed materials, for possible use in power station cooling water systems. Tony concluded by requesting that Dave should draw up a programme to get things moving.

Dave was both enthusiastic and excited at the prospect.

★

Sue's initial excitement with the move was quickly waning; she had thought that it would be so different. The countryside was lovely and more than matched her expectations, but the life itself? It had been over a month since the move but she had not settled and, with the girls starting their new school, things were likely to get worse. Dave didn't understand what it was like day in and day out in what, for her, was still a strange place. Hardly any contact with other people and those that she did meet were by and large – well! One of Dave's colleagues, Harry Slack, was nice enough and he had brought his wife Mary around to tea. Dave had encouraged Sue to accept Mary's invitation to return the visit, they were only just along the lane, which she finally had done. She bought a colourful plant from the village shop to take but, although she knew it was silly, she was apprehensive.

Through the front gate, the house was modest, typical of most of the village, but the garden was immaculate. That set the tone for everything else. Mary, a plump, fresh faced woman, was welcoming enough, a typical country woman who, with her husband Harry, formed one of the few local couples amongst the laboratory staff. The house interior matched the garden. It wasn't as spacious or elegant as her brother's house, of course, but it was a surprise being in this out of the way place and looking so ordinary from the outside.

"You'll have to take us as you find us," Mary had said as she ushered Sue into the parlour. My God, thought Sue, whatever had Mary thought of their place?

"Be with you in a tick. I'll just get the bread out of the oven, then we can have a cuppa."

Sue looked about her. Everything perfect. The row of books in an alcove was neatly aligned and, she noted, all in alphabetical order by author. There were half a dozen hunting prints around the wall and many of the ledges and shelves supported vases of flowers, the latter being home grown, no doubt. I bet she even vacuums under the sofa cushions, Sue thought maliciously. Sue, though by no means slovenly, had a pragmatic approach to housework; it was certainly not her mission in life. She was fortunate that Dave was sympathetic to this view and providing the house and garden had the superficial air of not being completely neglected, he was happy.

"Right, here we are at last," said Mary, entering with a tray bearing tea pot, cups and saucers. She went back into the kitchen and returned with scones, jam and plates.

"I do hope you'll like these, all home-made, of course, and what about some cream?"

"Gosh, no thank you, there's so much here," replied Sue, surprising herself with her genuine admiration.

"Well, if you're sure, but you'll need to work at it if you're going to fill out a bit. We village ladies won't feel that you're one of us till you've rounded out some."

The tea and scones were delicious and the conversation convivial. Sue relaxed a little. Although Mary did show some interest in Sue's affairs, for the most part she pressed on with matters of a domestic nature. Sue learned that Mary's washing was the envy of the lane and moreover, it was a pretty smart neighbour whose laundry was on the line before hers on a Monday morning. Following these instructive remarks, Mary outlined the social gatherings to which most of the village 'girls' subscribed. She felt sure that Sue would enjoy them and she would be happy to introduce her. With commendable self-restraint, Sue maintained a look which belied her horror at the thought of patchwork quilting, brass rubbing and the like, suggesting that she would certainly consider these pursuits when she had more free time.

As she made her way home, Sue, perhaps unfairly, suspected that all the other women-folk hereabouts were similarly indoctrinated. The sight of her own, less than perfect, interior was welcome indeed.

★

Dave sensed it. Sue, though to all appearances her normal self, was, to his internal radar, a little off key. Subtle signs, just a hint of brusqueness; a diminished enthusiasm in her responses as he eulogised over the minutiae of his work.

After tea Dave gently probed the reason for Sue's mood. His wife discoursed at some length the quite reasonable grievances of her present state, which really amounted to the lack of anything meaningful to do, certainly nothing locally.

"Just listen to this," she complained, picking up the current copy of the local weekly newspaper. "Bear in mind this is a front page headline; 'Wasp Nest Poses a Problem at Chippenham'. That just about says it all."

She had received ample confirmation of the limited horizons of most of the locals during her visit to Mary's. It may be that Harry Slack had always been accustomed to a devoted house slave but Dave could forget it.

"Surely there are some things that Mary isn't into," suggested Dave. He could see Sue's point, however, he was just taken aback at the sudden and unexpected outburst.

"Nothing very local," she replied. "Now that you use the car everyday it's more difficult."

"I could leave the car some days," supposed Dave. "I could travel with Gritty, we could share in turn."

"But it wouldn't be on a regular basis. There are times when you need the car without warning, such as when a sudden problem arises at one of the sites. I know that it's not your fault but you do see my point?" Dave readily gave his wife his understanding.

★

Time for the girls to start their new school. Although this was a tense time for them, it was even more so for their mother, who regarded herself the prime instigator behind the move down south. The wisdom of that decision would, to a large extent, be judged by how well the girls settled. The timing of the move was convenient as Jo was about to begin the build up to her 'O' level examinations. Although she wouldn't be sitting them this year, she had already been required to select her subjects. The head mistress of their new school had assured Sue that she had slotted Jo into her preferred choices.

Sue was nervous and went with her daughters to the bus pick-up point on this first morning. If they were honest, both Jo and Katy would have preferred that she hadn't. Becoming accepted by one's peers in a new place would be difficult enough and having Mummy as escort would do nothing to help the process.

The coach arrived. Sue's hesitant half-wave was resolutely ignored by the girls. The thoughts of Jo and Katy when they returned home after this first day or, indeed, for the next several days, were not made public, but Dave and Sue took comfort from the absence of any negative feedback. They assumed it would be unlikely that Jo would suffer in silence.

As the days went by Dave felt confident enough about the girls to surprise Sue with the suggestion of a few days away. He had arranged for her parents to come down and look after things whilst they took a short break. His assumption that this was just what Sue needed seemed justified judging from her excited reaction.

"All you have to do is put your best frock and some outdoor things into a suitcase and be ready to go first thing on Saturday."

As they passed through Minehead, Sue recalled their last visit to Lynton. Fifteen years, almost to the day.

"What a lovely surprise," she exclaimed, as they drove over Lyn

Bridge and up Church Hill, before turning right into North Walk. This was where they had stayed during their honeymoon. Sue jumped out and began to open the car boot.

"What on earth are you doing?" asked Dave, with some amusement. Sue stopped, looking rather hesitantly at her husband. "I just thought you'd like the view from here. They're probably fully booked anyway." As he said this he led her a little way back along the lane to the bridge over the Cliff Railway and pointed across the valley. The view, yes she remembered. When they had last been to Chough's Nest they had admired the view eastwards across to the wooded hill with the imposing Tors Hotel nestling amongst the trees.

"Come on then," chivvied Dave, "let's get on."

"You mean to say that we're not stopping after you brought me all the way up here?" Sue found difficulty in keeping the disappointment from her voice.

"You never listen to what I say, do you? I just knew you'd forget. What a memory."

Sue looked abashed. "What are you talking about? What have I forgotten?"

"The last time we were here, in 1954, I distinctly remember, as we were taking our last look across to the Tors, I said that the next time we came that's where we'd be staying."

Sue was flabbergasted but overjoyed. They unpacked in a leisurely fashion and later took a short stroll along the paths surrounding the hotel. Looking down upon the lower village of Lynmouth, at the toy-town cottages leading along to the small harbour, Sue recalled that, at the time of their honeymoon, the newly built road and the village itself had only just been reopened following the terrible flood damage two years earlier.

★

He stopped abruptly; began shaking uncontrollably as he relived the terrible moment. Just an ordinary day unfolding in the way so many had over the past four years. The early lunch – he was on afternoons that week. The two mile cycle ride, familiar faces and predictable banter with his workmates – just an ordinary day. The familiar routine, taken for granted, transformed in a split second. Not uncommon, it happened all the time, life changing in an instant, ordinariness twisted and disfigured into chaos – but always to other people. He could never return.

"Please accept our condolences and don't hurry, we've plenty of time," soothed the dark-suited chairman. Someone placed a glass of water at his elbow. Even sitting in the calm surroundings of the 'Raleigh Suite' of the Forest Lodge Hotel he felt overwhelmed. Beads of perspiration broke out on his forehead. He sat facing the panel of four with a younger man to his right taking notes, all exuding sympathy. It had been three days ago, but recalling the events faithfully – he was obliged to be accurate – was an effort of will. His pulse raced, it was impossible not to react, recalling the events meant reliving them and this was too distressing.

"Perhaps it would be easier to answer questions to begin with before making a formal statement?"

"Yes, if you will…"

The chairman leaned forward and spoke quietly.

"If you can tell us just where you were standing at the time of the incident. We have a plan view of the turbine hall on the board there and Mr Harris will mark the spot for you."

"I was between the west wall and Number 1 turbine, Sir, just alongside the L.P. cylinder."

"About here?" asked Mr Harris pointing to the diagram.

"A bit lower, yes, there. Just talking to Harry and then this almighty bang and whoosh… it missed me by inches… I just ran for cover… I left Harry… a good mate… I just ran… I… I… Oh! God."

The secretary rose to comfort the man who was sobbing noisily.

"I think that we're going to have to leave it for now gentlemen. Don't worry, Mr Winscombe, we can leave it until another time. We are likely to be several more days carrying out our enquiries."

★

It was going to be so good just to be able to relax for the next few days. After showers, the happy couple went down to dinner which, together with the wine, was excellent. They left the dining room feeling pleasantly full and slightly tipsy. And so to bed. The old married pair just lay for a while holding hands, each with their own special memories. This led to an increasing level of intimacy, which was considerably more assured than had been the case on their earlier visit.

The following days were pleasantly spent revisiting some of the places from their earlier stay, but this time they were blessed with beautiful weather. During the drive home they chatted about their new life. Dave reassured Sue that he was getting on top of the job and so he would now be working less overtime. This being the case, he thought that their next priority should be to see how they could work together to improve things for her. To Sue this was welcome news and seemed a fitting end to a wonderful break. She relaxed in her seat, at least until the Wiltshire border, when her concerns about the welfare of the family gradually infiltrated her mood. She had no cause to be anxious, she realised, when they arrived home and were showered with a week's worth of news. Both Jo and Katy had clearly settled.

3

"Before we begin formally, Mr Rolfe, may I offer you our condolences and add that you seem to have misunderstood our purpose. We are, at this stage, merely compiling witness statements of fact. There is no intention to interrogate witnesses. The only questions will be for matter of clarity."

"That's as maybe, but I want my union rep here all the same. Then there'll be no misunderstandings later."

"Perhaps before you begin you could indicate where you were positioned immediately prior to the incident."

"It was my responsibility to read the tachometer during the test. In order to fulfil my duty I was located at the governor end of Number 2 turbine on the west side of the high-pressure cylinder. I monitored the instrument reading as the speed of the turbine was increased. I would like to state at this point that it's my belief that there is an issue of safety arising here. Turbines can be dangerous pieces of equipment even at normal running speed, so it is obvious that they present an even greater risk during overspeed…"

"Mr Rolfe, please could you confine yourself to your factual statement. We are just recording where witnesses were positioned and what they observed."

"That's as maybe, but it would be a simple matter to close off the area during overspeed testing. Bill Winscombe and poor old Harry could also have been killed, along with Terry."

"Mr Rolfe, please."

"Well, the tachometer read 3,000 revs per minute while the turbine was still connected to the system. It gradually increased when the overspeed test started and we were just about at 3,250 revs when there was a loud bang. We *all jumped. From where I was sitting I saw a great gush of steam from near the top of the first low pressure cylinder and lagging flew off the steam pipes. A few seconds later there was an almighty explosion and flames shot up further along the machine. I joined the others in a rush to the control area away from the turbine. We were all shocked. It will be a while before some of them get back to work, I can tell you."*

★

It had been a timely break. They had needed it. Short but sweet. After the past three months of helter-skelter, Sue with all the hard work around the house and he getting into the job; yes, just what they needed. No phones, no papers, no TV. A second honeymoon.

He slowed as he approached the main gate. The gatekeeper waved him through. Something seemed strange. The lab car park was half empty. Dave entered the building. The first couple of labs were deserted. His office was next on the left. Hmm! Quite a pile in the in-tray – the downside of taking a break — then he saw the note on his desk:

'Take care of the shop – be in touch later. Tony.'

Tony – Dave's Section Head. How odd. Dave went out to explore the rest of the building. Not a soul about. At the end of the corridor was the rig hall where some of the big experiments were running. When he opened the door he found the reassuring hum of the operating rigs welcome. Even more welcome was the sight of Gritty and Geoff working on one of the fatigue testing machines.

"Where is everybody?" called Dave, raising his voice over the noise of the machines.

"Be with you in a mo," mouthed Gritty.

Dave returned to his office and was shortly joined by Gritty, who sat on the corner of the desk.

"They'll be glad to know you're back," he greeted. "Good break?"

"Fine thanks. Nice of you all to go to so much trouble to welcome me back here."

"Nothing personal," grinned Gritty, "just this West Winford incident, you know."

"What's that all about?"

"Come on Dave, don't say you're the only person in the civilised world that missed all the fuss? Even made the national press."

"Not a word. We've deliberately stayed out of touch during our break. It was such a pleasant change, not even TV."

"Well, to each his own. I can't imagine my Mary missing a single episode of her Coronation Street, not if we were in Timbuktu. Anyway, I better fill you in. Tony will be back later. He and Sweety are up at HQ this morning with some of the big-wigs, trying to sort out a Technical Investigation Committee and get the first meetings organised."

Sweety was the nickname for the Head of Scientific Services, Dr Alan Honey.

"The bare fact is that Number 2 turbine exploded during an overspeed test at West Winford. Went through the roof, some of the pieces apparently," added Gritty with relish.

"Anyone hurt?"

"Yes, sadly, one fatality and a couple of chaps with comparatively minor injuries."

"So Tony will provide the details later?"

"Right. I think he's going to ask you to look after our routine work here whilst everyone else is down on the Winford site. Could take months by the sound of it."

"Surely not everyone will be needed?"

"Almost. There's so much to do. They've already seconded people from other departments and got in quite a few on contract; photographers, engineers, non-destructive testers and so on. Mind you, from what I hear it's a tad late for non-destructive tests, apparently the place is like a bombed site. Anyway, best get on, I'll speak to you later." Gritty returned to the rig hall.

Dave realised that there would be a lot of stuff to be dealt with, even if he only did the absolute minimum to keep things ticking over. He was annoyed, as this would delay getting his own research project, on the sea water corrosion performance rig, started. He realised that any chance of promotion depended upon how well his project had developed by the time of his technical appraisal.

Geoff and Gritty joined Dave for lunch in the small mess room. They learned about his holiday and generally chatted about the early form of, recently promoted, Swindon Town under Fred Ford, their new manager, although Dave did not number amongst their devoted fan club.

"The skittles team will suffer if all the lads are away for long," grumbled Geoff. "It's difficult enough under normal circumstances to get a decent team out, but with so many lads away we shall be really struggling."

Mid-afternoon, Tony Richards' Triumph Sprite soft-top zoomed into the car park – he had a reputation for modelling himself on Stirling Moss. Staggering under the weight of paperwork, he barged into his outer office and dropped a pile of files onto his secretary's desk.

"Brenda, get David Harrison over here asap."

"Hi Tony, you wanted to see me? The balloon certainly appears to have gone up. I'd better not take any more leave."

"Well David, I hope you enjoyed it. You know the score I expect?"

"Only this morning. Sue and I have been out of contact with all the news whilst we were away, but Gritty has given me the gist."

"Good. I haven't got time today to go into detail. Suffice to say, it's going to be planning on the hoof for some time. I'd guess that it could be three months at least before we get any semblance of normality back here. I'm sorry about your own research, but we're going to have to keep our more direct practical services going for the present. You'll have Geoff Buswell and Gritty, of course.

Although they must keep the ongoing tests running, they should be able to undertake other jobs in between times. In addition, I am getting a couple of extras to help you. One chap over from Electrical Section and also a new lad called Ian who has asked for a secondment to us prior to a PhD course. Think you can manage?"

"I'll certainly do my best. Fortunately all the summer outages have been completed so, apart from Winford, the power stations should be fully up and running continuously through the winter. We should only get unscheduled stuff, which hopefully won't be too bad."

"I hope so. I'm afraid that you'll have to make the day to day decisions, as obviously my priority is going to be centred on the Winford investigation."

★

"If you will move into the Day Room the porter will bring Mr Fielding along directly," said the staff nurse. *The formally dressed, five-man inquiry team settled themselves around a space they felt adequate for an imaginary wheelchair – an incongruous spectacle – as they awaited Harry Fielding's arrival. After a few minutes the patient was brought along and wheeled into position.*

"Good morning Mr Fielding, we are pleased that you are well enough to speak to us, as we feel that it is important to gather the facts whilst fresh in the mind. May we offer our condolences before we begin?"

"I shall be pleased to help if I can, though I'm not sure that I shall be able to as it all just happened so quickly."

"We understand that you were with Mr Winscombe alongside Number 1 turbine."

"Bill. That's right. Just passing the time of day on my way to the loading bay when there was this bang, a real big 'un, and some flames. Then dust and lagging flew about and I was hit by something hard and down I goes and that's all I remember. I was so sorry to hear about poor Terry. A couple of the

lads came in last night and reckoned that it was a chunk of bearing housing that caught me. Must have ricocheted. Just a glancing blow, fortunately. Concussion, bruised ribs, broken humerus and this sprained ankle. Be back at work in no time."

★

Although Dave welcomed the challenge and set about his new role with vigour, it became evident that many hectic weeks lay ahead. His first task was to take a step backwards, assess priorities and direct himself and his skeleton staff in the most efficient way. Clearly there were only so many man-hours available, even including a more-or-less continuous overtime regime. He had sought advice from colleagues before finalising his plan. His ad-hoc team were advised, encouraged and exhorted and their response was tremendous. A collective determination seized them all.

A few days later, what at first appeared to be an early distraction arose when Dave was invited to accompany Mike Pearson to make his first power station visit. This proved to be anything but a distraction, as West Winford was the destination and the result was to give even greater impetus to Dave and his team.

During the drive southwards, Mike added to Dave's increasing knowledge of power station operation by explaining the turbine layout. Each turbine comprised three sections (cylinders) in which the rows of bladed wheels (rotors) were housed. Hot, dry steam from the boiler entered the high pressure (HP) cylinder and passed through the turbine blades, turning the rotor. The cooler steam was then divided through a twin system of pipes and directed into one of the two low pressure (LP) cylinders, where it passed through a second series of bladed wheels. The wet exhaust steam was then returned to the boiler.

The trip to Winford had become routine for Mike over the past couple of years and since the turbine failure, he had been at the site almost continuously, with the odd break to attend meetings. He was due to stay overnight again this trip and so Dave would be travelling back with a chap from the Engineering Department.

They checked in at Reception and then went onto the Mechanical Engineer's office to notify their arrival. During the journey Mike had advised Dave on the accepted protocol when visiting working sites. The turbine failure had made this visit particularly sensitive.

They next went to the locker rooms. Dave, taking his cue from Mike, found an empty locker. His pristine white overalls contrasted sharply with Mike's heavily soiled outfit as he followed him self-consciously into the turbine hall.

A vast, well lit space with a tiled floor and, in front of them, six blue turbine-generators stretched away into the distance. Dave took in the scene. The machines hummed and wisps of steam drifted from various vents. He was surprised to note that the areas surrounding the turbines were virtually deserted, with just one or two operators evident.

Recalling what he had learned from Mike's description, Dave could imagine, beneath the cladded exterior of the turbines, the large bladed wheels rotating as the hot steam flowed through. He took in as much as possible as he followed Mike past each turbine along the hall. He noted the tachometer instruments, which were reading a steady 3,000 rpm.

As they approached Number 3 turbine, halfway down the hall, they found a barrier had been erected across the full width of the building. The final three turbines were silent. Then the shock. The Number 2 turbine was badly scarred and the LP top covers had been removed, exposing the shattered interior. The surrounding area was littered with the damaged components; large battered covers, steam pipes, rotors, broken discs, bearing housings, bolts and much more, and within the exposed lower half of the turbine, masses of smaller items from who knew where? One LP cover had a large hole punched through it. Dave needed little imagination regarding the inner workings of the turbine in this instance, as the broken rotors and discs were exposed to full view. A frightening scene, indeed.

Looking upward at the turbine hall roof, which must have been over fifty feet high, Dave was amazed to see several large holes. What force had been released to cause such damage? Below the roof several large pieces of debris were precariously balanced on the overhead girders and netting had been extended below these for safety reasons.

The scene was of busy activity around the turbine, with men engaged on a variety of tasks. There were photographers, engineers, and technicians busily occupied with their own concerns. Away from the main area of debris, some of the larger fragments had been placed, and in some cases, partially reassembled as a giant jigsaw. Amongst these was a fractured LP rotor, identified in bold white paint as R/LP/GE, and an LP turbine disc, identified as LP/1AE which, Mike explained, were from the low pressure section. These had been reassembled from the fragmented debris and appeared to be virtually complete, apart from the outer blades of the disc. It was clear that the main fracture of the LP disc had originated in the keyway in the central bore and extended right across to the outer rim.

Just before half past twelve a gradual change came about. Dave sensed this. The workmen's chatter subsided to a murmur; cigarettes were stubbed out, followed by a shuffling of feet away from the turbine. Then, as these men withdrew, they were joined by colleagues from other areas. Slowly a wide perimeter of the station staff, including office workers, canteen staff, and others, assembled around the cordoned off section. Taking his cue from Mike, Dave moved out to join them. After removing their hard hats, the assembled group settled.

A gap through the crowd had been left near the doorway to allow access for a small party of visitors. Several smart-suited men and a clergyman escorted a middle-aged lady with two teenage boys into the area vacated. The group moved to a prearranged spot. A few words were spoken; it was a sombre moment. Working men, heads bowed, haunted looks, rough men, reverent, some in tears. A few minutes' silence, apart from the background hum of the turbines. All thoughts focused on the man – Terry, exactly one week on. A moment of quiet, a moment of dignity. Dave, a stranger, felt the emotion.

As the visiting party withdrew and the men stirred and slowly returned to their duties, Dave was confronted by a wide-eyed worker, clearly angry and emotional.

"It's a bit late you, in your smart white suits, coming down here, aint it? Should do your job in the first place, not come here when it's time to pick up the pieces. Engineers? I've shit 'em."

Dave was taken aback and made no reply as some of the man's colleagues helped him away with murmured apologies.

"Sad time for your first station visit," said Mike, "so different from the usual noise and banter."

Dave joined his engineering colleague for their return into Wiltshire. During the journey he reflected upon what he'd experienced on his visit. He was surprised at the devastated condition of Number 2 turbine. How could anyone hope to find the cause? At Fisher's Tubes he had come across failures of plant items involving their tubing, heat exchangers in particular, and had contributed to the investigation. However, a turbine was quite a different matter. Despite this, he had been hoping that, at some stage, he might be involved with the turbine failure enquiry and today's experience had reinforced that hope. His first duty though, was to continue to keep the day to day work progressing and he took some comfort from the fact that this was, in a small way, contributing to the West Winford effort in freeing up other staff members for the investigation.

4

Certainly, the demand did not ease and Dave continued to work long hours. Though difficult, he usually managed to get a couple of runs in during the week. His favourite route, when daylight allowed, was through the nearby Highwood Estate.

Gritty and Geoff undertook as much as they could fit in between their commitment to keeping the rigs running. Gritty was doing his best to look after the Fracture Group's work and the two secondments were surprisingly useful considering their lack of experience. The group did make time for occasional social evenings which, Dave felt, played an important part in engendering the team spirit between them. Despite all their efforts however, the backlog of work kept mounting.

Section members who were working on the turbine failure at Winford turned up at the labs occasionally to conduct tests as part of the investigation. Often they arrived, their car boots heavily laden with some large, distorted, metallic object which had originally been an integral part of Number 2 turbine. As Mike had explained the turbine layout to him, together with what he'd seen during his visit, Dave could appreciate much of what was arriving. He knew that the turbines operated at a running speed of 3,000 revs per minute and, once a month, each turbine was taken off the system for an overspeed test in order to check that the safety equipment, installed to control the speed of the turbine, was operating correctly. The test involved raising the speed of the turbine from its operating 3,000 rpm up to 3,300 rpm. The failure had occurred during an overspeed test on Number 2 turbine.

A detailed procedure had been established before items were removed from the Winford site. The first task was recording relevant details of the piece. An area was photographed untouched, then the larger fragments were removed, identified with a painted number or code, carefully replaced and re-photographed. It was not until an area had been recorded in this way that the pieces of debris could be taken away for individual examination. Work then moved on to another area of damage.

The next stage of the investigation was to examine the fragments to check whether any unusual defects were present. In most cases the piece could be confidently discounted as the primary cause. Others were less obvious and so the piece had to be put aside for more detailed inspection. An additional task was to attempt to identify where a particular fragment had come from and to try to rebuild some of the main components as a giant jigsaw. It was all very time consuming and the man-hours were building up. Dave understood perfectly, as he didn't know where his time went, there was just so much to do.

*

Time hung heavily for Sue, which she felt was ironic as she knew that she could not blame anybody but herself. She had been the instigator of the whole adventure. She reflected that as a young teenager she had been critical of the way many of the women she knew behaved. They were, for the most part, dedicated slaves and mothers. It annoyed her that their ambitions in life seemed to be limited to the traditional roles laid down by their mothers before them. She admired women that she'd read about who had not been prepared to settle for this mediocrity and had demonstrated that women could, and should, do more with their lives. She recalled the time immediately following her marriage when she had high hopes of moving away from the city and taking up a more meaningful career, whilst Dave found an equally fulfilling position. Her sister had married a nice steady boy in Pete, but he was so limited, so parochial. When she and Jenny were girls she had been the one who suggested joining the tennis club, belonging to a theatre group, spending the day at the Lickeys and so on. Her sister seemed to be happy to mooch around the house or hang about the local shops.

Just stop it. Stop it now Susan Turner! Words so familiar in the mouths of her schoolteachers, now seemed to be fully justified in the present case. Only she was going to alter the situation. She had always intended to get herself sorted out once they had settled. The fact that Dave was now so busy, so rarely at home, and when he was he was so tired, had brought things to a head more quickly. Tomorrow she would act.

★

Dave was finally awoken by the insistent phone. It was six thirty-five. It was Mike Pearson, clearly excited.

"Dave? Bit early I know, but can you get over here asap? We're in the rig hall. Got something that will interest you."

"Er. Okay. I guess I'll be half an hour."

"Come on, chop, chop. If you drive like Tony, you'll make it in ten minutes."

Having shaken off the remnants of sleep, Dave was excited and intrigued. There were half a dozen already in the rig hall when he arrived. Mike, of course, with some of his Fracture Group colleagues, plus a couple of technicians, but most surprisingly, Tony Richards.

The group was gathered around a large piece of metal. Although not badly distorted, the item was clearly a fractured piece of the

Number 2 turbine from West Winford, as it displayed its characteristic debris identification, LP/1AE, in bold white paint. Dave was invited to examine this. Mike pointed out a feature on the fracture surface of, what he explained was, part of the LP turbine disc they had seen on site. He reminded Dave that at its centre was a hole which allowed the disc to be slid onto the turbine rotor. Along the length of the hole was a groove (a keyway) which enabled a steel key to be fitted to locate the disc precisely into position. Whilst most of the disc surface was covered with a smooth, black oxidised layer, the fracture was clean, bright metal. Mike pointed to a small, though distinct, patch of discolouration near one edge of this clean surface.

"We think that's it," he enthused, "the cause of the failure. What do you reckon, Dave?"

"I think that you can say that this discoloured area was present before the main fracture occurred. It comes from the keyway, so it's likely that this was cracked to that depth before the whole thing disintegrated."

"Exactly," agreed Mike. "If you remember, the main crack that we saw in this disc during our Winford visit started from the keyway. This section is just one side of that crack. The small piece that has been cut out is being prepared for the electron microscope. It contains part of the discoloured section. We called you in to take a butcher's for us. I should think the vacuum level is OK by now." Mike led the way to the electron microscope room. John Bolton, the main man when it came to electron microscopy, was seated at the consol. The room was dark with just a small desk-light on to indicate the control positions. John acknowledged Dave with a nod and shifted to his left to allow Dave to wheel up a seat beside him. The eerie, greenish, display screen glowed, showing the sample taken from the LP turbine disc at low magnification. The variation between the discoloured and bright area of the fracture was obvious. However, both showed a 'crystalline' surface even at this magnification.

"I'll bump it up a bit," said John, turning up the magnification dial, and after refocusing, a clearer picture of the fracture surface emerged. The section visible at this higher level was from the brighter area of the surface and the crystalline nature of the fracture was obvious. This indicated that the fracture path had followed the grain (crystal) boundaries of the steel.

"Certainly brittle," said Dave, "I suppose that that would be expected from such a thick section of steel. It's remarkably clean."

"What about the discoloured area?" asked Mike, leaning forward over Dave's shoulder. John manipulated the specimen carriage until the discoloured area came into view.

"Ah!" breathed Dave. "Interesting. You can see the discolouration is typical of an oxide coating, mainly iron and chromium oxides, I expect. The other thing of interest is that this part of the surface is also crystalline and so whatever caused it also went for the grain boundaries."

They returned to the main laboratory. Tony asked for Dave's opinion and the others waited eagerly. Dave pointed out that, based upon this preliminary examination, there were some useful indications. As he had not examined any of the other, goodness knows how many, hundreds of pieces of debris from the turbine, he had to accept the judgement of those who had, that this portion of LP turbine disc was the site of the actual fracture which probably caused the turbine failure. Given that proviso, it looked as though a crack, which had formed in the keyway area of the disc bore, had extended during turbine operation – the discoloured part of the fracture – until it had become deep enough to cause the rest of the disc to fail – the bright part of the fracture. It was likely that the failure of just one disc of this size at operating speed, would account for the extensive consequential damage noted, including the break-up of other discs. The surprising thing was that the depth of the initiating crack, that is the discoloured part of the surface examined, was so tiny; he guessed that it was not more than an eighth of an inch. He sat back to await comments.

"Wow!" exclaimed one of the technicians, "Are you saying that the bloody bomb site that we've spent the past couple of months picking through was all down to a sodding tiny crack of an eighth of an inch?"

Before Dave could answer, Tony asked the more pertinent question of how the initiating crack, small though it seemed, got there. Mike responded. He had spent many years looking at fractures and he thought that this one was likely to be due to some form of environmentally assisted cracking. It certainly was not caused by simple overloading, and metal fatigue, another possible candidate for cracking under these circumstances, was different, as the path of the crack would be through the grains rather than around the grain boundaries. He looked to Dave, hoping to receive confirmation. Dave supplied this.

"I agree with Mike. I would plump for stress corrosion myself. It may be significant that the failure occurred during a routine overspeed test, which is when the stresses on the disc would be greatest. Better get the views of others though."

"Naturally," replied Tony. "I shall be onto the Technical Committee chairman shortly, but I wanted us to have an opinion, albeit only a preliminary one. I better let Sweety know first, he'll be really chuffed. Good news at last."

★

Having completed her essential chores, Sue just had to get out. A good walk would be the antidote for her mood. She set off and chose a route that would take her away from the lane and onto the Highwood Estate. The footpaths here were little used on weekdays, only the occasional jogger or dog walker. Just what Sue wanted, a couple of miles or so of quiet; time to think. She felt it ironic that she had been so anxious about how well the rest of the family would settle, but she had had no doubt about her own ability to cope. She had realised that the first couple of months would be taken up with getting the place just how she wanted, which she had more or less achieved. Her concern for Dave had proved unnecessary as, clearly, he was happy in the new job. Katy had also settled well. She had taken to rural life and made several friends. Even Jo seemed less of a problem than she had envisaged. Girls of her age were prone to be rebellious wherever they were and she didn't think that Jo was unusually unsettled. As for herself? Well, she was surprised.

The house was fine, as were most of the villagers, although some of the older residents did seem to require at least a forty year tenure before complete acceptance would be bestowed. Becoming involved in village activities as they came around, church fetes, summer fairs, and so on, would no doubt hasten their integration. This reminded Sue that she had volunteered herself and Dave to help at the school's Christmas bazaar/concert. However, these events were few and far between, so just what else did they all do? The village seemed to be stuck in a time-warp, activities and attitudes remaining unchanged since the nineteenth century. Sue needed something more challenging intellectually. The younger mothers seemed to fill their days with routine jobs interspersed with taking and fetching their offspring from the village infants' school. Maybe there were some women that she hadn't yet met who were in a similar position to herself. She could only hope. She realised that she was spending more time alone than was good for her.

She had to admit that it was wonderful countryside, some of the autumn colours determinedly hanging on. October had seen something of an Indian summer. Walks, such as these were fine, but it was the interaction with other people that she missed. She had been spoilt in that respect in Birmingham with her parents and her sister living locally. Being alone in the house all day was tiresome and this was made worse with Dave usually working late. She understood, he had to get on top of the job, but now this Winford thing had come along. What about her English Literature course work? She had been working through a correspondence course until a year ago. Perhaps she should look the stuff out.

She came to a fork in the path; if she kept to the left it would wind back to her starting point at the lower end of the village. The path to the right took the shorter route to the lane and through the village itself. As she was tired, having kept up a brisk pace, she decided to take this route. The first building at this end of the village was the pub. She wondered? As she felt warm, having been sheltered from the wind for the last mile, a drink would be welcome. Why not? Inside, the bar was quiet.

"Hello, Mrs Harrison," greeted Sam, the landlord. "You're very welcome and luckily we've still the odd seat vacant," he said, extravagantly waving his arms around the virtually empty room. "What's your pleasure?"

"Thank you. Just a half of shandy please."

"Are you all settled in now?"

"Pretty well and everyone's been so kind."

"Aye, they're not a bad lot, though they expect newcomers to conform to all their funny ways."

"Yeah! You soon found that out when they vetoed your plans for a brothel upstairs."

This wry comment came from a weather-beaten rustic perched upon a high stool at the far corner of the long bar.

"You just ignore him, Mrs Harrison, he's what you might call our local wag. When he's finished his training he'll be our fully-fledged village idiot."

"God Sam, make it a stiff one, I'm knackered." This request was made from the doorway by a smartly dressed woman.

★

Dave heard animated chatter coming from the Fracture Group's office next door.

"You have a look then if you don't believe me."

"You're having us on? What, really? Old Honey Bear?"

"Yep. Just like I say, bright yellow."

"What's all the excitement?" asked Dave, moving into the room where half a dozen were gathered. "It's not difficult to see that the Winford work is more or less sorted, with you lot having a mothers' meeting."

"Well, according to our section newshound here," said Gritty, indicating Geoff, "old Sweety's up to something. He's dressed up to the nines and all topped off with a yellow bow tie."

"Saw him in the bogs, combing his hair. He looks like an auctioneer or an artist," chuckled Geoff.

"More like a bookie's runner, I'd have thought," suggested Gritty.

On further inquiry Geoff's rumour was confirmed. It seemed that although Sweety was anxious to keep out of sight, spending the best part of the morning beavering away in his office, the odd trip to the lavatory had been unavoidable, in fact more so than usual. No reason for the upgraded sartorial elegance of Dr Alan Honey could be gleaned from enquiries made to the prim Mrs Murray, his secretary, who reminded her interlocutor that her job title was Confidential Secretary. This being so, Geoff was pressed into service in his dual role as department socialiser and part time womaniser, to elicit information from his lady friends in the typing pool. He did not disappoint. The whole story tumbled from Janet's lips at the mere suggestion of Geoff's irresistible smile. Although Janet was the office new girl, she had already been fully assessed by the chaps during their lively debates in the smoke-filled mess room and was now top of their poll as 'the girl they would most like to give one to'. A dubious honour indeed.

It seemed that Sweety had been delegated to face the press on the Authority's behalf. The media interest in West Winford, which seemed to have diminished since the first week following the failure, had, it appeared, been rekindled. A cynic might feel that the timing of this, with the likelihood of a general election only months away, may not be entirely coincidental.

During the afternoon a memo was circulated to all staff informing them that, in response to a request from the press, the Authority felt that this was an appropriate time to provide an update on the significant progress made on the West Winford Turbine Failure Inquiry. It had agreed that Dr Alan Honey (Head of Scientific Services Department) would be made available. Staff will be interested to learn that Dr Honey's report will be covered by BBC Television News and screened by the local 'Points West' evening programme.

"Blimey! That should cause a power surge around Devizes," said Gritty to a full mess room at afternoon tea.

"Yeah!" agreed Geoff, "When everyone rushes away to make their supper. Mind you, he can count on me to watch."

Dave arrived home to find Sue in a more cheerful mood than recently and he later learned of her outing. Both girls also seemed to be in harmonious mode as they sat watching television side by side on the sofa – not unprecedented, but certainly a rare occurrence.

"Hi! Kids, I hope that this doesn't go on much longer as there's a real treat on the local news shortly."

"Hi Dad!" was the unhelpful response.

The programme began with the opening montage of West Country activities. Then the predictable images of local landmarks faded, giving way to a brief summary of the programme contents. There was another demonstration of sibling unity, as with a synchronised exclamation of 'boring', Jo and young Katy left the room.

It was towards the end of the programme before the West Winford topic was addressed. The camera panned across to the far side of the studio where the lead presenter sat facing a barely recognisable, Sweety. Geoff had been right. A regular swell. He looked the part, the hint of the scientist cloaked in a senior manager's persona. The camera moved into closer focus.

Presenter: "Thank you for agreeing to this interview, which is of great public interest."

Sweety: "Not at all. We in the Strategic Supplies Authority accept that we are ultimately responsible to the electorate."

Presenter: "Would you agree that the West Winford failure is both costly and raises doubts about the safety of the plant?"

Sweety: "We accept the seriousness of the failure and have taken steps to prevent a recurrence."

Presenter: "What the public is concerned about is that such a thing could happen at, let's face it, a modern power station for which you, the SSA are responsible. Isn't it the case that inexperience is a factor?"

Sweety: "Yes, the plant is modern, but no, it is nothing to do with inexperience, as with all our acquired assets, we have, wherever possible, retained the previous management and operators."

Presenter: "But surely you must admit that, to the public, it appears that standards have slipped during your tenure?"

Sweety: "The public can be assured that we are working to exactly the same standards and safety codes as the utilities did and still do."

Presenter: "But, with respect, there must be some reason why it happened?"

Sweety: "Clearly – and that is why we have mounted this huge investigation. The utilities could certainly not have undertaken a task such as this so comprehensively."

Presenter: "The public are asking how safe are the other turbines at West Winford and indeed elsewhere. It is particularly worrying that this is, after all, a nuclear installation that aroused strong opposition to its construction right from its inception."

Sweety: "May I say that the question of the nuclear issue and its irrelevance has been dealt with on numerous occasions and it is quite inappropriate for you to raise unnecessary worries. As to your other point, I repeat that we are looking into all these aspects and lessons will be learned."

"Good for you Sweety," encouraged Dave from the armchair.

Presenter: "It seems a little ironic, I'm sure you will agree, that you are supposed to be THE Strategic Supplies Authority, where integrity of supply is paramount, but it would appear as though the cheap and cheerful, good old utilities are more reliable after all."

Sweety: "Fortunately our strategic planning is sufficiently robust and we have enough capacity even with this prolonged outage to meet our current and foreseeable future commitments. I would point out that even now we are exporting surplus power to the national grid."

Presenter: "Perhaps we can get a final comment from the Conservative MP representing the Winford area, who is in our Southampton studio."

MP: "I admire Dr Honey's complacency. This most serious incident is completely unacceptable and the public will not be reassured by Dr Honey's bland responses. There was a great deal of opposition to the setting up of this, inappropriately named, Authority and this concern now appears to have been fully justified."

Sweety: "With the greatest…"

Presenter: "I'm sorry but we have to leave it there. Now over to Gordon for the weather."

"Well they cut that short, and no mention of the progress made in the investigation," grumbled Dave, getting up to switch off the set.

"That's the media for you," replied Sue as she went off to prepare their evening meal. Dave followed to offer some help. Sue hummed a recent Beatles song as she worked.

"You seem pretty pleased with yourself tonight," he remarked, giving her a squeeze. Sue then surprised him by confessing that she had had a pretty adventurous day, including going into The Marden Arms alone. Dave made a face of mock horror. "Gosh, you're becoming a regular boozer." Sue laughed and told him of her invigorating walk and how friendly Sam had been. She enthused over her meeting with a woman named Pam who had just burst into the pub as though she owned it. At last, she had met someone who had actually acclimatised to life in the twentieth century. She was a breath of fresh air.

Dave was pleased with the evident change in his wife. He asked what was so interesting about this woman. What had they talked about? "Well, that's the strange thing really," Sue told him. "It wasn't anything special but rather her whole attitude, which was different to any I have so far encountered."

It was a rare family meal; complete harmony. Perhaps it was the nearness of the festive season that was a factor. Later Sue related more details of her day. It seemed that Pam also found the locals generally dull and she spent as much time as possible in London, where she had a flat. "But the main thing," Sue went on, clearly animated, "is that we've arranged to go out for the day next Tuesday, to Bath." Dave was enthusiastic. It was just the thing that Sue needed. At last she looked so pleased.

"So that'll be the Christmas shopping sorted out then?"

"Maybe, but really I'm just hoping for a good day out in good company."

5

Dave received a pleasant surprise when his section head brought him up to date with the latest developments in the Technical Committee's West Winford investigations. Tony laid special emphasis on the decision to set up a new sub-committee in which he wanted Dave's involvement. Recent evidence had shown that there was an environmental aspect to the LP turbine disc failure and so it was necessary to look into that side of things. In retrospect it seemed remiss that this was not considered earlier, when the other sub-committees were formed. This was going to be an important part of the investigation as all the evidence pointed to corrosion as being a significant factor.

"The sub-committee is to be chaired by an independent member from some unconnected body," Tony continued. "There will be someone from the turbine manufacturer involved and, as you would expect, a representative from our own Central Research Labs, at Slough. As I mentioned, Sweety has put you forward to cover our interests. I share his confidence that you will hold our end up excellently."

Dave returned to his office, full of enthusiasm for this new opportunity. He called on Mike Pearson, who had made a major contribution to the initial Winford failure investigation, particularly the mechanical aspects. As he anticipated, Mike agreed to share anything of interest with him. Mike then told Dave about a recent development. He explained that, as the LP turbine disc failure had not been due to any obvious shortcoming in the particular disc itself, worries about the condition of the other turbines at West Winford had been expressed by safety officers and the unions. After all, they had argued, the conditions under which LP turbine discs operate are very similar. These concerns had been increasing even before Sweety's TV interview. Numbers 1 and 3 turbines were a particular worry as they had been in service for a similar period to the failed turbine. The other turbines, Numbers 4, 5 and 6, had accrued less service hours. In view of these concerns and the unacceptable consequences of another failure, including the risk that this posed for operating staff, an overspeed test was to be carried out on an apparently sound LP turbine rotor of the same design. This rotor had been held at the Winford site as a spare. Significantly, it had previously been in service in Number 1 turbine and had completed just over 30,000 hours of operation.

In addition, it had been decided that turbines Numbers 1 and 3 would be withdrawn from service until the results of this test were known. The spare rotor had been delivered to a turbine maker's works in Runcorn which was equipped with a test rig capable of running such an overspeed test on a full size LP turbine rotor. That test had just been carried out.

★

Runcorn – a few hours earlier.

The noise was deafening as the steel turbine disc burst, flinging fragments from the spinning rotor; huge chunks of high energy shrapnel released, some burying themselves deeply into the concrete walls of the test pit.

Several seconds elapsed.

"Bloody hell, what a show. That's just about wrecked the bloody test rig."

"Yeah! Spectacular wasn't it? Still below normal overspeed test level. They'll never believe it."

Despite their apparent nonchalance, it was clear that both technicians were deeply shocked. The relative ease and the catastrophic nature of the failure of this turbine disc was as spectacular as it was unexpected.

Fortunately, the automatic trip cut off the power.

★

"Any results yet?" asked Dave.

"I'll say. One disc burst. It flew off the rotor in a similar way to how we imagine the disc from our Number 2 turbine did. Haven't all the details yet but it was bad, and it happened before it reached the 10 per cent overspeed level. This has meant the cancellation of all overspeed tests. This disc will be examined and compared with our findings on the failed one."

★

Sue was looking out through the sitting room window wondering if Pam had forgotten their arrangement. She had been up early, excited at the prospect of, if not exactly an adventure, at least a change from her customary weekday routine. She was about to turn away when an impressive car drew up outside. Pam gave a cheery wave as Sue joined her.

"Sorry. A bit late. A spot of blasted plumbing, I'm afraid. The old man disappeared at the crack of dawn leaving Yours Truly to sort out the bloody ball-cock, yet again – men!"

With this greeting Pam sped away at a rate that would have impressed Tony Richards, possibly even Stirling Moss. Sue assured her that she had only just got herself ready and anyway she assumed that they had no fixed agenda. Although Pam agreed that their time was their own, her driving suggested otherwise as she fiercely accelerated to beat the change from amber to red at the Corsham cross roads. Soon they were speeding down the hill past Brunel's Box tunnel and shortly afterwards they were amongst the elegant Georgian buildings for which Bath was noted. Evidently Pam knew her way around the city, as she soon drew into a spacious car park.

"I suggest that we begin at the top of Milsom Street and make our way down towards the Abbey. I've arranged for us to have lunch at the Francis Hotel in Queen Square at one. Will that be OK?"

"Fine, I'm in your hands, it's just so nice to be here on my first visit to Bath," replied Sue, looking about her with great interest and anticipation. Pam was so unusual – quite a lark!

With Pam aggressively leading the way, Sue was transported down various streets and passages invading a number of stores and shops en route. At first Sue was overawed as Pam led her confidently into two exclusive establishments dealing in antique furniture. The staff at both, perhaps taking their cue from Sue, hovered in the background as Pam carried out a detailed examination of various items. She had an authoritative manner which the staff clearly recognised as they responded to her queries regarding provenance and cost.

"I may call back," she announced as she guided Sue from the premises.

Then, to Sue's relief, Pam's mood changed. It seemed that her purpose had been served and now it became a more frivolous lady who swept Sue into the kind of stores with which she was more familiar. Their tour included shoe shops, gift shops, clothes shops and finally a hat shop where, at Pam's prompting, Sue modelled a variety of the most improbable headgear. They both thoroughly enjoyed themselves as they giggled their way southwards.

Sue lost track of time and her bearings. Entering Queen Square, Pam ushered her along the south side where an imposing ornate Victorian canopy reached forward onto the pavement welcoming them, through the revolving doors and into the spacious interior of the Francis Hotel.

"Ah! Pamela, my dear, there you are," greeted a middle-aged man, rising from a well upholstered leather chair. He gave Pam a welcoming hug. "And not alone I see."

"Ever perceptive. This is my friend and newly adopted clothing model, Sue."

"Charmed Sue, I'm Charles and I too have a friend," he said, moving aside as the other man rose. "Peter, this is Pamela and her friend Sue."

Peter smiled and shook hands. He was younger than Charles, maybe forty. They all settled in at a table.

"Drink ladies?" Charles asked as a waiter approached.

"I'll say," enthused Pam lighting a cigarette, "G & T."

"Just a lemonade and lime for me please," said Sue.

Over their light lunch, they chatted. Initially Pam led the conversation as she explained that her companion was a recent escapee from the land of the dark satanic mills. She added that, despite this, it was a pleasure to find that they had much in common, in particular a need to make contact with the strange alien life forms away from the village. Sue was surprised as she felt no awkwardness with these unusual people in such unfamiliar surroundings and she happily joined with Pam in relating the fun day that they were having.

Whilst awaiting coffee, Pam and Charles became more earnest as they talked together and this left Sue and Peter to concentrate on each other.

"May I say that you both seem to be enjoying your day out," began Peter.

"It's just so nice to be away from home," said Sue, a little too eagerly she thought, retrospectively. She hurriedly explained that perhaps that sounded awful. What she meant was that she was finding life in the country, well, not what she had expected.

"Ah! In tinsel trappings," murmured Peter.

"Pardon me?"

"George Crabbe. It's from a poem. It contrasts the difference between real country life and the perception that many people have, who've not experienced it."

"I'm afraid I'm not very well up on poetry," confessed Sue.

"And what of books?"

"I seem to have fallen out of the habit, though I did begin an English Literature course, but, you know, family life?"

"Well, not really," replied Peter, "I plough my own lonely furrow. Which authors appeal to you?"

"Several, though I wouldn't say that I was well read. Trollope and Dickens, of course, but before our move down here I was just making a start on Virginia Woolf and George Eliot. I wanted to read them partly because they were women who didn't conform."

"Did you get around to Middlemarch?"

"No. I understand that it is a real classic."

"Indeed it is and another reason why you should read it is that you would meet women of contrasts therein," explained Peter.

Sue thought that she would do as he suggested, after all she had plenty of time on her hands these days. Pam broke into their conversation to say that she and Charles had to go off on some minor business for an hour and asked if Sue would like to go with them. If however, she preferred more shopping they could meet up later. Sue was rather taken aback by this and before she had made any reply Peter invited her to spend the time with him. He had something which may be of interest to her in mind. Sue was annoyed that she could not cover her confusion. She had found Peter's company interesting and agreeable but she nevertheless surprised herself by accepting his invitation.

"Back here at four then," said Charles.

Sue explained that, as this was her first visit to Bath, she would need to rely upon Peter's navigation. He agreed as he led her down

Barton Street, stopping briefly to point out the Theatre Royal, where Ibsen's 'Peer Gynt' was being staged. From that point on Sue lost track of their movements, though she recalled passing the soot-blackened front of the Mineral Water Hospital and then the Abbey. Later they stopped outside an elegant Georgian house set behind ornate railings. Peter ushered Sue towards the imposing doorway and rang the bell. He pushed the door open in response to a buzzer.

"Ah! Welcome Doctor Fenner, and how are you this fine December day?"

This greeting was addressed to Peter by a short, distinguished looking man. Sue was surprised to find herself, not in an exclusive bank as it first appeared, but in a book shop, although shop was perhaps too common a word. There was a wealth of mahogany – desks, bookshelves, tables and chairs. The bookshelves were mostly glass-fronted and contained an enviable collection of expensively bound books. An array of leather bindings in brown and red, most with gold-leaf lettering.

"Hello, Mr Croft. Perhaps something classical for my friend here to begin with. What about Dickens?"

"The very thing sir. Come young lady and examine this edition of Bleak House," smiled Mr Croft, carefully removing a volume from a cabinet and handing it to Sue.

"How lovely," she exclaimed, carefully turning the pages.

"Just twelve pounds for that one; a real beauty, you'll agree Doctor?"

"Don't settle for that, Sue, he'll let it go for a tenner to a friend," said Peter with a smile. He had a nice smile.

Sue almost dropped the book with shock. After they had had their amusement, Mr Croft returned it to its place. He told Sue that he and Peter had to attend to some brief business. Would she like a coffee, or she could just look around. In response to her hesitation, he explained that there was a large selection of less expensive books downstairs and she was welcome to browse. Such a contrast. A cellar with more rudimentary shelving, but still an amazing collection, ranging from cheap page turners to many first editions. The prices, Sue noted, were more moderate. She found several copies of Middlemarch, the price reflecting the particular book's condition. She selected one of middle quality which was reasonably priced.

Her return to the upper room was well timed as it coincided with Peter concluding his business with Mr Croft. Sue's faith in Peter's navigation proved to have been justified as they met up with the others as arranged. She thought Bath a lovely city, this fleeting glimpse had whetted her appetite for a more leisurely tour in the future. They made their farewells, and then, despite the onset of darkness, a repeat of the morning's journey as far as recklessness level and speed were concerned, only the direction was reversed.

Sue breezed into her house, tired but exhilarated, and flopped into an arm chair. She could hear the girls upstairs – who was making all that racket? It sounded as though Jo and Katy were not alone. She was looking forward to their evening meal together as it would be a nice change to be the one to have something to chat about other than domestic matters.

6

Dave was keen to review the key features of the turbine failure. If he was going to represent the department he didn't want to appear ignorant, especially in front of people from outside of the SSA. He had chatted to Mike and read some of the papers produced. He made notes of the main points he had learned during his visit to Winford, together with his examination of the failed LP turbine disc in the lab. The telephone interrupted his musings. It was a meetings secretary from the SSA London Headquarters. She had been asked to check his availability to attend the first meeting of the West Winford Corrosion Sub-Committee. The first week in January had been suggested. Dave said that would be fine with him – he was keen and as far as he was concerned, this was his top priority. Was he being childish? He could hardly wait for the New Year.

★

"You're in my way Dad," was Katy's greeting as he tried to get along the brightly lit hallway.

"Well let me get into the house. What are you two doing anyway?" Katy's school friend, Rosy, was with her.

"It's for the Christmas bazaar at school on Friday. You are coming aren't you?"

"I wouldn't miss it for the world. Are you both performing?"

"Of course we are."

"I shall be on the edge of my seat," enthused her father, managing to squeeze past the coloured banner. He found Sue in the kitchen.

"Hiya, my lovely. I've had an interesting day. I'll tell you about it over tea."

"Hello love. Not until you've heard of my adventures, you won't."

"Oh! I'd forgotten. How did it go with your funny lady friend?"

"Wait until tea, and anyway she's not funny, she's remarkable."

★

Friday, the twelfth of December, saw Sue helping her daughters with their final preparations for the bazaar, which was primarily intended to be a sale of Christmas related goodies to bolster school funds, together with a short carol concert for friends and family. This also served to give the pupils much needed practice before they toured the local hospital and old folks' homes the following week.

Dave arrived in time to help load the car with a collection of colourful parcels and the long 'Welcome to Our School' banner which Katy and Rosy had put together. They found the school hall busy with parents, teachers, and pupils, milling around setting up stalls and decorations. With the help of Jo, Katy and several of their school friends, it didn't take long to transform the room into a festive scene. Dave, Sue and Rosie's parents prepared their stall.

The head mistress was making her rounds and she stopped off at the Harrison table.

"Hello! Mrs Harrison, I'm very pleased to see you, and this must be Mr Harrison, hello! Welcome. I must say that you are making a wonderful display here. I'm glad that your daughters have settled so well. I am having to hurry around everyone as I am expecting Lady Marden from Highwood House any moment. She's kindly agreed to open our little enterprise. Ah! Excuse me here she is now." She moved over to the open doorway to greet her guest of honour. Sue had just returned her attention to unpacking the last of the boxes when she was surprised to hear a familiar voice. Such a characteristic combination of authority and enthusiasm, it just had to be Pam. She looked up and saw it was indeed her new friend. More surprisingly, she was responding to the head mistress's greeting. Pam? Lady Marden? Pam waved as she was being escorted to the stage and mouthed that she would be over later.

The evening went splendidly, the music and singing was well performed. As promised, her duty done, Pam came over to chat to Sue. She laughed loudly at Sue's expression of awe and her exaggerated curtsy. Pam was introduced to Dave and the girls and it was difficult to tell who was the more self-conscious at meeting a Lady. Pam told Sue that she would be in London over the festive season but she would call her in early January. She suggested that they have another day out, if David didn't mind. Dave, who was a little captivated by Pam, assured her that he would not object. In truth he wanted to encourage this friendship between the two women, as clearly the first trip had benefited Sue enormously.

Back home they settled down with coffee.

"Well you *are* mixing in high society," Dave teased.

Sue smiled.

"Did you like her? What a surprise, Lady Marden and she lives over at Highwood House. I can't believe it."

"I did like her. I just knew that the whole village couldn't be all fuddy-duddy."

Christmas Day was upon them. They spent the day at home and travelled up to Birmingham to mingle amongst the Turner clan on Boxing Day. Though the holiday was enjoyable, both Sue and Dave were, for different reasons, eagerly awaiting the New Year.

★

The Materials Section was busy. Many of the research officers were taking the opportunity to make progress on their research projects. Dave had more immediate concerns. The first meeting of the Corrosion Sub-Committee had been set for the eighth of January.

★

Sue viewed 1970 with optimism. She felt more energised and knew that it was largely due to Pam and, to some extent, to Peter, who had encouraged her to renew her reading. She had loved Middlemarch, such a feast of activity, rather than just a single storyline. She had made a conscious effort to study the leading women in the novel in response to Peter's remarks. She empathised with Dorothea Brook; bright, intelligent, but married to that dry old stick. Despite Dorothea's potential and her frustration with the situation, her sense of duty compelled her to support, in a very servile way, her husband's fruitless labours. Not, Sue hurriedly checked herself, that her Dave was anything like Casaubon. Any similarity between herself and Dorothea was confined to feeling frustrated and unfulfilled, but not for the same reason.

Sue, contemplating her next novel, wondered what Peter might recommend. This thought triggered a spark of guilt. She had told Dave about meeting two men friends of Pam's in Bath but not given any details. She wondered when Pam would call.

★

"Hi! It's Pam. Happy New Year to you. Sorry not to have been in touch earlier. I got back from London a few days ago but had to pay the piper and do a bit more slogging away here. Anyway, when I got up this morning I thought sod it, I'll just tidy up a few ends and then get out of here. So, fancy an afternoon out?"

"Happy New Year to you too. What a good idea, Pam, I'd love to."

"I thought perhaps Marlborough. A short wander around the town and tea." After lunch Pam arrived at 'Beechside'. The fifteen miles to Marlborough sped by, as seemed to be the case wherever Pam was driving. Nevertheless, even at speed Sue enjoyed the views as they travelled eastwards along the A4. The White Horse at Cherhill, the open fields and Silbury Hill. She made a mental note that nearby Avebury would be a good idea for a family visit.

And so to Marlborough with its red-brick college buildings and wide High Street. Pam braked sharply and steered aggressively into a parking space barely allowing time for the departing car to escape.

"You've got to be quick on your feet around here," she explained. "Sod it!" she added, as she bumped her hand on the steering wheel. She shook it and when she removed her glove Sue was surprised when she saw the damage. Pam's knuckles were grazed and bloodied.

"Pam! What on earth have you done? You hardly touched it."

"No. It was earlier, hit it with a bloody lump-hammer knocking down a wall. I'll pick up some Elastoplast at the chemists."

Sue smiled in spite of her surprise. Pam was just – well, so full of surprises. Pam, Lady Marden, Lady Lump-hammer! They had a great time checking out shops in the High Street and in the odd alleyways. Antiques a plenty here. They finally settled themselves in a spacious tea room where Pam ordered cream tea.

"Oh! I've a message for you from Peter Fenner. You remember him?" Sue gave a start. "Yes, but goodness knows why he should send a message to me."

"Whilst I was in London Charles called. He asked me to let you know that if you wished to have a better look around Bath sometime, Peter had offered to escort you. Obviously you made a good impression on him."

Sue coloured slightly, and this annoyed her. "Well, I am surprised, but I don't have any plans at present. Do you know anything about him? Doesn't he have a job?"

Pam smiled at Sue's discomfort. "As you know, I only met him

THE WEST WINFORD INCIDENT

when you did but, as I thought that you would be interested, I asked Charles what he knew."

"What do you mean, interested?"

"Well, I was even if you weren't," replied Pam. "Apparently he lives in Corsham and he is not short of money. Family I suppose. He's an academic and has many interests. At present it seems that genealogy is taking up most of his time. If you did want to take up his offer you could come along with me as before. I shall be going over there, on and off, for two or three months yet." Sue thought that it would be unlikely, but agreed to think about it. Their order arrived, they settled back and chatted amicably about Sue's children whilst Pam gave more details of her work at Highwood; a daunting programme of DIY by the sound of it. Delicious but filling was Sue's verdict on the tea as they settled the bill.

Arriving home Sue was surprised to find Dave already there. Even more surprising was to find him making token preparations towards tea. He had decided to get off early, which was unusual as his work load had not diminished as he had predicted. Although he had relinquished his temporary job of overseeing the section's work, this had now been replaced by his new responsibility on the Winford inquiry. He felt under pressure to learn as much as possible about power plant generally and West Winford in particular. So much stuff! His meeting was coming up but he thought that he needed a break in order to absorb some of the information. Just piling it in was causing confusion. Though he welcomed Sue's improved social life, he was slightly put out that she wasn't home when he had made his decision to be early. He did his best to overcome this irritation and asked about her day. Sue gave a brief resume, adding that she certainly would not want any tea herself as she was very full.

★

An early start. The train was crowded. Dave was surprised to find that a first class ticket did not guarantee a seat. Luckily he was well placed to get a seat at Swindon where a few passengers got off. He dug out the paperwork relating to the meeting, which was being held at Walton House, the London Headquarters of the Strategic Supplies Authority. He read that the group was to be chaired by Prof Henry Fletcher, Technical Director at British Steel Products. Dave had not met him but was aware of his standing as a metallurgist specialising in the field of corrosion. The representative for the turbine manufacturer was Joe Griffiths, and two (!) members, Dave noted, from his own organisation, representing the Central Research Laboratories. He had met neither Drs McCann nor Collingwood, although he knew Dorinda McCann was an expert in stress corrosion cracking. Having both Prof Fletcher and Dr McCann attending, the committee had impeccable credentials for their task.

Paddington already. Dave was unsure of himself and somewhat in awe at the prospect of meeting his fellow committee members, so he certainly did not want to be late. He hurried to Lancaster Gate underground station. This was on the Central Line, as was St. Paul's, his Walton House stop.

He was greeted at reception by a Miss Pauline Sage and learned that Joe Griffiths had already arrived. The young lady escorted him up to the fifteenth floor, by express lift, and into one of the conference rooms. After making the introductions she returned to the reception area. Dave estimated that Joe was probably in his early forties. He was short and stocky. They shook hands and shared their respective experiences on the rail network, whilst taking in the marvellous view over St. Paul's, Tower Bridge and far beyond. Joe had travelled down from Nuneaton. The next to arrive was the Chairman. He greeted both of them warmly with, what Dave thought was, a slight Scottish accent. He was a tall man with grey hair and appeared to be in his mid-fifties. Dave, although not himself an expert on environmental cracking, was familiar with some of Professor Fletcher's work on alloy steels going way back to when Dave was still at college. He had an international reputation. It soon became clear that Henry, as he asked to be called, was modest, friendly, and did not stand on ceremony. Shortly afterwards the final two members arrived. Dorinda McCann and Henry, who had met at various conferences, chatted easily together. Dr McCann was a similar age to Henry whilst her colleague, James Collingwood, was clearly the youngest of the group, being in his mid-twenties. Dorinda McCann was generously built though not fat, she had a cheerful, ruddy complexion, grey wiry hair and had not completely lost her Irish brogue, even after thirty years away pursuing her professional career in both the USA and England. Her junior colleague, Collingwood, fresh faced, bespectacled, had only recently joined the Central Laboratories.

Henry Fletcher poured coffee and they settled around the table. Almost immediately, they were joined by Miss Pauline Sage who, it transpired, had been appointed sub-committee secretary. She declined Henry's offer of coffee as she efficiently settled, notebook at the ready.

After formally opening the meeting, Henry introduced himself and asked the others to do so for the record. He continued by saying that, although he wanted this and subsequent meetings to be as informal as possible, they would have to observe certain formalities, particularly with regard to paperwork and reporting. Fortunately, he announced, Miss Sage, despite her youth, had a wealth of experience in committee matters and he felt sure that she would keep them in order. Indeed, this looked like being the case as she had already put into place a document recording system, which she outlined.

Henry explained, possibly with some modesty, that he was unfamiliar with the details of the power plant and the circumstances leading up to the turbine failure. He wondered if Mr Griffiths would be the best person to give a brief outline of these. Dave was impressed by Joe's response. He gave an excellent review from which it was clear that he was knowledgeable in matters of steam turbine design and operation, in addition to his metallurgical expertise.

Henry then went on to discuss the allocation of work required to identify the cause of the LP turbine disc failure. Dorinda McCann offered her Department's help in undertaking a worldwide literature search into any relevant information on localised corrosion of steels, together with preliminary laboratory tests, to determine the failure mechanism. Joe said he would collect together the background on any relevant previous failures of steam turbine components. He also announced that his company were intending to carry out laboratory tests on LP turbine disc steel, in a high-purity steam rig, in an attempt to reproduce the cracking observed.

The meeting adjourned for lunch. Miss Sage led the way up to the dining area on the seventeenth floor, where an even more spectacular view of London greeted them. Over lunch they all chatted amiably on a variety of topics, though this did not include technical matters. Dorinda and James were good company, which was a pleasant surprise for Dave and led him to wonder whether his predisposed suspicion of them was perhaps unjustified. Certainly, there was a general paranoia within SSD concerning the Central Lab staff at Slough; a wariness regarding their reputed tendency to cream off the high profile jobs, leaving the more mundane, routine problems, for their Wiltshire colleagues. They returned to their meeting room.

Dave had the uncomfortable feeling of being surplus to requirements, as he had not made a significant contribution to the meeting. However, Henry had clearly given some thought to his possible input, as he highlighted the clear need for some investigations directed towards establishing the particular operating conditions at West Winford. He pointed out that an important aspect of the whole investigation, in his view, was why West Winford? It was evident, from Joe's earlier submission, that there were similar steam turbines at other locations, both within the Strategic Supplies

Authority and at numerous utilities around the world. In many cases these had been operating for longer than the failed turbine. Why then, had they not suffered any problems? The rest of the members listened keenly as Henry developed his point. He didn't believe that a more detailed consideration, of the actual conditions at West Winford, could be avoided and he thought that Dave was the person to take on this essential part of their work, as he was the local man. They all agreed. Dorinda suggested that one important area of work would be to obtain a detailed analysis of the steam quality at Winford, especially checking for contamination. Dave was pleased to be able to accept this project as he knew that both Tony and particularly Sweety, would be happy to get their department involved in this high profile investigation. Three of the Winford turbines were still in service, though routine overspeed testing had been suspended.

7

Dave was awaiting Tony Richards early the following morning when the sound of an aggressively driven car announced his Section Head's arrival. Laden down as usual, Tony breezed into his office. He listened whilst Dave summarised the proceedings of the inaugural Corrosion Sub-Committee meeting. Tony was pleased to learn that they were to have a clearly identifiable role, rather than just providing labour for the Central Labs, and he agreed to clear things with Sweety.

Back in his own office, Dave put in a call to 'Bunsen' Goss from the Chemistry Section, and also to Alan Smith from Engineering, to see if they could meet after coffee. They both agreed. Bunsen was an analytical chemist, working on a project developing improved sampling techniques for the measurement of impurities in steam down to very low concentrations, whilst Alan Smith was a chemical engineer, who took on the design of test rigs for the department.

Dave outlined his ideas for obtaining an analysis of the LP steam at West Winford and asked Bunsen if it was feasible. His plan was to have continuous measurements made of the steam on its entry into the LP turbine. Bunsen almost glowed at the prospect. Indeed, he said, it would be possible and was something that he would willingly undertake. He explained that his lab research project on a novel steam sampling system was nearing completion and had performed well under laboratory conditions. His next logical step was to persuade some enterprising Station Superintendent to allow him to site-test his prototype sampler. This West Winford proposal, if approved, would avoid the need for him to go, cap-in-hand, around the stations looking for a patron.

Alan Smith was asked if he could foresee any problems fitting the sampler into the power station's LP steam system. He knew the layout and steam conditions at Winford and confirmed that it would be feasible. Dave, encouraged by the interest shown by the two men, broached another idea. Would it be possible to incorporate a test vessel into the sampling system, through which the sampled steam could be passed? Again Alan foresaw no problem. Finally, Dave explained that the job would need to be given top priority, as everything would have to be ready for the outage of Number 5 turbine in a little over six weeks.

His phone rang. It was Tony confirming approval. There was an ample budget for the inquiry work, the costs were miniscule compared to the potential costs of more failures. He asked Dave about his first thoughts for tackling the work proposed. Dave explained what had been suggested at the sub-committee meeting, as well as his discussions with Bunsen and Alan. He stressed his wish, yet to be put to the sub-committee, to have a vessel included in the test circuit. His plan was to have specimens, manufactured from the failed Winford disc material, put into the test vessel in an attempt to reproduce the type of cracking found in the failed disc. Tony was enthusiastic and could foresee no problem in getting approval for this extra item. Dave was excited with the prospect of, at last, making a contribution to this important investigation. After months of covering for his colleagues, it was now his turn. He returned to his office and set about drawing up a detailed proposal.

"Can we count on you tonight?" Geoff stuck his head around Dave's door.

"What's that?"

"Skittles, eight thirty."

It was mid-afternoon, and Dave was still at an early stage in his planning.

"Not very convenient. I've masses to do here."

"Oh! Come on. We really need you. It's against the 'Roaring Lions'. They're top of the league. We have no chance unless we get our best team out."

"It's no good trying flattery, I know you must be getting desperate if you need me to play."

"You may be cynical but, fair play, you're correct. I'm afraid a couple of our stars have had to go off to Thornton and I'm down to five, so you must come," coaxed Geoff.

"Well OK, but put me on first, then I can leave early. Sue will kill me if I'm out late again."

At home, Sue was preparing the evening meal. She was going through the motions of a regular recipe, which was just as well as she was thinking of what to do about Peter's invitation for a tour of Bath. She had enjoyed his company but was undecided about accepting. Certainly he was charming and interesting but, no, she ought to refuse. Dave arrived home and, kissing Sue, remarked that the meal that was in preparation looked appetising. Would it be long, he wondered, as he had to go out. Only for an hour though, he added. Sue was not pleased, after another long day at home. She had imagined that now Dave had settled into his job and that the work in the department was almost back to normal, he would be spending more time with her. However, this was far from being the case, now that he had been thrust into the Winford inquiry work.

"Well, dinner won't be long, but I hope it will only be an hour. You're seldom home these days. Is it important?"

"Well, Geoff tells me it's vital as he's short for skittles."

Sue resisted the temptation to take the discussion further.

The game was away at a pub near Devizes. Gritty had offered Dave a lift. The skittle alley was at the rear of the main building. It was dark, but they were aided by the shafts of light streaming through the windows as they made their way to the door. The room was full of noise, smoke and the smell of beer. Dave hadn't played for the team before, though he had joined in an informal game at a lab social evening. In the West Country, skittles was played on short, narrow wooden alleys and not anything like the ten-pin bowling alleys that were so popular in the USA. In fact there were just nine pins and the bowling balls were plain wooden ones and smaller than their transatlantic cousins.

Dave was greeted eagerly.

"You're on first old chap," said Geoff encouragingly. "Just take it easy, nice and straight, don't force it. I'll get you a pint. What about you Gritty?"

"Only shandy, I'm driving."

Dave and Gritty were due to play the first pair, but the plans had to be changed at the last minute when John Bolton rushed in and announced that he had to get back home early, as one of his kids was ill. This necessitated a reorganisation of the team order, with the result that Gritty was moved to play in the middle pair. Geoff and Ian would be the 'anchor' pair.

John went first and scored a respectable seven and Dave was pleased and surprised to do the same. Their opponents scored eight and six, so all even. The next five rounds were eagerly contested with John and Dave coming out the unexpected winners, by one pin. Dave had been spurred on noisily by Geoff and his other team mates.

"Forty Two, that's terrific," cried Geoff excitedly, "I'll get you another pint."

"No. Beginner's luck. I'll get the drinks as I'll not be around long. Just as soon as Gritty's finished," replied a very relieved Dave.

Dave collected his round of drinks and returned to find the middle pair in action. As he drank his pint, he chatted to a couple of chaps from the 'Roaring Lions' team. Their conversation was interrupted periodically by cheers or groans, as one side or the other gained or lost an advantage. This middle match was also evenly balanced and high scoring with several 'spares' being posted. The sticker-up was certainly earning his fee. Eventually the 'Lions' edged in front. This gave them a two pin lead in the match. Very close.

Gritty came off the alley looking pleased with himself. More beer flowed as the opposition's last pair were preparing themselves. The final game began and the spectators became more animated. Cheers echoed around the alley – 'Spare'.

"Great stuff, Ian," Geoff roared. "Make the last one count."

Ian steadied himself as the sticker-up reset the pins. He took a careful aim – five. Gritty cheered, the highest single total so far.

"Oh! Come on Dave. You can't leave now. Did you see that, fourteen?"

Dave succumbed to the general revelry and agreed that another pint to celebrate would be fine. He shouted encouragement to Geoff, who was about to bowl.

Against all the odds, 'The Boffins', the SSD team, won. In spite of their defeat, the opposition were hospitable; it had been an excellent match, they agreed, and they bought a round of drinks for the victors.

It was late when Gritty dropped Dave off. He was happy. He was pleased with himself. He was late. How late he was not sure, but certainly if Sue hadn't been asleep she would have been keen to let him know!

★

Sue called Pam early the following morning to say that she would like to take up her offer of a lift to Bath when Peter was available. Pam was pleased and said that she would be meeting Charles in the next few days and would see if Peter was free.

Following the call, Sue experienced a mixture of emotions. Her first reaction had been bold defiance. Should she be the little wife to wait around and accommodate her husband's work and social interests? No. She had learned that she could not be content to accept the confines of the village either. Pam was her only established conduit to the real world, and Peter? He was so different from most of the men she knew. This resolute mood was, however, undermined periodically by the whispers of convention. Family life, in her experience, generally accorded with the traditional ways of her parents and siblings. Nice, safe, settled. The thought of her sister going to a pub alone was unthinkable and to meet a man. Oh God!

By the following Tuesday, Sue's nervousness was gaining supremacy over her defiance as she awaited Pam's arrival. Perhaps a little car sickness she thought as, leaving Corsham, she gazed briefly on the panoramic view of the sunlit By Brook valley.

Pam and Charles were, Sue learned, due to meet up at the car park and then travel on in Charles' car. They would leave Peter and Sue to do the tour and they would all meet back at the car park. Greetings were exchanged and Charles and Pam drove away.

"I'm so grateful that you could find the time," said Sue. She was amazed that now she was here with Peter her doubts had disappeared; she felt comfortable. Peter said that he had been looking forward to seeing her again and that the good weather was an added bonus. He suggested they begin in the lower part of the city and perhaps, after some refreshment, tackle the stiff climb northwards.

The Pump Room and the Roman Baths were first on their tour and Sue was surprised to find, even at this early time of year, plenty of other tourists crowding around their guides or strolling in small groups, cameras at the ready. A couple of buskers were already settled, entertaining a crowd of French schoolchildren in Stall Street, as well as a pavement artist. As they made their way through the narrow streets, Peter exchanged a word here and there with acquaintances. Sue was impressed by Pulteney Bridge and the weir. The design of the bridge, Peter told her, had been inspired by the Ponte Vecchio in Florence. Their next stop was the Abbey with its impressive Eastern window, illustrating scenes in the life of Jesus.

Sue gazed for some time at this sunlit, colourful display, attempting to interpret which biblical incident was being depicted in each of the various segments. Exiting into the startling brightness of the Abbey courtyard, they found an odd mix of people sitting around on the benches. Amongst the tourists taking a rest, schoolchildren filling in their question sheets and a romantic couple, were two elderly ladies feeding pigeons, plus half a dozen, bobble-hatted, rough sleepers hugging their bottles of beer. Across from the courtyard Peter led the way along a narrow passage to a pub. The Crystal Palace, though less spacious than the Francis Hotel, seemed more appropriate today; more compatible with their tourist mood, though it would be a few weeks before the main season began.

They chatted together with an ease which surprised Sue, given her earlier misgivings. Peter added more detail about the city and what they had seen so far. She asked, without any self-consciousness, what he did for a living. He smiled and said he assumed she could guess that it was nothing physical, such as on a building site or down a coal mine. Actually, he said, it was nothing very definite, but rather he dabbled and for the past few years he had devoted a great deal of his time to genealogy. This, he continued, began as just a hobby but now, although not lucrative, was almost a full time job. He related to Sue some of his experiences with evident enthusiasm. It sounded fascinating.

"I've often wondered about my own family history," said Sue, "but we're just ordinary folk."

Peter replied that that was no barrier.

"Everyone has a family and just digging around is usually very rewarding, not financially by any means, but it gives one a sense of local history and one's place in it."

"I wouldn't know where to start. I suppose you need professional help."

"Not at all. There are books, but be careful to choose one that's simple, straight forward and, most importantly, up to date."

"Could you recommend one?"

"Ah! I can do better than that," smiled Peter, drawing a small package from his shoulder bag. "For you." Sue was startled. She opened it and found a small book inside. 'Family Trails' by Peter Fenner. "I've just collected a few pre-release copies," Peter explained. "That's what my short meeting was about when we were at the book shop last month."

"Oh! No, I'm sorry Peter, I can't accept it." Though Sue was surprised and discomforted at this development, her reply was decisive. She was conscious that since becoming involved with Pam and Peter, she was in danger of becoming beholden to them and this she would resist. Peter sensed this immediately and did not press the matter.

"Very well, Sue, but I'm sure you will not object to borrowing a copy." He took from his bag another copy of the book which showed clear evidence of having been used. "You will find a few pencilled comments here and there, but it should suit your purposes, I'm sure."

"That's very good of you, I'm sure I'll enjoy it."

Peter, glancing at his watch, suggested that they should make their way northwards.

Sue recognised Queen Square as they passed through, taking the pleasant route along Royal Avenue. Although most of the trees were bare, there were plenty of evergreen bushes and the odd conifer lining the route. And then the view. To the right, the grassy slope upwards with the imposing sweep of the Royal Crescent at the top. This was the impressive scene that most people associate with Bath. They walked along the cobbled way past the row of houses stopping mid-way to gaze over the city at the view to the south. Rows of houses climbing up the far hillside. Another architectural delight was the Circus. Sue was impressed. Although having no special knowledge of architecture, she could appreciate the wonderful symmetry of the colonnaded buildings circling a huge grass-covered island. In the centre of this were five towering plane trees which, she imagined, when in full leaf would add to the whole, awe-inspiring, effect. After dwelling briefly around this upper area they descended, in the gathering dusk, towards their 4pm rendezvous.

Pam and Charles were waiting and they said their farewells. Sue assured Peter that she was looking forward to reading his book and that she would be sure to return it.

8

The usual morning routine – a scampering irritability of girls disrupting the more measured approach of the adults.

Clatter, scrape, bump, slam – silence.

Sue hurried through her chores and settled down with Peter's book. After reading a few chapters, she had to agree with Peter that it was very straight forward. It gave an easy guide into tracing one's family history and was interspersed with interesting and informative examples. Sue found the subject fascinating and was surprised that it had not occurred to her to ask her parents about their family background earlier. Some of the anecdotes in Peter's book were compelling and made her wonder why so few people were interested in genealogy. She supposed that it could be time consuming, but in her own case that was part of its appeal. She was particularly struck by Peter's suggestion that for anyone beginning a quest, speaking with elderly relatives was the first and most urgent task. Documentary evidence was particularly useful. Birth certificates, photographs and family papers were a bonus. Following the information obtained from family members, one should attempt to draw up a speculative family tree. This should enable the researcher to see what information was missing from their recent past. The next step would be two-fold. Firstly, attempting to confirm the information given verbally and secondly, endeavouring to fill in missing items. This normally entailed obtaining evidence from civil registration sources in the form of birth, marriage and death certificates, which usually required a visit to Somerset House in London.

"Hmm." Sue put the book down. Goodness, was that the time already? She went up to make the beds. She reflected that almost all her living relatives were still in the Birmingham area, as far as she knew. She would phone her mother. During the rest of the day family history matters dominated her thoughts. The obvious thing to do was to make a trip to her family home. The thought came to her suddenly; half-term was only a few weeks away, which would be a good time. It would be nice for Jo and Katy to be with their cousins again.

★

The second meeting of the Corrosion Sub-Committee was set for the eighteenth of February. Dave felt that he must make some progress before that. A store had been set up at a sub-station close to the Winford site where the failure debris was now being housed. He arranged for Gritty to collect a sample from the failed LP disc material.

★

"Dave, that's just so annoying," was Sue's response when she learned that he had to go to London during the half-term break. "Surely you have a say in when the meetings should be held. You are one of the members, not the filing clerk." Dave winced. He was still not confident of having paid off his bad debt associated with the skittles match. Sue was right. He should have an input when meeting dates were decided, but he still felt in awe of his fellow sub-committee members, as well as feeling favoured by his own department in choosing him to represent them. He was prepared to accept any date that was proposed, rather than rock the boat or to have a meeting take place without him. These people had international reputations; their time was valuable. He was a comparative novice from Fisher's Tubes who had trained at the Birmingham College of Technology, for God's sake. He was flustered.

"Of course I'm consulted. I was happy with the date. How did I know you were planning something?" He hoped that he sounded convincing.

"Half-term? Surely that's the most likely time we'd want to do something as a family," Sue snapped, also a little guiltily, as her own planned research was hardly something the rest of the family would enjoy. "I'm surprised that the other members don't wish to spend time with their own families," she added. Some might feel that the catastrophic failure at a nuclear power station was a tad more important than a stroll around the Bull Ring, Dave thought, but sanity prevailed and he just agreed that, indeed, it was surprising. Sue was not to be easily placated and trusted that they could rely on him for transport.

The following morning, Sue was still feeling aggrieved at Dave's selfishness. Since moving here she believed that he had changed. In Birmingham he had struck a happy balance between family life and work. As far as she knew he had been conscientious in his job, but this had not prevented him being pleased to be at home and actually having fun with her and the girls. Nowadays his work was clearly his main priority, perhaps his only priority, if you didn't count skittles. No, that wasn't quite fair, she wanted him to have a social life, but it did seem that she and the girls were seen as, more or less, obstacles to his ambitions. Maybe it was just a phase and things would eventually return to how they used to be. In the meanwhile she had to get on with her own life.

She made two phone calls, the first to her mother to make arrangements to visit. She thought it best if, whilst she stayed with them, the girls could go to Velma and Barry as it would be much more fun for them to be with their cousins. This suggestion seemed to be accepted. Sue mentioned her intention to do some family research and would be glad if her mother could think of who she ought to visit whilst she was there. There was evidence of teeth being sucked at the other end of the line. It might be tricky, her mother thought. Some of the family were still of the opinion that such matters were nobody's business but theirs. Sue left it with her mother to think about. Her second call was to Pam, partly for a chat, but primarily to see when she was next seeing Charles or Peter, when she could return Peter's book for her. Pam said that she was going to be in London for a couple of weeks – 'the bloody DIY can wait'. She had Peter's telephone number if Sue wanted to arrange something directly with him.

Her mother rang back just before lunch to say that she had made the arrangements. As far as her queries on family history were concerned, her mother guessed that, since Auntie Clara had died, her best hope, on her father's side, would be her Uncle Stan, her father's brother and for her side of the family, she probably knew as much as anyone. Uncle Stan lived in Sparkbrook, which wasn't far. He wasn't on the phone but she had his address.

"Thanks Mum, that's really helpful. The whole idea sounds intriguing, I can't wait to make a start. Could you just give me some information to be going on with?"

"Oh! Dear. It would be better to wait and let me think about it properly."

"Well, just tell me your mother's maiden name, that would be a start," wheedled Sue.

"Daniel, surely you already knew that?"

"And when did they marry?" Sue persisted.

"I'll need to check, just after the turn of the century I think. Look, I've got to get your father's lunch. You won't have to wait long before I see you." And with that her mother rang off. Sue decided to write to Uncle Stan, but first, she was like a child, she grabbed the telephone pad and began to sketch out the first, of what would be many, embryo family tree diagrams.

★

Half-term, and not before time from Jo and Katy's point of view. It wasn't that they disliked their new school, but the prospect of seeing their cousins again was exciting. Sue was eager to be back in Birmingham because it was home, but now this was reinforced by the exciting prospect of taking her first steps into family history.

★

Wednesday, the second meeting of the sub-committee. Dave was in a more relaxed mood as he had now met his fellow committee members and this time, he had something useful to contribute, in addition to having a better appreciation of the whole problem. Same floor as last time. Express lift for the three of them. Dave had met up with Dorinda McCann and James Collingwood in reception. Henry Fletcher and Joe Griffiths were helping themselves to coffee as they arrived. Pauline Sage followed, laden down with paperwork comprising photocopies of correspondence and other documents which had been generated since their first meeting – so much already! They settled around the table and Henry opened the meeting. Pauline, unconsciously exuding an aura of efficiency, passed around copies of a variety of papers which, Dave noted, all had their assigned document number at the top right hand corner, WW/CSC/1 being the minutes of their first meeting. When the time arrived, as it inevitably would, when the value of this sub-committee's work was assessed, at least it looked as though they would get good grades for record keeping.

Henry outlined his activities since they last met, which had been largely of a procedural nature. Dorinda McCann reported that she had found nothing of relevance in her literature search. As far as their own investigations were concerned, she would leave that to James to report as he was much closer to the laboratory than herself, these days, she said, adding ruefully that she had been reduced to not much more than a paper shuffler. James explained that he had carried out some crude tests using metal cut from one of the Winford LP turbine discs. These specimens had been subjected to a variety of tests, the results of which were consistent with the earlier suggestion that the turbine disc failure had been the result of stress corrosion cracking. The nods and murmurs of the folk around the table as they scanned the accompanying photographs reflected general assent. James concluded by commenting that their intention was to undertake more detailed testing.

Joe was asked about his research into previous histories of steam turbine failures. He said that though other failures had occurred, none were similar to West Winford. Dave began his report by saying that he was pleased to be able to offer to investigate the steam conditions at Winford to check for contamination. This could begin quite soon as he'd learned that Number 5 turbine was due to have a brief shutdown at the end of the month. The necessary test equipment would be installed during this outage. He surprised the others by adding his intention of including a test vessel in which he could expose specimens to actual West Winford steam. This was welcomed by Henry and the others. Joe thought that such tests would be useful and would complement his laboratory steam-rig tests, which he'd mentioned last time. It would be ideal if they could use similar specimens so that the results from the two tests would be comparable. Before leaving, Dave made arrangements to visit Joe Griffiths in Nuneaton to discuss the specimen design for their tests. A very satisfactory day was Dave's conclusion as he travelled home.

★

Dave's first job the following day was to bring his Section Head up to date with the sub-committee developments. Later, with added motivation, he visited Alan Smith to check what progress he had made with the design of the steam test rig. Yet more good news when he learned that everything was on track for the end of month deadline.

Gritty was waiting when Dave returned to his office to report that he had delivered the Winford turbine disc material to the workshop. The design and number of the test specimens seemed to be the next step. Dave had some ideas, but he needed to make the trip up to Nuneaton to discuss his thoughts with Joe Griffiths.

9

Jo and Katy were enjoying their return home, as they still considered it. Snow had arrived with a vengeance and although causing immense problems for commerce, it only added to the fun for the girls. Travelling was difficult, but they were able to visit the local cinema to see 'Carry on Again Doctor' as well as calling on old school friends. They were also able to get on to the edge of the local golf course and hone their tobogganing and snowballing skills.

The snow did not hinder Sue as she began her oral family history. Her mother, initially with reluctance, but later with growing interest, informed Sue of her maternal ancestral background. On the face of it this did not appear to offer the promise of high intrigue or adventure, at least at this early stage, as she learned that all of her immediate relatives including her grandparents, had been born in Birmingham. In addition, no family member had moved more than a few miles from their birthplace during their lifetimes and their occupations had been essentially of the manual kind. Sue's mother had been a Boughton and her maternal grandmother, Florence, had been a Daniel. Sue's mother had her own parents' marriage certificate, which, after perhaps a moment's hesitation, she let Sue have. She also, after a long search, found a box of memorabilia on top of a wardrobe.

As Mrs Turner reminisced her excitement grew and she enthusiastically plucked dog-eared, fading, photographs from the box with appropriate exclamations such as, "Oh! It's Dot Walker, we used to go to Sunday school together. She was a laugh. Up to all sorts," or some similar comment. In spite of Sue's keenness to press on with strictly family matters, she indulged her mother, as it seemed to her a small price to pay in view of the evident pleasure she was deriving. It was a long time since she had last seen her so animated.

"It says here that Granny and Granddad Boughton were married in 1902 and that both of their fathers were named Thomas. Do you know anything about them?" asked Sue.

"No, I never knew my grandparents on the Boughton side. They both died before I was born."

"No family gossip?" persisted her daughter.

Her mother gazed in front of her, clearly searching her memory. "Well, I seem to recall that my dad was one of about five children, which wasn't a big family then. They went in for big families in those days you know."

"What about your mother's father, the other Thomas?"

"No, he died early as well."

Sue sighed and carried on looking through some of the other papers spread around her mother's chair.

"Now your great grandmother, Granny Boughton's mother, I think that I met her," announced her mother, as if awaking from a dream. Sue was all ears and asked her what she could remember about this lady. Her mother replied that she only had a very vague memory of an old lady living at the home of one of her uncles.

"I went to visit them with my mother once, a grocer's shop in Sparkbrook, yes, that's right. She did seem very old sitting there outside the shop, but I suppose that I was very small, so they all seemed old to me." Mrs Turner relaxed into the back of her chair as though exhausted from some great effort. Despite her inclination to push forward, Sue realised that this was proving to be something of a trial for her mother and it would be unfair to probe deeper at present. She thanked her and said what a great help she had been and, whilst her mother rested, Sue picked through the 'treasure chest' and put aside some items of particular interest.

Sue's other planned interview was with her father's elder brother, Uncle Stan, the following day. This was a case of déjà vu as Sue left her childhood home and walked the half mile along the snow covered pavements to the No.44 bus terminus. Goodness knows how long it had been since she last made the journey. Fifteen? No, sixteen years. Before her marriage this had been her regular route to work, for five years, catching the bus from Lincoln Road North, through Acock's Green to the Serck factory in Greet. This morning she was travelling further towards the city to the Mermaid pub. She was pleased to find that her mother's directions were uncomplicated and soon she was being welcomed by her Uncle Stan. Another memory test. This time she reckoned that it had been at least twenty years. Her uncle, though his hair was much greyer, was still tall and upright as he led her into his tiny sitting room, the remnants of cigarette smoke catching her throat. Seeing her expression, he explained that since her Auntie Marion had died, he didn't need so much room and so he'd done a house swap with a young married couple. The phrase 'in need of a woman's touch' sprang to mind as she surveyed the tell-tale signs of this deficiency.

"Sit yourself down over there by the fire and get thawed," he said, indicating an arm chair, "brrr, I reckon it's almost as bad as sixty three. I've sorted out as much as I could for you to have a look at." There was a shoe box near the opposite chair and as he sat down, he announced, "First thing is this." He passed over a fading sepia photograph. Sue saw that it was a family group comprising two adults seated on chairs. The lady had a baby on her lap. Three other children were present, two in front of the adults, and an older lad, in a huge white collar, standing between.

"I reckon that it was taken about 1904." Sue looked towards her uncle with expectant interest and he continued, "That's your Granny and Granddad Turner, with their first four surviving children. Maud is the one on Mum's lap." Her uncle paused to light a cigarette.

"Now, although our dad was born in Birmingham, your granny, whose maiden name was Loomes, came from London. She was born in Paddington and they married in Southwark. Our Jim, Clara and I were born in various places around London. Maud and your own dad were born here in Birmingham.

"That's so interesting."

"Oh yes, we were forever moving house and there were a few more excursions before we finally settled in Brum. Our Elsie was born in Sheffield and Edgar in Blackpool." Listening to her uncle, Sue thought that this side of the family appeared to offer more interest than her maternal line. Uncle Stan took out a pencil and, squinting through his tobacco smoke, sketched out a rough family tree from memory, which he passed to Sue. He perched on the arm of her chair and she noticed his hand was trembling as he pointed to his sketch. "Our Jim was born about 1895 and as he was the eldest, I suppose Mum and Dad married around 1894, which means, I reckon, they would have been born, what, in the early 1870s?" Her uncle's knees cracked as he returned to his seat.

"What were they like?"

"Well me and your father you know about. We worked together with Dad for a long time – various engineering firms. I suppose Maud had the brains in the family and she was very artistic, good at drawing and such. Took after Mum's side of the family, she did. Mum was very artistic too."

"Oh! That's interesting. Jo, our eldest, is good at art. She's hoping to go to Art College after school, assuming that she passes her 'A' levels. Do you know anything about your grandparents?" Sue's optimism was rising.

"I only really remember Dad's mum," her uncle broke into a fit of coughing, but retained the remnants of his cigarette in the corner of his mouth. "She was called Emma Perkins. The others were all dead, or near enough, when I was born." As he talked, her uncle continued leafing through his box and, after a cursory glance, he laid the various items aside. "Ah! Yes. On Mum's side, the Loomes – it was a big family I believe – Mum was the eldest girl and was named Caroline after her mother, but second names were becoming popular amongst ordinary folk just then and so she was Caroline Jane."

Sue was busily noting down all her Uncle said in a hurried scribble. "So my great grandmothers were named Emma Perkins and Caroline something who married a Loomes. That's so useful. Thank you so much, this is just the sort of thing I need in order to get copies of their birth certificates, unless you've got them that is?"

"No 'fraid not. Maybe your Auntie Clara had, but I don't doubt that she'd have kept them well hidden."

Sue's uncle then offered her tea and she accepted, but insisted he stayed in his chair whilst she did the honours. Later, she bade him a grateful and fond farewell, promising to visit again once she'd progressed their family tree. She felt that she had achieved more than she could have hoped for from her visit. She was in high spirits when she returned through the slush to her parents.

★

Half-term over. Time to collect the family. The journey hadn't been difficult as the road-gritters had finally got themselves organised after a week of traffic chaos. Dave parked outside the nineteen thirties semi; the headquarters of the Turner dynasty. After a brief chat with his father-in-law, he was treated to another tour around the house to approve the latest decorations.

"Is it your lot who've been causing a stir around here with this rumour of an atomic power station to be built at Stourport?" asked his father-in-law.

"No it's the utility who have applied for planning permission, but you're not on your own, they've also applied for one near Chepstow."

"Well, I dunno where it will all end. There's enough funny folk around here as it is without any little green men turning up."

"I shouldn't worry too much just yet. There's a long way to go before any permission will be given, if ever."

After tea, Dave and Sue left to make their next stop at 'Uncle' Barry's, to collect Jo and Katy. It was only after promising to return soon, that the Harrisons were able to make good their escape. Even that did not prevent Katy's sniffles for a mile or so. The chance of another trip to Birmingham would suit Sue as she could look forward to delving further into her family history. Working around the girls' schooling would be the main obstacle.

Settling back as they made their way southwards down the Fosse Way, Sue gave Dave a summary of her chat with her mother and Uncle Stan. Naturally this had to be interwoven with equally enthusiastic reports from the girls on their perambulations during the week, including the dubious claim of fabricating the world's biggest snowball. Difficult to verify was their father's opinion now that the thaw had set in. Dave thought that Sue's research seemed to have been successful as she told him that she had obtained information about her grandparents and some on her great, grandparents.

"Well, that's good after just one trip," he encouraged.

So, for the Harrison clan this had been a particularly agreeable week. In the case of both adults, jobs well done.

10

Sue, alone again, stared at the phone. Following the excitement of the previous week she was feeling her isolation more keenly. She had spent part of the morning sketching out another family tree diagram with her newly acquired information added. She couldn't wait to make another trip home to glean further details. She was keen to chat about her early results with someone – anyone. She felt so energised, almost bursting with excitement, although she realised that she was being childish. Oh! To hell with it.

"Hello, Peter? Is that you?"

He confirmed his identity and his pleasure at hearing from her. Sue related her family history finds with hardly a pause for breath. Peter congratulated her on what he thought was great progress. He suggested that her next step would be to obtain copies of each grandparent's birth certificate and to do that would probably require a visit to London.

★

"Mum! Guess who has come to live near us," cried Katy excitedly as she charged into the house making Sue jump. Jo followed at the more dignified pace befitting her developing maturity. Sue, startled from her reverie, asked what all the fuss was about. Katy explained that the house along the lane that had been empty for a while had been bought by the Potters. Her mother's puzzled look prompted Katy to explain that it was Rosy Potter's family. "My best friend from school. They moved in over half-term." It will be nice for Katy to have someone to play with locally, Sue thought. Katy happily agreed and said that she had invited Rosy over after tea. Maybe her brother Sam may come as well. He was in Jo's class.

"He better not," said Jo, "he's a real swot."

"Well we all know you'd rather it was the luscious hunk Simon Heath who'd moved here don't we?"

The interested observer would be forgiven for concluding that there was some truth in Katy's remark from her sister's, less than dignified, reaction. A lightning lunge, a dodge, a flurry and weave followed by a race upstairs, finally rounded off by a slamming of doors.

★

Dave had escaped the confines of his office. He was on the Fosse Way again but this time travelling northwards on his way to visit Joe Griffiths in Nuneaton. Joe represented his company, who were the manufactures of the steam turbines at West Winford. Dave had been eagerly awaiting this meeting. It was the next logical step along his test-programme flow chart.

He put his foot down. Dave liked the Fosse Way. The good old Romans knew how to build roads, they didn't give a bugger about planning permission or public enquiries – straight as a die. The only slight irritations were the increasing number of main roads to cross as he got further north. This however, did nothing to spoil his buoyant mood. He reflected that this was almost a permanent state these days and little wonder. Everything was going so well. He loved his job, the personal freedom he enjoyed to get on with it without the continual necessity of seeking approval. This was so different to Fisher's Tubes, where his time and his work method had been strictly controlled. There was also the increased status. He mixed freely with his managers and had personal dealings with senior people at the various locations. Added to this was the interaction with his highly respected and renowned co-workers on the Corrosion Sub-Committee. On the home front, Jo and Katy had settled much better than he had anticipated. It had been an added bonus that the Potters had moved into the village. Sue, though a little down to start with, now seemed in a better frame of mind since meeting Pam and taking up her family history quest. As for the location, he had known from the outset that for him it was a dream come true; living in a rural setting had been a long held ambition.

Joe met Dave and took him on a tour of the laboratories. He was shown the partly constructed steam test rig, which was progressing well, before returning to Joe's office to discuss the programme, in particular the type of specimen to be used. Joe felt that the evidence was mounting in favour of the failure of the Winford disc having been caused by stress corrosion, in fact he said that in his view there was no doubt. Accordingly, as his rig capacity was limited, he was in favour of using test specimens in a stressed condition. Dave agreed and had planned to do the same in his on-site steam rig. If the specimens for their separate tests were taken from the same disc material and were of similar design, they should obtain a direct comparison from both test rigs. After lunch, they settled down to consider specimen design.

It was Joe's view that a lot, maybe all, of the evidence so far obtained was leading to the, he thought inevitable, conclusion that sodium hydroxide contamination was necessary to cause cracking in the medium strength low alloy steel from which the LP discs were made. It was possible that some sodium hydroxide, which was known to be present in the boiler water, had been inadvertently carried over with the steam into the turbine. This contamination may only have been present for a short time, but long enough for a small pit or crack to develop in the disc. Joe's view was that such a defect, once formed, might later deepen during operation in normal 'uncontaminated' steam and penetrate into the disc at the keyway, where the stress was highest. It could become deep enough to cause failure under the operating stress of the steam turbine – increased during overspeed testing.

Dave listened carefully as Joe developed his point, nodding occasionally at the faultless logic. What Joe had in mind, given what he'd said, was the use of a specimen design that incorporated a preformed defect. In summary, he recommended using specimens containing a defect, in the form of a sharp crack, which would represent the sodium hydroxide damage that might have occurred in the actual discs. These specimens would be fitted with a bolt in such a way that a stress could be applied to the crack, the amount of stress could vary in the various specimens. Each specimen would be x-rayed before starting the test to obtain a picture of the starting crack. The specimens would be put into the test rig, through which high purity steam would be passed. Each specimen would be removed and x-rayed again to check for any increase in crack depth. Afterwards they would be returned for further exposure.

Finally, Joe had a pleasant surprise for Dave, as he had sufficient specimens, machined from the failed disc, for Dave's on-site tests as well as his own. Dave was delighted, even more so to find that they were already loaded up to the required stress intensities and each had been x-rayed. All Dave had to do now was to get his own test rig installed at Winford. He hoped that it could be ready to go by early March.

★

Dave left Nuneaton and travelled the short distance into Birmingham. He had arranged to stay with his parents overnight in order to call in on his old workmates the following day.

He submitted to the customary inquisition as they sat around the tea table. His parents lived quietly these days and were glad to learn of their son's progress. Mrs Harrison was unapologetic in her quest for information, as she was always keen to have something with which to impress her neighbours. Mr Harrison, though more diffident, was also proud of his son and enjoyed learning of his work. Later, as his parents settled down to watch television, Dave phoned Sue.

"Hello love, I'm glad you called," greeted Sue, "how did your meeting go?"

"Fine, thanks. How's everything back at base camp?"

"All quiet now and I'm relaxing after a couple of boisterous hours with the Potter kids here. Betty has just collected them. She'd been invited out for the day so I agreed to look after Sam and Rosy."

"That's good, but you will have to be careful that you don't become a regular child minder," cautioned Dave.

"Yes I will, but it would suit me if, between us, we could set up an occasional sharing system as it would mean that I could get out now and again with Pam and so forth. Incidentally, on that subject, I would like to go up to Somerset House to do more family research and there's a chance for me to get up there in the next couple of weeks if it's OK with you."

"Sounds a good idea. Be a nice change."

Sue seized the opportunity. "I'd hoped you wouldn't mind as the chap who lent me a copy of his family history book – you remember?"

"Yes, Peter somebody?"

"Peter Fenner, that's right. Well he's offered me a seat in his car when he goes up to London for the day. Apparently he takes several of his family history circle regularly and they each go off and do their own thing. Although he has two regulars, the third seat is often free. It would be handy for me and economical too."

"Sounds great," enthused her husband.

"That's where an arrangement with Betty Potter would be good, as she'd look after Jo and Katy and, together with Sam and Rosy, get their homework hour organised."

"That would be ideal."

"Thanks love. Now I've got some good news for you – well for both of us really, and no, before you ask, I'm not pregnant. Gritty popped in to let you know that your request for a contract-hire car has been approved. It seems that the cost is mainly borne by the Authority, so hopefully, we should be able to afford to keep our Morris as well." Dave agreed that it was good news. He rejoined his parents feeling pleased with himself. It was likely that Sue would be much happier now, having the extra freedom the car would give. Hopefully he could put all his efforts into achieving his own ambitions without feeling too guilty. The future did indeed look bright.

★

How dingy it all seemed. Dave was welcomed by his former lab colleagues, as he had been by the familiar faces that he'd passed on his way through the main workshops. He had forgotten just how noisy and frantic the place was. He had some good mates here. The lab was busy as ever and most of his former colleagues nodded a welcome or exchanged a quick handshake, before returning to their work. Dave didn't resent this. He could remember the pressure they were under to turn around the work quickly.

A couple of his closest friends broke off what they were doing and led him into the quiet of the chemical balance room for a chat. They brought him up to date with the gossip concerning mutual friends and appeared keen to hear of his progress. The three of them had been together for many years. As new school leavers they had joined Fisher's training scheme. They had embarked upon part-time day release courses at college and night school, desperately working through the various stages of the National and Higher National

Certificate courses, followed by the professional institutions' examinations, the dread of having to repeat a year ever present. But good times for all that. They had played in the company's football and cricket teams and been especially active in the pursuit of girls and even now, as they relived some of the incidents, the hint of competition was still alive. After a cup of tea, Dave took his leave, promising to keep in touch.

Back in the car, Dave reflected upon those earlier times. His working life now was so different from that of the many people, bright people, working in numerous industrial labs around the Midlands. Even after obtaining their professional qualifications, the work for many was undemanding and repetitive. The chemists had maybe a hundred routine samples to analyse each day, whilst the metallurgists spent hours carrying out repetitive tensile strength or hardness tests on batches of components. All run like a production line really. Occasionally, an unusual job might turn up, perhaps a component failure to investigate but, for the most part it was a boring routine. Despite this he had been happy and contented and he admitted that, left to himself, he would probably have remained at Fisher's all his working life – lack of ambition, imagination, or just plain inertia? He was pleased that, largely thanks to Sue, he had taken his opportunity. As a result he felt that now he had a chance to make his mark and was sure that very many of the lads at Fisher's and elsewhere could do equally well given the chance. He was, after all, just one of them. The industrial landscape of Bolton and Watt gave way to pastoral Shakespeare country as Dave made his way home.

11

An unusual calm hovered, albeit precariously, as Katy and Jo grudgingly completed another assignment and Sue buried herself in her book. Dave's arrival was an excuse for all three to take a break.

Dave heard of their various activities, in particular Sue's preparations for her family history trip, which was due within the next couple of weeks. She was intending to obtain copies of the birth certificates for her grandparents. These were held at Somerset House. It seemed, however, that it was necessary to carry out one's own searches through the records. She was comforted in the knowledge that she would not be alone, as one of her fellow passengers on the trip was also visiting Somerset House and, as she was an old hand, would probably be able to get her started. Peter and the other woman were planning to visit The Society of Genealogists.

*

Dave learned that the manufacture of his test vessel was complete and being delivered to Winford. He made plans to travel down to the site with Gritty, to organise its assembly into the steam turbine pipework. As this would be a two day job arrangements were made for an overnight stay in Lyndhurst.

Dave asked Ian to store the pre-cracked specimens which he had received from Joe Griffiths. He also mentioned his own intention of including some extra specimens that did not contain cracks. The purpose of these was to determine whether cracks could initiate under normal 'uncontaminated' steam conditions without having any pre-existing defect present. He accepted that this was extremely unlikely, but it would eliminate any lingering doubts that cracks could form during normal turbine operation. He regarded this as good science.

What he required were specimens to be manufactured from the Winford LP disc material, in the form of long bolts, loaded into an open steel frame through which steam could flow. The specimens would be stressed using locking nuts. He sketched what he had in mind. Ian, being both intelligent and resourceful, would, Dave was confident, be able to get the frame with its loaded specimens organised by the time the on-site test vessel was ready.

Dave arranged to pick up Gritty en route to Winford. He started early. Gritty was waiting at his front gate, ever keen and reliable. They arrived at Winford and were in high spirits now that the long tedious preparation period was over, things were now on the move. But not for long.

"No chance of a fitter until after lunch," Dave was told. So he and Gritty spent the morning checking the test site around the steam inlet to the LP section of Number 5 turbine, deciding where best to position the test vessel. They found a suitable space on the turbine operating floor.

It was four o'clock when the fitter arrived. Although this was annoying, as far as the experiment was concerned, a short delay was not a problem as the length of the test was likely to be several months. Dave's concern was that Number 5 turbine which they'd been allocated for their experiment, was due to return to service the following evening and, as the Senior Maintenance Engineer had so succinctly announced, 'It's steam-to-set at five o'clock tomorrow even if you're inside the bloody thing'.

"Right you are gents," said the fitter on his arrival, "where's the permit?" It was following this remark that a naive Dave was instructed on the 'permit to work' system which every power station operates. In brief, he learned that it was a safety system organised by the permit office, who issued permits, locks and keys to the person undertaking the work. The plant item covered by the permit was disabled and could not be operated until the permit had been returned. So Dave needed a permit for his work on the LP steam system. The fact that Dave couldn't fault the logic did little to soothe his temper. The final straw was the queue of people awaiting attention in the permit office. Naturally this was always busiest during overhaul periods. So as Dave and Gritty made their way to their digs in Lyndhurst, they could reflect that all they had achieved in one full day was finally obtaining a permit to do some work.

★

Sue was delighted when Peter called to ask if she was free the following day as they were having to bring their London trip forward. One of the ladies had a hospital appointment on the original day, he explained. Sue, having confirmed that Betty Potter could take Jo and Katy after school, had agreed.

★

It was an early start, but Sue found no difficulty in getting out of bed. Her interest in family history had been building; gradually dominating her thoughts. Even during sleep the subject had not been completely erased with the result that, before becoming fully conscious, a ghostly vision of an imagined ancestor hovered around her bed, beckoning; urging her awake.

It was a pleasant drive up to London with an abundance of chatter on all things genealogical between the two elderly women. Peter had been quiet, which may have been due to the need to concentrate on negotiating the rush-hour traffic. However, during a lull in the conversation, he explained to Sue that he would park the car under the Hammersmith flyover and they would pick up the tube from there.

All four took the District Line, with Peter and Beryl getting off at Gloucester Road, as they were visiting the Society of Genealogists' library, whilst Sue and Kathleen stayed on until Temple. The two of them climbed the hill up to the Strand and turned left to Somerset House. This building housed the birth, marriage and death certificates of all residents of England and Wales who had been registered since July 1837.

It came as a shock to Sue that she would not be searching through certificates, but through indexes and she was disappointed to learn that she would not have anything to take home with her that day. Any copies she ordered would be posted on to her.

★

Dave's patience was sorely tried early on his second day at Winford. He had thought that, having obtained the permit to work and having his fitter and mate, all would be well, but then another obstacle – the safety man – made further difficulties. The test vessel, he was informed, could not be sited where they had planned – 'a clear hazard if ever he'd seen one'. Therefore, it would have to be positioned further away between two existing steam pipes, out of the main walkway. An additional requirement was that the test vessel and all its associated pipework, would have to be insulated to protect other workers, as these items would be hot when operating. Having thus spoken, he consulted his clipboard, scanned down its itemised list, before moving on to spoil someone else's morning.

After some head scratching and intakes of breath, Dave's fitter measured up the various pipe runs and identified suitable valve positions before returning to his workshop to begin cutting pipe to size. Later, he informed Dave, he would be back to sort out the routing and bending of the pipe sections required to bring the sampled steam, from the overhead LP turbine steam inlet supply, down to the test vessel's new location. Gritty and Dave were left to survey the test vessel and consider how best to position it in the area now required by the safety officer.

"It's going to be a tight squeeze," Gritty observed, and Dave agreed. Between them they attempted to manoeuvre the vessel, which, in effect, was a large diameter, stainless steel cylinder with flanges top and bottom, several pipe entry bosses and fixing lugs. It was cumbersome and surprisingly heavy.

★

"I do believe they are getting heavier," observed Sue to her companion as she carried another large volume and set it down with a thump on the sloping shelf. The other woman smiled in silent agreement.

The indexes of births, through which Sue was searching, were large, heavy, leather-bound volumes stretching seemingly endlessly along the shelving which lined the walls. The three separate sections, births, marriages and deaths, were divided up by narrow balconies. Each section began in July 1837 and ran chronologically up to the present day, every year being divided into quarters.

Sue began her search of the indexes looking for her grandfather, Harry Boughton. As she knew his age was twenty three from his marriage certificate in early 1902, she started with the January – March Volume for 1879, but without success, so she had to progress through the rest of that year and then into 1880 – another four heavy volumes – with no sign of Harry Boughton. Oh dear, this wasn't going to be as straightforward as she had imagined. Sue decided to try the years either side of the two years she had searched through and then, in the second volume, April – June of 1878, she found his entry. Despite feeling self-conscious, she experienced much joy at this, her first find. As she was to learn, this reaction never seemed to diminish, each success producing the same jolt of pleasure. Sue completed the application form for a copy of the original certificate, noting down his name, the place of registration (Aston), the volume, date and quarter plus an index reference number.

She next moved on to Harry's wife, Florence Daniel, in Birmingham, but another problem arose when she found several entries of that name in the indexes for the likely years and no obvious way of knowing which was her ancestor. She felt that it would be more useful to use the remaining time by moving on to her paternal grandparents Tom Turner and Caroline Jane Loomes, hoping to find a Caroline who was born in Paddington. She was less certain of the dates for these, as she had only the guesses that Uncle Stan had made to go on and it was very many books later – arms tired, back sore and feeling hot and sticky – before she found the likely entries and completed the request forms. Sue handed these in with the fee (7/6d each) and after self-addressing an envelope, she was finished. She realised that there was the possibility that the people that she'd identified might not be her ancestors. There could be other Tom Turners, for example, born in Birmingham around the same time as her grandfather. There was no way of knowing from the indexes alone and so she would have to wait until the copies of the certificates arrived. As she made her way back to the tube, she checked the time and was surprised when she found how long it had taken just to complete these first few steps.

★

"This will take forever," complained Dave, giving the test vessel a violent shake, for the umpteenth time.

"Dave. Dave. Let's just leave it for a minute," advised Gritty, stepping back and wiping his brow on the sleeve of his overall.

They had been struggling unsuccessfully for almost half an hour, the turbine hall was noisy, hot and humid, and they were both sweating profusely. The turbines either side of the one upon which they were working were operating and the floor throbbed with the vibrations created. There were plumes of steam emanating from vents here and there, adding to the humidity.

The situation was a tantalising one as, although it appeared that the test vessel would just fit into the space between the two large pipes, it simply refused to go into that position. Was it an optical illusion? The lugs welded to the sides didn't help, but even so it seemed possible that it should fit.

Dave succumbed reluctantly to Gritty's entreaty and they both went to the mess room for a drink and a well-earned break. Gritty, ever sensible, was right. A five minute rest and reflection was likely to be more beneficial than continuing the struggle.

They discussed progress, or rather the lack of it. It was not only the problem of getting the test vessel positioned, but the construction of the necessary steam piping was not progressing well either. The fitter and his mate had appeared periodically from their workshop with variously shaped sections and, as often as not, after shaking their heads they returned to their lair. Time was running out quickly, as Dave regularly reminded anyone who cared to listen. Gritty could sense how short Dave's temper was becoming, with outright rage only just beneath the surface of his colleague's sweaty, grimy, exterior. Although they had removed most of their clothing beneath their overalls, it still felt as though they were working in a tropical rain forest.

"Right, back to it. It's almost two o'clock," urged Dave, lifting himself stiffly from a stool.

A surprising sight greeted them when they returned to the waiting turbine, with half a dozen men cheerfully working away above and below the turbine floor level. The mate explained that all the necessary piping had been cut and shaped and Fred (his fitter) had persuaded some of his colleagues to help with the assembly and fixing. A bit of good news at last.

Dave felt under particular pressure as this was his first major job; the first real test of his management skills. He thought that he had performed well since joining the SSA and in that respect, had been appreciated by both his Section Head and his colleagues. That, however, had been the kind of work for which he had been trained and had practised for many years at Fisher's Tubes. This was different. It was larger, in every sense, than laboratory based work. He was in charge and having to deal with practical men under on-site conditions. It was new to him, but was the kind of operation that he was expected to be competent to cope with. He had his test facility to get organised at Thornton Power Station when this investigation was completed, which, he assumed, would require similar qualities.

Well, at least things were now moving along, though he and Gritty had not made much progress themselves. Yet another half an hour, feeling physically drained, they had still not succeeded. The tempers of both men were fraying and, as Gritty gave the test vessel an unwelcome tug just as his colleague had his side positioned, Dave exploded in a torrent of expletives which the ever willing Gritty certainly did not deserve. Dave then proceeded to push – pull – shake and twist the vessel as violently as his waning strength and sweating palms would allow until his temper was assuaged. Gritty took up the struggle manfully, tugging and kicking, but with equal futility as his comrade. To the casual observer, this must have presented a comic scene reminiscent of Laurel and Hardy in the days of black and white films. They had to let it go. Their energy spent.

"Bastard thing," Gritty observed with feeling, offering a final puny kick. "It's not helping having to hold it above floor level. When Alan designed it he imagined that the vessel would be supported by its pipe connections, but it would have been better to have had some feet welded to the bottom so that it could rest on the floor."

Dave nodded. "It's too late for that now," he replied wearily, "they're beginning to seal up the turbine. The steam is due to be on in less than three hours. It's clear that we're going to have to get those lugs cut off and then re-welded on after we've got it into position," he added with evident resignation. Once the turbine was returned to the operations department it would be kept running for eighteen months unless something major occurred.

He felt sick; a wave of complete dejection passed through him. He had been so pleased to have been selected to represent the department upon this prestigious committee – his first chance to really impress. He felt that this had been an opportunity to take his place amongst the other well respected scientists, but now, when confronted with actually making his only real contribution to the investigation, he had failed. Joe and the scientists from the Slough labs were obtaining useful, probably vital, publishable results and what had he got? Nothing.

"Hang on a bloody minute," exclaimed Gritty, jumping up from the impromptu seat he had made of a flange on the turbine casing. "We are being bloody stupid. It's the bloody woods and trees thing. If we're quick we can save the situation."

He went on to point out the – blatantly obvious when you came to think of it – solution, at least for the time being. Their pressing problem was that the turbine had to start operation shortly, whilst their test didn't. A day or two here or there didn't matter to them. Lateral thinking maybe, but all they needed to do was to get a length of pipe welded into the LP steam line before the turbine went back into service. The pipe would have to be fitted with an isolation valve, which would be kept closed whilst the turbine was operating, until they had their own test vessel and Bunsen's sampler attached. So the turbine could start up as planned and they could get their test rig assembled over the next day or so. It could be connected to their isolating valve whilst the turbine was running and when they were ready, they would open the valve to extract their steam and begin the experiment.

After a certain amount of rushing around, the pipe and isolating valve was fitted into the main steam line, just before they were ordered to return their permit (the last one out!) to the office. With sighs all around, the turbine was gradually brought into operation according to system plans.

Dave and Gritty left Winford, both of them keen to get home. The situation had been saved and, although they were pleased, the rigors of the past two days had taken their toll.

Their journey back into Wiltshire was made in good time and, after apologising for his show of temper, Dave dropped Gritty off. It was dark but Dave was surprised to find his house also in darkness. Not the welcome for which he had hoped. The house was empty and cold and he had only just turned the heating on when the door burst open.

"Daddy, will you tell Jo off, she's been so mean to me?" whined Katy, throwing her school satchel on to a chair. She flopped onto the sofa pouting.

"Katy, I've only just got home myself. Where's Jo and Mummy anyway? And get your satchel off there and take it to your room."

"I'm here," called Jo from the hallway. "We saw you drive past. We were at the Potters' and don't take any notice of old misery drawers there, she's been a pest all day."

"Not true, fat face."

"Never mind that, where's your mother?"

Jo told her father that Sue had gone up to London, which came as an unwelcome surprise, as he thought that her trip wasn't planned for another week. He supposed that he would have to get his own tea. Jo said that they had been fed by Mrs Potter.

Dave was cold, the heating had been off all day. He felt irritable as he sorted through the fridge to find something to eat. A few minutes later Sue arrived. She was immediately accosted by Katy, who reiterated details of Jo's meanness. Sue placated her daughter and greeted Dave pleasantly.

"Sorry I'm a bit late, but it was worth it."

She was tired and achy but she had had a good day.

"How did your work go love?" she enquired, putting her arm around Dave's waist as he sawed away at a loaf. Dave muttered a response. Despite his best efforts, his irritability surfaced and he complained that he hadn't known that she was going to London, adding, rather unnecessarily, that the house had been freezing when he got in. Sue, noted his manner, but decided to maintain her bright mood.

"Never mind love, we're all home now and it's warming up already. I'll make us a hot drink shortly, after I've had a quick shower. You can't imagine how hard I've worked today."

Rather stiffly Dave replied that his day had been quite hard too.

"Well, you can relax now and put your feet up," she persisted.

This didn't ease her husband's ill humour, which was not improved when the hostility between the girls, who had been sitting on the sofa making faces at each other, escalated into a pinching competition, with accompanying verbal abuse.

"Will you two just clear out?" shouted their father above their cries.

The girls obeyed, though a pushing-pulling match, beginning in the doorway, persisted up the stairs until the slamming of two doors signalled the end, for the present at least.

"It seems from your mood that your work didn't go so well," Sue observed.

"Things were just very hard for a couple of days, that's all," Dave grumbled, "and then to find you out with your friends…"

"What? Just what's that supposed to mean?" Sue was deviating from her soothing mode. "You knew that I was going up to London sometime. It just happens that the day was brought forward, that's all."

"Well, not to a very convenient time."

"Convenient for whom? For Christ's sake, Dave, I've been stuck in this house, more or less continuously, for weeks and then when I get the rare chance to go out and do something other than baking bloody tarts with the WI, it doesn't suit your convenience – well bloody tough luck." Having made her point, Sue went to the doorway with the intention of taking her shower, but before she got through, she decided that Dave required a further insight into her thoughts.

"Do you fit any of your jaunts around me? I know that you are keen to make progress at work and I support you in that, but it seems that you'd rush off and do any fiddling, piddling, job you liked, without giving a second thought to how convenient, as you call it, it is to me, and that even includes bloody skittles too." Having got those thoughts off her chest, Sue went for a tearful shower.

Dave was surprised by the suddenness and ferocity of his wife's fusillade. He felt aggrieved and it was the reference to skittles that stung most. It was a few days later before the Harrison household returned to something like normality, though a suggestion of residual resentment still lingered.

12

The return to a more harmonious household was greatly assisted by the coincidence of two, seemingly unrelated, incidents. Though unrelated, each played their part in lifting the spirits of both man and wife. Unsurprisingly, it was positive developments in both the Winford investigation and the Turner family history quest that were responsible.

It was with eager anticipation that Dave and Gritty travelled to Winford to start up the test rig. Initially, they partially opened the inlet valves a small amount, so that the flow of steam, from the turbine into the vessel, was low. This allowed all the components to warm up slowly. The pipework sections groaned as they expanded and adjusted to the rise in temperature. Later, they opened the valves fully and the steam flowed unhindered from the LP turbine pipework and through the test vessel. They noted the temperature and pressure. Dave had decided to delay installing samples until the system had been 'steam cleaned' for a few days. Leaving Winford, both Gritty and Dave experienced a mixture of pleasure and relief.

Meanwhile, thanks to the combined efforts of the General Registry Office and the postal service, Sue received her eagerly anticipated certificates from Somerset House. She cleared away the remnants from breakfast to make table room for her studies. She checked her certificates:

Harry Boughton b. 27/4/1878 Father Thomas (Maltster), Mother Martha (formerly Eccles). Born Aston.

Caroline Jane Loomes b. 17/4/1872 Father James Henry (Servant), Mother Caroline (formerly Potten). Born Paddington.

Tom Turner b. 18/4/1873 Father George (Tin Plate Worker), Mother Emma (formerly Perkins). Born Birmingham.

"Yes!" she gasped. It all seemed to fit in with what she knew. Thomas' job tallied with her information and Caroline Jane's birthplace was confirmed as Paddington. Her mother's name was Potten. The certificate for her grandfather Turner was also almost certainly the correct one. She had covered many years during her search through the indexes and although there were several Thomas', this had been the only Tom and his birthplace was as expected. Sue felt that she could now start building up her family tree in earnest. She couldn't wait to pay another visit to London and do more searching, tiring though it was.

When Dave arrived home he found Sue to be, if not overwhelmed by his return, at least, not overtly hostile. He was able to add to the improvement in relations by announcing that he was due to collect his contract-hire car the following day. Sue was pleased, as it meant that she would now have the use of their Morris, which would give her much greater independence.

The evening could have passed pleasantly between the two, as Dave's combined satisfaction of having his test rig up and running, plus the new car, should have made him amenable. Initially he showed an interest in Sue's recent family history 'finds', but he could sense that she would go on and on about them unless he cut her short. He attempted to conceal his increasing boredom.

"So what's your next step?" he enquired, after looking at her grandparents' documents.

"Well, for the moment I'll concentrate on the three couples that

I've found and try to find details of their parents' marriage in the indexes. Now that I know the maiden names of my great grandmothers, it will be much easier."

Whilst Sue paused briefly with this thought, Dave took his chance and went into the hall to collect his briefcase.

"Well, must get on myself."

Sue was disappointed. She was so enthusiastic, but it was clear that her husband's priorities lay elsewhere. She was not deceived by his apparent interest in her family history, she realised that he was patronising her. As long as he was not diverted from his own interests he was happy. His attitude saddened her, as one of the pleasures of any activity was being able to share the successes and failures with others.

A few days later Sue phoned Pam to see if she could be persuaded to put down her hammer for the day, as she would like to take her out, it being such lovely weather.

"It's my treat. I've got the car from now on and it's to say thanks for the lifts that you've given me over the past months."

"You should know by now that it doesn't take much for me to down tools. The old man will probably have a tantrum and have me thrashed by his manservant when I get back, but I'll just have to put up with that. Actually, I'm beginning to enjoy this rough treatment, but then Cummings does have something of the Mellors about him, so that's OK. What time?"

It was an hour later when Sue drove through the ornate gateway and along the tree-lined drive, to the eighteenth century house. The sun slanted through the beeches and, as she neared the building, an abundance of snowdrops lit up the imposing frontage. There were masses of them, including numerous large islands on the lawn in front of the main doorway. Crocuses were also making a determined effort to compete. She gave the archaic bell-pull a good tug and was disappointed when the door was opened by a frail lady and not the Mellors look-alike. Perhaps another time. Pam almost knocked the old dear off her feet as she brushed past her.

Sue's suggestion of Salisbury was fine with Pam, who relaxed, as best as anyone with her background could, in a Morris 1100. Strangely, Pam found that it was a pleasant change to be a passenger. Sue would have thought that someone in her friend's exalted position, would be used to being chauffeured everywhere, even to the local shops. Not so apparently.

They took the journey sedately. Wiltshire was a lovely county and Sue was, from now on, going to make every effort to enjoy it. Through Devizes and onwards to the open plain – wonderful. The rolling hills either side, the odd stand of beech and the sunshine. Later, having turned right just before Stonehenge, they passed a cluster of burial mounds and gradually descended towards Salisbury, instantly recognisable even though still some way off, by occasional glimpses of the cathedral spire.

Sue and Pam's day followed their well-established format of a pinch of culture (easily satisfied by Salisbury's treasures), a purposeful assault on the retail outlets and, favourite by quite a long way, the pub lunch. This long savoured finale was this day enacted at The County Hotel, adjacent to the River Avon, which Sue liked as much for its ambiance, as the food it served. It had, she thought, something of Trollope's Barchester about it and she could imagine the likes of Mr Harding, Mr Slope and Mrs Proudie sitting in this dining room, though obviously not all at the same table. This thought epitomised her feelings of the differences between her new home and Birmingham. She preferred the old fashioned, genteel air; the slower pace of life that pervaded Bath and the small market towns locally. She still felt herself a Brummie and was at home amongst her humorous, good natured, fellow citizens, but the life in the city was so hectic by comparison.

The meal was enjoyable. They drove home slowly, succumbing to that companionable mood that characterised their relationship.

"Keep your fingers crossed for me. I may escape Cummings' beating," said Pam as they drew up at the huge doorway, "but on the other hand, I may be lucky," she added with a twinkle in her eye. Sue drove the short trip home smiling. Dear Pam, she was priceless.

★

This was the third meeting of the sub-committee and Dave felt a keen anticipation now that he had a meaningful contribution to make. In addition to being able to report upon the on-site test rig, he had information from the Non Destructive Testing Group's site investigations.

After Henry and Pauline had combined to bring everyone up to date, Henry asked Dorinda McCann to report upon their work and, in particular, to introduce the memo that she and James Collingwood had prepared. Dorinda did this with, Dave thought, an unnecessary amount of formality. In essence though, it was really the tidying up of the information that they had presented at the last meeting, with a few more test details.

It was evident that they were firmly decided that the disc failure was the result of stress corrosion cracking caused by sodium hydroxide, which had been carried over with the steam from the boiler, into the turbine. Dave, though he accepted this was the most likely explanation, believed that other, admittedly less likely, possibilities should not be discounted. Though not having the university background of the others, he felt that his open-minded approach was more appropriate at this early stage.

Joe was next. He reported that he had produced two sets of pre-cracked specimens which he had loaded up to two separate values to obtain, at least a rough idea of the effect of stress intensity. He had also supplied Dave with similar specimens. His own tests were underway using laboratory produced 'pure' steam.

Henry expressed delight at the progress being made. He, of course, felt himself, as independent chairman, to be responsible for the overall work of the sub-committee. It was to him that the

Technical Committee, overseeing the whole investigation and ultimately the board of the Strategic Supplies Authority, would look to provide answers.

Dave was pleased to report that his on-site test rig had been manufactured and installed on Number 5 turbine and that it was currently being steamed out to clean the system. The pre-cracked specimens he had received from Joe would be placed into the test vessel within days, together with his own specimens. These were un-cracked specimens in the form of plain, small diameter bars, made from LP disc steel, under stress – in effect just long bolts.

Dorinda interrupted him, saying that it was ludicrous for anyone to imagine that alloy steels, of the strength level used for the manufacture of turbine discs, could possibly suffer from stress corrosion cracking in high purity steam. She had been studying the phenomenon since her post graduate days, which was longer than she cared to remember. She had contributed to and attended virtually every major conference on the topic. She could say, with confidence, that the small number of chemical solutions that could cause stress corrosion cracking of these alloy steels could be counted on the fingers of one hand and she added, warming to her argument, a pretty small hand at that. James Collingwood added the final point in their argument which was that the credibility of the whole sub-committee would be undermined if it became known that they were pursuing any odd fancy, when there was an urgent job to be completed. Dave was chastened. He was not in a position to refute Dorinda's superior knowledge, yet he still thought, though did not express his view, that it was good science to include the less likely possibilities, even if only for the purposes of elimination. He sat awaiting Henry's final judgement.

Before Henry could make his, probably damning, remarks, Joe came to Dave's rescue in a way that surprised and pleased him. He said that he accepted much of what Dorinda had said but, on second thoughts, it could be that Dave may have a valid point in this instance. Everyone looked across to him for elucidation. After a pause, Joe went on to say that, at this time, everyone seemed to agree that the most likely cause of cracking of the Winford disc and therefore the turbine failure was contaminated steam. Further, it was generally agreed that cracking in normal 'high purity' steam was an extremely remote…

"Impossible in my view."

Following Dorinda's interruption, Joe continued by saying that this being the case, there remained the slight possibility, though remote, that contamination might still be present at Winford. If this was accepted, then the inclusion of some un-cracked specimens in the trial could be justified. If the chemical analysis of the steam during these trials, which Dave was monitoring, found evidence of contamination, it would give added weight to Dorinda's hypothesis if the plain specimens did crack.

Some seconds of silence followed Joe's comments. You're a real star, was Dave's unspoken thought. Henry, clearly relieved by Joe's observation, was pleased to be able to satisfy, to some extent, all parties.

After lunch, Dave passed around a summary of the results of non-destructive testing. A number of apparently sound discs had been removed from the LP rotors of the failed turbine. These had been tested for surface cracking around their bores and keyways, using a magnetic technique. Widespread cracking had been found in some of the discs. It was the pattern of the cracking which Dave thought instructive. The discs that had been positioned near the inlet of the LP steam were the most badly cracked, whilst those nearest the exit from the turbine contained no cracks. In general, cracking of the remainder diminished moving along the turbine rows towards the exit.

It was known that the steam conditions varied along the LP turbine, being just slightly wet near the inlet and becoming increasingly wet along the machine, until the final discs were operating in a continuous shower of water. Furthermore, the fine balance of the steam conditions near the inlet end, was such that it could be either just wet, or just dry, depending upon operating conditions.

Dave summarised, the disc cracking was worst where the steam cycled between being wet and dry and it was absent where the discs were completely wet. It could be postulated therefore that cracking occurred predominantly when the disc surfaces were alternately wet and dry which, he had to admit, fitted in with Dorinda's idea of contamination. One could imagine the gradual build-up of salt/impurity concentration as the wet/dry cycle took place, rather like the formation of a salt tidemark on a part of a beach, where the sea water evaporated as the tide went in and out. Henry thanked Dave for his contribution.

Dave was pleased with the eventual outcome of the meeting, but the residual tension caused by the argument about his work, with the implied suggestion that he was an idiot, made him weary and this feeling persisted during his journey home. He was less than pleased to find the place a bit of a mess, as well as being very noisy – the Potters' kids were there again. He was glad that Jo and Katy had friends, but these two were particularly boisterous and this infected his daughters, which meant that when the four were together, he knew that he would have to resign himself to two or three hours of disruption.

Sue seemed to take it all in her stride. Of course, the bilateral agreement with Betty Potter suited her. This arrangement, plus the car, had led to a great improvement in her quality of life and she was no longer dependent upon Pam, who had been away quite often lately anyway.

★

During idle moments Sue had wondered about Pam and her relationship with her husband. Although she had not met Lord

Marden, she had seen his photograph in the local paper in a variety of roles, including cutting the ribbon across the front of a new block of flats and pink-clad on horseback at the local meet. He appeared to be older than Pam, but still an attractive, imposing figure. On occasions, Sue also contemplated Pam's precise relationship with Charles. Pam had, to Sue's knowledge, had several meetings with him, including at least one in her London flat. She wondered? Her thoughts then turned to Betty Potter and what her reasons for wanting to be away from home so regularly might be. A man?

Oh! Susan, do stop it. Inexplicably, Peter then came into her mind. What would people be thinking about her? Had anyone from the village seen them out together, say in the Crystal Palace in Bath? What would they be saying? She shook her head dismissively. It was nonsense. Peter was nice, charming and good company and that was it. She didn't care what other people made of it.

"Just how long are those bloody kids going to be here?" Sue was shaken out of her reverie by Dave's outburst. "They're becoming a blessed nuisance," he continued.

"For goodness sake, Dave, they're kids, they're enjoying themselves. It seems you've forgotten what that was like since you've been down here." Having said that, Sue went into the kitchen to prepare the evening meal. She was annoyed, partly with herself for her reaction to her husband's irritability. Her mood had been altered in just the few minutes that he'd been home. In recent times, there had been periods where an uncomfortable atmosphere simmered just below the surface between them and this was the case for the remainder of that evening. He was so completely focussed upon his investigations.

A couple of days later, Peter called to say that another London trip was planned shortly, did she want to take advantage of it? Sue responded enthusiastically saying that she would be delighted but she'd have to check with Mrs Potter. The arrangements were subsequently confirmed.

13

Dave called Ian into his office to learn how he was progressing with the extra set of specimens for the Winford rig. Ian reported that they were all loaded into the test frame and ready to go.

Tony Richards phoned to remind Dave that it was their turn to present an item for the departmental monthly seminar. He wanted him to make a presentation on the latest developments in the Winford investigation. He suggested that the main theme should be a general introduction to stress corrosion and its particular relevance in the case of the Winford LP disc cracking.

★

As Gritty was involved with an urgent job for the West Bay water treatment plant, Dave elected to go to Winford alone the following day. He was keen to get his on-site tests started. His first job on arrival was to climb the temporary scaffolding up to the Number 5 turbine LP steam inlet pipe, where the manifold valve arrangement had been fitted. He turned off the steam supply. When the vessel had cooled he removed the internal stainless steel trays and after loading his specimens, he replaced them in the vessel. At last, he thought, he could begin the test in earnest. As on the previous occasion, he only opened the steam valves partially to allow the specimens to warm up slowly. Later he turned the valves fully open, checked the temperature and pressure and was pleased to note in his pocket book:

TEST COMMENCED 1415 12th March 1970.

Now that really did feel good. He had also been pleased to note that Bunsen's equipment was working; the various monitoring instruments clicking away, as the ink markers plotted their readings onto paper charts. At last he felt part of the investigation, such a major investigation too. He couldn't have imagined it a year ago – no, six months ago, even. He was in his element, doing real research of great practical value, not just an academic exercise.

His thoughts moved on to his family and his relationships with them. This part of his life was not going so well at present. The demands of this project had, he admitted, made him increasingly irritable, but Sue was being unreasonable as well. She was the one who had wanted the move and yet she had spent most of the time since complaining about her lot. He was working for the family, for goodness sake, and on the odd occasion when he socialised with his workmates at skittles, or whatever, she seemed to think it was unreasonable. Well, his chance had come, he had to grasp it, and he would. It may be that Sue's brother-in-law was under the thumb – but no, not for him.

*

The conference room was crowded. He hadn't thought that this topic would have been so popular. He supposed it could be that people wanted an excuse for a break from their own work, though he assumed that at least some had come along out of genuine curiosity. Although some of the staff, particularly the engineers and chemists, would have heard of stress corrosion, it could be that they had only a vague notion of the process.

The background chatter died down as Sweety rose to open the seminar. He reminded his audience that these meetings were held for good reasons, other than just getting away from desks and labs for forty five minutes' rest on a Friday – laughter. One reason, he continued, was to bring a project up for discussion when the research officer responsible felt that his work was in need of some fresh impetus, or where the future direction of the research was in some doubt. It had been found that comments from colleagues, from quite different backgrounds, had often given a new perspective, from which the project had later benefited. Today however, this was not the case, he told the audience. David Harrison of the Corrosion Group and his colleagues appeared to be progressing well with their investigations into the cause of the LP turbine disc failure at West Winford power station. He for one was looking forward to learning a little more about the process of stress corrosion cracking, which seemed to be the agreed mechanism responsible for the well-publicised incident. So, over to you David.

Dave began by saying that, as it was a cosmopolitan audience, he wanted to keep things simple. He hoped that those who were familiar with the subject would excuse him if he over compensated as he generalised. He went on to suggest that when the word corrosion was mentioned, most people thought of old cars, corrugated iron structures, seaside piers and so on. In other words things made of iron or steel, exposed to rain or seawater. "Surprisingly, in many cases, these do not present a serious technical problem. Certainly, the discolouration of the surface and an alarming amount of corrosion product – rust – appears to suggest a major loss of metal, but often this is superficial. This does, however, provide early warning, allowing timely action to be taken to avoid failure."

He continued by asking his audience to consider a different situation where there is a sudden leak of a hazardous substance from a pipe, with no warning and no obvious evidence that corrosion has been taking place. No rusting, no unsightly brown surface deposit – nothing – just bright shiny, metal. This may be a vital part of some equipment, such as a transcontinental gas pipeline which has cracked completely through.

"The process of stress corrosion cracking, although less common than general corrosion, takes this insidious form of attack and is therefore potentially a much greater threat than the usual forms of corrosion, with which people are familiar." He continued, "Stress corrosion is caused by the combined action of stress and corrosion resulting in the development of fine, usually deeply penetrating, cracks. This is not a new phenomenon, one of the earliest recorded instances being the cracking of brass cartridge cases at the time of the Indian Mutiny in the late 1850s. At the turn of the century, another series of stress corrosion failures occurred in steel steam boilers, due to the presence of sodium hydroxide in the boiler water." He went on to say that some of the audience might be wondering why stress corrosion is not more common. The reason is that only a few chemical solutions cause this highly localised attack in just a few alloys. These solutions need to be sufficiently aggressive to cause some corrosion, but not so aggressive as to cause the attack to spread out as happens in the case of iron or steel in damp conditions, which he had mentioned earlier.

"Stress corrosion cracking often occurs in normally corrosion resistant alloys, such as brass or stainless steel, which possess good protective surface oxide films. If this film is damaged and corrosion results, the oxide film usually reforms quickly and prevents the attack from spreading laterally though, in the presence of a stress, it may continue to penetrate into the metal. Common solution/alloy combinations causing stress corrosion cracking include ammonia with brass, chloride solutions with stainless steel and sodium hydroxide with ordinary steel."

Dave suggested to his audience that they would be relieved to know that he was nearing the matter in hand, at last; the Winford turbine disc failure. The discs were made from a medium strength, low alloy steel and from what he had already said, they could probably guess that the most likely cause of the stress corrosion cracking was sodium hydroxide. The boiler water at Winford, he reminded them, did contain some sodium hydroxide which, ironically, was added to prevent corrosion within the boiler itself. It was thought that at Winford some sodium hydroxide had been inadvertently carried over in the steam and entered the turbine, perhaps during some unusual boiler operation. This contaminated steam would have passed through the HP turbine as normal, as the steam would have been hot and dry at this stage. However, as it cooled and entered the LP part of the turbine, some wetness would have been present and droplets of contaminated moisture could have been deposited in the disc keyways and crevices. Although the concentration would have been very low, this could have gradually increased, as the steam in this area cycled between wet and dry depending upon turbine conditions. As the centre of the discs, that is the bore and especially the keyway, was under stress, all the conditions for cracking were present. Dave concluded by briefly mentioning his Winford test programme.

★

Peter's car drew up outside but before he had turned off the engine, Sue was half way down the front pathway. In just a short time she had become a practised genealogist, at least as far as the addictive behaviour was concerned. She joined her fellow enthusiasts. The morning was overcast and there were a couple of light showers during their journey, but it began to brighten as they neared London. Having parked at Hammersmith, the previous routine was followed with Sue and Kathleen retracing their steps to Somerset House.

Soon Sue was settling into her morning's exercise with the heavy index books – lift – turn – across – thump – search – return. She picked up the rhythm quickly. This time she was in the marriages section, searching for the marriage of three of her great, grandparents, firstly the Boughtons. She worked her way methodically through the quarters knowing that their son, Harry, had been born in 1878, so she needed to start at that year and work backwards through earlier years systematically. The search was on. The area in which she was working was crowded and this slowed her progress.

It turned out to be a long search, which entailed checking through twenty odd volumes, to find the entry she wanted; Thomas Boughton's marriage to Martha, which she found indexed in the April volume of 1872. The next marriage – that of James Loomes to Caroline Potten – took almost as long and so she had to abandon her search for the third marriage, through lack of time. She still had to fill in the request forms and pay her fees. She felt tired, hot and grubby after the hours of searching. So much for glamour, she thought, checking herself in the mirror in the Ladies, before meeting up with her travelling companions.

The four of them regrouped at Hammersmith and settled for the drive home. As they drove along the A4 past the White Horse at Cherhill, Peter said that he would prefer to take a different route from the morning one, which meant dropping off Kathleen and Maureen first and leaving Sue until last. He was, he explained, due to put in an extra session with his indexing team at St. John's in Bremham, which was more convenient for him. Having dropped the others, he stopped at Sue's and accepted her invitation for tea. They had just settled when Jo and Katy burst in with the customary sound track at full volume. This was reduced considerably when they found an unknown man sitting on the sofa. Strangely shy, considering that it was their home, they acknowledged their mother's introductions, though they kept their eyes on her the whole time. Quite soon and with the minimum of fuss, they were closeted in their rooms.

"Well, Peter that's one advantage of inviting you in that I hadn't anticipated," smiled Sue. "A significant noise reduction, plus an early start on their homework. Perhaps you could call in every evening?" Sue placed Peter's tea, together with a selection of biscuits, on a small table beside the sofa.

Shortly afterwards, Katy peered around the door chewing the end of her pencil. "Mum," she said, glancing shyly in Peter's direction, "can you come here a minute?" She was half in and half out of the room. Sue smiled and asked her to come in as Peter was unlikely to bite her. Katy did as she was asked and moved slowly into the room, passing quickly by the sofa containing the funny man, as she went to her mother's side.

"Do you know what – er" glancing at her homework book, "a palindrome is?" She seemed surprised when her mother said that she did.

"Why, what do you want to know?"

Katy leaned rather babyishly against her mother's knee and replied that they had to find as many as they could for school. As a special incentive, Mr Evans had said that there would be a prize for the child with the most.

"And have you got any yet?" asked Sue, trying to get Katy to stand away from her so that she could read what was on the page of her exercise book. "Yes, you've got deed and pop, bob, and level. That's a good start. Now try and think of some more."

"Ooh! Mum, help me with some," weaselled Katy.

"Erm, well there's madam and rotor and civic," suggested Sue.

"How do you spell civic?" asked Katy, making a note of her mother's contributions. Sue spelt the word for her and added that it was really her homework and it wouldn't be fair on the others if she did it for her.

"Oh! Just one more then, please Mum."

"Why don't you ask Peter? I bet he will know a good one," replied her mother, looking across to him. Peter was touched, watching the charming family scene, of which he had no experience. He had a couple of nephews but rarely saw them.

"You ask," said Katy from behind her book.

"Certainly not, it's your homework."

Peter spared Katy further embarrassment by asking her if there were any extra prizes for the longest palindrome. Katy, still leaning against her mother, looked sideways and with a shy smile, shook her head.

"Well, in that case you won't want mine."

"Oh, anything would do," she coaxed.

Peter said that he would need her pencil and paper, so Katy decided that this was worth following up and she moved across to him. Peter wrote on the loose piece of paper that Katy gave him, as she climbed upon the sofa to see what he was writing. He pulled away from her to prevent her seeing. Sue watched with amused interest. Katy took the paper when Peter offered it and, with a puzzled frown, went back to her mother.

"What's this, Mummy?" she asked, showing Sue what Peter had written.

"That's a super one, isn't it?"

"But what is it?"

"Well you can read, so what does it say?"

"Was it a cat I saw? But what does it mean?"

"Well, it isn't just a single word, it's a sentence, but if you write all the letters backwards they will be in the same order as forwards, so it's a palindrome just the same."

"Goody, Goody," giggled Katy bouncing up and down before going gleefully upstairs. As if by magic, Jo appeared just as Sue was going into the kitchen and, without so much as a glance at Peter, she followed her mother. Jo, it appeared, also needed help as she had to write about Fox-Talbot at Laycock Abbey – her class was due to visit there soon. Sue wasn't sure of the details, she just knew that it had something to do with photography.

"Ask Peter, I bet he'll know," her mother suggested.

"No, I can manage it on my own, I suppose," grumbled Jo and she went back to her room.

For the next few minutes Sue and Peter chatted and she asked him what his indexing meeting up at Bremham was all about. He explained that very shortly, given the progress she was making with her research, she would be needing to check census and parish records. When she did do that, she may often come across the difficulty of not being able to find out where a person was at a particular time, say at the time of a census, or perhaps, not having any idea of where or when some ancestor had been baptised, for instance. There were so many records. Census returns were based upon addresses, for example, and so in order to find someone, you needed to know the person's address at that time.

"Now supposing that you had an index of names to consult," he said, "it would be so much easier to locate your ancestors."

Sue could at once see the benefit of such an index. Peter continued, by explaining that there was a growing collaborative programme, amongst groups of genealogists all over the country, aimed at providing such indexes. Lots of volunteers were busying themselves regularly, in organised groups, working their way through local records. Gradually, indexes were becoming available for parish registers and census records, he continued. It was a very long job, which required a lot of dedication. He said that he had accepted the task of overseeing this work for a few of the Wiltshire parishes and the nearby parish of Bremham was the first to be tackled. His group was small but they were keen, which was the main thing, and also they were very precise. They usually met on Fridays. He ended by saying that if Sue felt like joining them, they would be very pleased. Sue thought that she could spare some time and it would be nice to feel useful and also meet with other family history folk locally. She would think about it and let him know. Peter was pleased and said that she would be welcome to pop in one Friday to see what it entailed.

Katy returned, homework completed presumably, and when her father arrived he was surprised to find her on the sofa, chatting unselfconsciously to a complete stranger, whilst Sue was busy in the kitchen. Introductions followed and a brief friendly chat, before Peter left for his appointment and Dave went out for his run.

14

Friday couldn't come quickly enough for Sue. During the week she had met Pam for a couple of hours in Chippenham, but otherwise she had been unsettled. At last, the postman arrived. Earlier she had resisted the foolish urge to go down to Home Farm, at the end of the village, and hijack the poor man. Eventually her patience was rewarded. A long brown envelope, bearing her own handwritten address, dropped amongst lesser items onto the hall floor. She checked the two marriage certificates and was pleased to find that the details, for her great grandparents, were as expected, with one of the marriages having taken place in Birmingham the other in Kensington, which was very close to Caroline Jane's birthplace, Paddington. Of particular interest, was the additional information provided, including their ages at the time of their marriage, which would help in obtaining their birth certificates. A real delight was learning the names and occupations of her great, great grandfathers as this took her 'tree' back another generation. She was excited, though perversely, this information had the negative effect of fuelling her appetite for more. Goodness, where would it all end? Her next step was to find the births of these great grandparents, which would necessitate another visit to Somerset House. She could hardly wait to get to London again.

★

The next sub-committee meeting was arranged for the following week and Dave was preparing a few notes, upon recent developments, when he received a phone call from Dorinda McCann. She told him that he may be interested in witnessing some of the work they were doing. They were colleagues in the same organisation and she had been thinking since the last meeting, when they had had their minor differences, that it might be better if they kept in closer touch and attempted to resolve such differences between themselves, rather than washing their slightly soiled linen in public. Dave agreed and arrangements were made for him to visit Slough, following the London meeting.

Dave decided he would treat himself to an overnight stay at The Bonnington Hotel in London, with whom the SSA had special arrangements. Having this organised, he went to check on Bunsen's progress with his Winford project.

The white-coated Bunsen was his enthusiastic self, bustling about the lab like a two year old. He greeted Dave with a wave, whilst swirling around a large flask containing a hot, probably aggressive, blue solution in his other hand as though it was a cocktail. Dave advanced, though he kept a respectable distance from the frothing mixture.

"Dr Jekyll, I presume?"

"Greetings David. Want a swig?" Bunsen quipped.

Dave was pleased to hear that all was well with the chemical sampling and measuring equipment at Winford and that all steam impurities were within prescribed limits and not significantly different to any other power station in the country – no evidence of contamination.

★

Sue decided to call Peter. She knew that she was being silly, letting all this family history assume such significance for her, but she couldn't help herself. She had been taken aback by Dave's reaction at finding

Peter at the house. He said that he had been pleased that she had found an interest, but he didn't expect it to result in him coming home at night and finding some bloke playing fathers with his daughter. She thought that this was more evidence of Dave's attitude to her new found interest. It was clear that he didn't mind her amusing herself with, what in his view was, a silly pastime, providing that it didn't impinge upon his own life. This was particularly galling after she had made an effort to show an interest in his every move.

Peter answered and Sue told him of her news and where her next step lay. She said that she was impatient to make progress and this would require another trip to Somerset House. They chatted for a while, during which Sue agreed to visit his indexing group.

She was still despondent however as, despite having her new friends and her interest in family history, she was still spending many hours alone. She calculated that it was something like forty hours a week. She had checked through the classified section of the local paper, for job vacancies, several times since Christmas without finding anything suitable, but now that she had transport there was a wider selection from which to choose. She had seen two possibilities and written off. The prospects did not seem good as her CV had that ominous fifteen year gap, in addition to her age. These days it appeared that over thirty was over the hill. Her pessimism had been justified, as she was not granted an interview in either case. She had since circled another two and now settled down to apply to both, then, with some effort of will, she directed her attention to her other role in life as housewife and mother and got on with her chores. Goodness, Dave and the girls would be home any minute.

★

Dave arrived home and went straight out for his run. Since the evenings were drawing out, he was able to go over the paths crisscrossing the Highwood Estate, which he much preferred to the winter runs along the dark lanes.

After tea Sue mentioned that her certificates had arrived and so she now knew where her next steps lay, which meant another trip to London. Her delight, when she learned that Dave was going up shortly, was quickly quenched when he added that he'd be staying overnight.

Unusually, Dave travelled to London by car, as this was convenient for getting to Slough the following day. Unlike Sue, he was not familiar with the Hammersmith car park and so as he approached London, he decided to look for an underground station where he might leave his car. He turned north at Chiswick and, after passing Chiswick Park station, he found a suitable place.

The meeting began with Henry, ably assisted by Pauline, doing the usual honours of presenting documents received since the previous meeting. These were the subject of discussion. One gave details of the progress being made with the refurbishment of Number 2 turbine at Winford, which was going well. Some new discs had been manufactured, whilst some of the existing ones had been modified, by removing the keyways and devising a different form of attachment to the rotor. The intention was to carry out a complete refurbishment of all LP turbines. This would be a long term programme involving a huge amount of non-destructive testing.

Joe gave an update on his tests, which were the highlight of the meeting. His steam rig specimens had completed 1,000 hours of exposure and had been removed for inspection by x-ray. He believed that some increase in crack length had occurred, though this was quite small. This caused a ripple of excitement around the table. If confirmed, these results meant that, surprisingly, cracks in disc steel could grow, or deepen, whilst operating in 'pure' steam, in other words, during normal turbine operation. Thus, just a small 'crack-like' defect in a disc, say an original fault, could extend during service and cause the disc to fail, as the Winford one had, so dramatically, done.

Following lunch, James Collingwood gave an update on their work at Slough. They had examined the discoloured portion of the fracture surface taken from the failed Winford disc and had found something significant. There was evidence of a series of narrow lines of deformation, which may have arisen, one by one, at each monthly overspeed test. As the dates of these tests would be in the station's records, it might be possible to use these lines as a method of dating the development of crack progression during service, in a similar way to that used with rings on trees. Another observation was that there was evidence of staining on the surface, producing ripples, which could be the residue of an impurity, such as sodium hydroxide, from water droplets in the steam.

Dave's contribution was a collection of small advances. He reported that Bunsen had examined some of the steam analysis data from Winford and that, so far, no evidence of contamination had been found. He went on to say that he had received information from their Fracture Group on the mechanical properties of the failed disc and Pauline had circulated the details. It was evident that this disc had been in a very brittle condition. In addition, there was significant segregation within its structure, including the distribution of impurities in the form of sulphide particles, though the number of these was about normal. All one could say from this, was that the poor mechanical condition of this disc was probably the reason why it had been the one to fail. It was known, from the examination of other discs removed from the failed Number 2 machine, that several contained cracks. It could be that some of these could be deeper.

The meeting broke up early. When Dave went down to the ground floor he saw Pauline standing near the door surveying the incessant rain beating down upon the pavement.

"Going to have to make a run for it," he grinned.

"I'm meeting a friend later. I was wondering about a taxi."

Dave said that he was going up to Holborn and would just dash to the tube. Pauline surprised him by saying that Holborn was where she was meeting her friend. Perhaps they could dash together? Pauline's superior knowledge of the Walton House layout, was put to good use as she was able to lead Dave through the complex of corridors, which minimised their exposure to the rain in getting to St. Paul's underground station. As Pauline was not due to meet her friend until later, she accepted Dave's invitation for a drink at The Bonnington, which he hoped they could get to without actually drowning.

Little lasting damage was sustained and the experience had the benefit of overcoming any reserve that either might have felt. After ordering drinks they settled and chatted comfortably. Pauline and her friend were thinking of seeing a film, though they hadn't decided which. She asked Dave about the hotel food. He didn't know but said that one of his colleagues recommended an Italian place just along the road. Pauline enjoyed Italian cuisine. Impulsively, Dave wondered if she would like to join him when he next stayed over. She accepted enthusiastically. They lingered over their drinks as Pauline had almost an hour to kill. They chatted about their respective home towns, of Birmingham and Chichester and their family backgrounds, the most interesting revelation being that Pauline was half Italian on her mother's side. She thanked Dave for his company and the drink before leaving. After a shower, he sought out the local restaurant.

He drove to Slough the following morning and met James, who was to be his escort, as Dorinda was in a meeting. She would join them for lunch. James gave him a tour of the labs. Dave was struck by the contrast between this laboratory and his own. Even though they both belonged to the Strategic Supplies Authority, this was so different. Here there was a proliferation of long hair, beards and pipes with, it seemed, sandals being *de rigueur* in the footwear department. The laboratories were free from the assorted plant items, chunks of metal and the general clutter that he was used to and an air of quiet unhurried calm pervaded.

Eventually they arrived in the Surface Sciences laboratory, which was where corrosion related problems were confronted. In the microscope room a sample from the Winford disc was loaded in the microscope. This had been cut from the same disc section, which Dave had examined five months earlier. He was able to see for himself the features on the fracture surface of the failed disc that he'd heard about at the meeting. Dave could see the features, to which James had referred, but he did not feel that the significance Dorinda and her colleagues were attaching to them, could be justified with any confidence. He expressed his reservations. There were no hard feelings and, following lunch, Dave left.

Back home he read on the message pad a reminder of the skittles match at eight. Sue, without any outward show of displeasure, prepared an early meal. It was with a great effort of will that she resisted the temptation to complain, though this further example of her husband's insensitivity was mentally noted.

The following day Dave told Ian that, during his visit, he had learned of two technical publications, which he wanted him to add to their regular reading list. Some weeks earlier, he had asked Ian to go through a selection of scientific publications on a regular basis and make notes, in a card index, of anything of relevance to their work.

★

"Here we are Sue. The office." Peter led the way into a dingy vestry room which smelt of dust, damp and decay. It was not well lit. Amongst the clutter, the room contained several old wooden chests and a couple of modern metal cabinets. Around a refectory table in the centre of the room, sat four characters who, Sue would later describe to Dave, seemed to have escaped the pages of a Dickens novel. Peter introduced them; Barbara (Miss Flight?), Liz (Sairey Gamp?), Margaret (Miss Haversham?) and Richard (Mr Pickwick?). The women looked up from their work and smiled or nodded according to their custom. Richard stood up and smiled over his thick spectacles.

"This is Sue, a friend of mine, who is interested in seeing what we get up to on a Friday." After a mixture of murmurs and nods, the four returned to their work.

"Let me show you what goes on here," said Peter, leading Sue over to the metal cabinets. He began by explaining that the parish registers of St. John's were begun in 1547 and parish events, notably births, marriages and burials, had been recorded since then. He opened a cabinet and removed an ancient volume. Heavily bound with thick, off-white pages which, in spite of some evident water damage, were clearly identified as the Parish Register for St. John's. Bremham – 1547. Even in the early pages of this first volume, the entries were clearly written in sections under the heading of Baptisms, Marriages, or Burials. However, the writing was difficult for Sue to interpret as the style and spelling of the entries was unfamiliar. She could see that the 's' was often written as a long 'f' and she could guess some of the old spelling of certain Christian names 'Johannes' – John? She realised that it would require greater concentration to transcribe, than would be the case with the more modern volumes.

"How wonderful," she commented. Her feelings when handling the precious volume, all those years old, were difficult to put into words. Peter took the book from her and carefully replaced it in the cabinet. Rather unnecessarily, he pointed out how valuable such an original document was, adding that this was the reason for locking the older registers in the steel cabinets. Unfortunately, there was insufficient room for them all and the more recent ones were kept in the wooden parish chests, at present.

"As I mentioned, together with other teams around the country, we are trying to do our bit in preserving these original registers by producing copies. In this way people who wish to consult the records, family historians and so on, can use our copies and thus reduce the wear and tear on the originals. There is a bonus for these scholars as, whilst we are copying the records, we also provide a surname index to the entries, which will make finding a particular entry much easier."

Sue looked over to the 'team' who had suddenly become animated and were crowding around Barbara. She gave Peter a questioning look.

"This is probably our biggest problem, trying to decipher some of the writing, especially in damaged areas. Often, if we can't agree, we check other records, such as Bishops' Transcripts, to see if there is any information relating to the entry."

After a closer look over people's shoulders, Sue got a better idea of how they worked. She declined their offer to join them for lunch, as she had agreed to have a drink at The Marden Arms with Pam.

15

Sue joined the quaint members of the indexing team the following Friday at Bremham vestry. Soon she got into the swing of the action, although she did find that it was an effort to maintain the required concentration. How these elderly old dears managed was a wonder to her. Everyone worked well with each other. It was a team effort.

During her second visit, a week later, Peter mentioned that he would be going up to London on the following Tuesday, which delighted her. Although she had been trying to busy herself with other things, such as the indexing work, her own research in waiting was never far from her thoughts.

Tuesday arrived. Sue was, as usual, ready early and had time to look through the information that she had so far amassed. Even at this early stage, she was conscious of the difficulties she would encounter in dealing with the expanding list of direct ancestors, as she moved backwards through the generations. Soon, even if her searches were only partially successful, the amount of information could become unmanageable. Clearly she would need to be selective. The problem could resolve itself naturally as some of her family surnames became difficult to trace. This had already begun, insofar as she had only managed to trace two of the four marriages of her great grandparents. She decided to defer any decision until later. Her immediate task was to search for the birth details of at least some of her great grandparents and so, she would once again be amongst the birth indexes at Somerset House.

Peter arrived. He had one passenger with him, a man unknown to Sue, who she learned was a member of the local family history group. They were both intending to visit the Newspaper reference library. Sue travelled from Hammersmith alone, which pleased her, as she could be flexible about lunch.

She entered into the search routine with the air of a regular, which of course, she now was. She had details from the two marriage certificates which, in addition to the ages of her great grandparents at the time of their marriage, included the names and occupations of their fathers. She began her search through the birth indexes around the likely birth dates, based upon their age at the time of their marriage, although she had no idea of their places of birth. She was rewarded with promising results for two of her great grandfathers, finding birth details which seemed appropriate. The first was born in Woolpit in Suffolk and the other in Kensington. Her first real dilemma arose with her great grandmother Potten, when she found two Caroline Pottens in the index born in 1846, which was the likely birth year she had deduced from her great grandmother's marriage certificate. She thought this perverse, as it was an unusual surname and there were no other Caroline Pottens listed for several years either side of this date. Both were registered in Brighton. She decided to apply for both certificates and then later attempt to determine which of the two was her great grandmother.

On the journey home, Sue mentioned her problem to her more experienced fellow travellers. They agreed that she had done the sensible thing in applying for both certificates. She should be able to confirm which certificate was her great grandmother's, by checking the name of her father. She already knew, from Caroline's marriage certificate, that the one she sought was named Thomas, who was a carpenter.

Back in Wiltshire, she was pleased to find everyone at home. The girls and the Potter kids were, making the most of the lighter evenings, playing an improvised version of volley ball using a makeshift net strung across the front lawn. Dave, having returned from his run, was in the kitchen making a start on preparing the meal. It seemed that he wanted to eat early as he had work to do. When hadn't he?

A few days later the four certificates which Sue had ordered arrived. She was pleased to find that her great grandfather, Thomas Boughton was born in 1842 in Woolpit, Suffolk, and that his father's name was indeed James. She had similar details recorded on the next certificate, which was for another great grandfather, James Loomes, who was born in Kensington in 1848. His father was John, a house painter. So far so good. Next she turned to the first of the certificates for Caroline Potten. Of course, she knew from the earlier marriage certificate, that Caroline's father was named Thomas and he was a carpenter. She was delighted when she found that this was the case for this first Caroline, who was born in Brighton in May 1846. Caroline's mother's name was Elizabeth Baker. The address was given as number forty one, Upper North Street.

From this information Sue could see the next part of her research, regarding these three families, would entail checking the census returns for 1851 as the next generation, moving backwards, would have been born, perhaps even married, before civil registration had been instituted in 1837. As she now had the addresses of two of her great grandfathers, at least at the time of their birth, she could start at those locations in her census search, hoping that they hadn't moved home. She imagined that, as Woolpit was likely to be a small village, the Boughton family should be easy to locate. She decided to start there and then move on to Kensington to seek out the Loomes. As for her great grandmother Caroline, she would check number forty one Upper North Street.

She put her certificates into her wallet folder and, almost as an afterthought, checked the certificate for the other Caroline Potten out of interest. She read through this with an increasing sense of shock:

Caroline Potten b. 7th Nov 1846, father Thomas, mother Elizabeth Worth, father's profession – carpenter.

She couldn't believe it, same name, same place and year of birth, both fathers were carpenters named Thomas and both mothers were named Elizabeth. This second Caroline was born in Chichester Street. She was stunned. She had not resolved her difficulty and still had no way of knowing which of the two was correct. She could only hope that Peter might be able to advise her.

During a break from the laborious indexing work at St. John's, Peter and Sue sat a little apart from the 'Dickensians' – as Sue thought of them – and Peter went through her Potten birth certificates.

"Hmm! The road not taken it seems," was his comment.

"Pardon me," asked Sue.

"Oh! Sorry. Robert Frost. It's a poem," Peter explained.

"But will his poem help me?"

"No, it's just a bad habit of mine, I'm afraid. I can't suggest anything positive just now, nothing that would definitely resolve your dilemma. However," Peter thought for a moment, "I believe that for the present you should regard them both as your great grandmother. It could be that they are descended from a common ancestor, they could be cousins. It's quite an unusual surname after all. If they were closely related, then you could construct a family tree for both and carry on back from there, possibly finding them joining up to a common ancestor. It may be that later, when you've used other sources of reference, you will know which is correct." Once again she couldn't wait to be on her travels.

★

Dave was back on the Winford road again. He was intending to carry out an inspection of his on-site specimens. Bunsen was with him, providing a constant stream of lively chatter. It seemed that almost any incident or any object that they passed could spur him into some tale or anecdote which stirred in that buzzing brain of his. He really was, Dave thought, the absolute stereotype of the mad professor that many people call to mind when thinking of scientists. In amongst his observations Bunsen did include, for Dave's benefit, a potted history of boiler water chemistry and how this had changed over recent years. The two basic strategies to prevent corrosion of the metal components within the water/steam circuit were the removal of oxygen and the maintenance of alkaline conditions, within the circuit. During the early period of operation at Winford, the boiler water had been dosed with sodium hydroxide, but in recent times, the chemical hydrazine was mainly used with sodium hydroxide only as an occasional back up.

Bunsen explained that today he was planning to check the steam quality readings. He would also collect the first few weeks of completed instrument charts and recalibrate his reference standards. In order to save time, Dave had arranged to have the steam to his test vessel turned off a couple of hours before he was due to arrive, so that he could get access to his samples immediately.

After signing in they changed into their overalls. Whilst Bunsen went to meet the Station Chemist, whistling tunelessly along the corridor, Dave made his way to the turbine hall to open his test vessel. He was pleased to see that the pre-cracked specimens on the top tray had acquired an even, shiny, black surface coating, similar to that found on LP turbine discs after service. He made a mental note to ask Joe if this was also the case with his laboratory steam rig specimens in Nuneaton. After removing the pre-cracked specimens from the vessel, Dave inspected each one for signs of crack extension. He was only using a visual check this time and not x-ray, as he didn't want to lose exposure time in the test rig, which would be the case if he wanted to take them away for more accurate measurement. It was early days and the extent of extra crack growth, if any, would be very small. He had a magnifying glass with its own light source which he used to aid his inspection – and yes, yes – he was sure. He could just detect the smallest suggestion of growth on several of the specimens. Next, he examined his own extra samples, those without pre-existing cracks, and was pleased to find that they were also oxide coated along the whole of their test length. Dave could not detect any surface features that would suggest cracking or even pitting, but he accepted that this would be unlikely using normal visual methods alone. After making his notes, he replaced the specimens into the test vessel, closing the lid securely. He returned the rig to service before checking on Bunsen's progress. Following a canteen lunch, during which they chatted with station engineers, Dave returned to the turbine hall to make a note of the temperature and pressure readings in the test chamber, whilst Bunsen clambered up the scaffolding to inspect his instruments.

They managed to get away from the station early, which suited Dave as he wanted to get back to work in time to make a start on his contribution for the forthcoming sub-committee meeting. How quickly these seemed to come around.

Back at his desk he phoned Pauline to check on a couple of agenda items and he took the opportunity to let her know that, although he would not be staying overnight this time, he trusted that their dinner date would still be valid when he could make the arrangements. Pauline assured him that, although she hoped he wouldn't feel that she was being too forward, she was intending to hold him to it. Dave hung up and sat back in his chair with the smile of the middle-aged man who apparently hadn't lost all his charisma.

The meeting day arrived and the members assembled. A routine meeting was anticipated but this was to turn out not to be the case. Proceedings began normally enough as Joe was invited to begin the members' progress reports.

His main contribution was to confirm that the cracks in his specimens had definitely extended during his tests, though the growth was small. Dorinda thought that this was an important result, though she pointed out that crack propagation would only be a problem if there were defects already present in the discs in the first instance. She believed that the rigorous inspection techniques employed, both at the manufacturer's works and by the customer's own inspection engineers, should guarantee that no such defects could be present in LP discs before entering service. This struck Dave as being a particularly significant point. It implied that some surface damage must occur whilst in service, before cracking could occur in high purity steam.

Dave followed Joe, presenting his latest results, including the suggestion of crack growth, of the pre-cracked specimens in his test rig, though it was early days. James, clearly pleased with himself, followed by reporting that at Slough they believed that they had made an important breakthrough. He thought that, when they heard the details, the committee would agree that a credible explanation for the turbine failure could at last be presented to the main Technical Committee. The other members, excepting Dorinda, were clearly taken by surprise at this statement and were intrigued to learn details. James, perhaps betraying his youth, was eager to enlighten them and with something of a flourish, produced copies of a draft report which, after assigning a number, Pauline distributed.

James began by saying that he had spent many hours poring over the power station records and had found what he believed was credible evidence for possible sodium hydroxide contamination of turbine steam, during the station's commissioning period in 1965. Difficulties during commissioning of the sodium hydroxide dosing equipment, had resulted in several periods of considerable overdosing into the boilers. The Winford chemistry staff had been conscious of the need to maintain alkaline conditions during this, most important, early stage in the life of the plant. The presence of these high values, albeit only for short periods, at a time when the operation of the boilers was also being fine-tuned, could easily have led to sodium hydroxide being mechanically carried over in the steam. As the routine at the station settled down these problems were rectified. Consequently by the time Number 3 turbine was operational, the boiler water chemistry was strictly controlled and the turbine steam of high quality. He paused at this point awaiting comments.

Joe was the first to respond and he said that he was pleased that at least the possibility of contamination of the turbine steam could be envisaged, which would support the suggestion that sodium hydroxide was responsible for the failure. It suddenly occurred to Dave that Joe, with the best will in the world, might not be completely unbiased. He represented the turbine manufacturers, after all, and it was in their interests to support the view that an operational problem was responsible for cracking, rather than any shortcomings at the turbine production stage. He did not voice this thought, however, but said that, though he agreed that James' suggestion was interesting, he felt that it was likely to be just one of a number of possible explanations and he would wish to await the results of the various tests in progress before going public. Henry characteristically did not hurry his response. He was a thoughtful man. When Dave had finished, he thanked James and acknowledged that his observations were important and may prove to be pivotal in the failure scenario. However, he went on to add, he was not clear how this latest information fitted in with the features on the fracture surface to which Dorinda and James had attached such importance previously.

"Well, now then," began James in a rush. He was almost beside himself with his enthusiasm. Clearly this was just what he'd been waiting for. He reminded the others that he had spoken about features on the fracture surface of the failed Winford disc at the last meeting. These, he said, had been further examined and in the case of the overspeed 'markers', there was some evidence to suggest that approaching the crack tip, which was shortly before the final failure, the distance between these increased. This, he continued, indicated an increase in crack growth rate. There was a rustling of papers as everyone found the page. Additional support for this suggestion, he added with relish, was seen from a similar pattern of increased spacing between the staining marks. He'd also mentioned these at the last meeting as evidence of a chemical deposit build up, probably sodium hydroxide. This could possibly trigger an increment of crack growth. Using the overspeed 'dating' markers on the crack surface, he had been able to estimate the actual period when the crack growth rate increased and, comparing this with the details from the Winford Power Station's operating log, this would correspond with a suspected operational error late in 1968.

James' excitement increased as he made this announcement and it was only with an effort of will that he managed to contain himself. The others waited in silence as he recovered his composure.

He explained that the error mentioned in the log related to a trial that was being undertaken on Number 2 turbine at that time, which entailed dosing hydrazine directly into the LP turbine steam inlet pipe. By 1968, the dosing of hydrazine into the boiler water, in order to remove oxygen and increase alkalinity, was well established at Winford.

He continued, "This chemical is prone to dissociate within the boiler system and loses its effectiveness later on in the steam cycle."

The trial mentioned was being conducted to evaluate the benefit of replenishing the hydrazine just as the steam entered the LP turbine. As this was only a temporary set-up for the duration of the trial, the dosing tank and pipework was not well labelled and colour coded in the usual way.

"We suspect that on the evening shift of 14th November 1968, one of the junior chemists may have accidentally contaminated this temporary hydrazine dosing tank with a small amount of sodium hydroxide solution, which was intended for the adjacent permanent sodium hydroxide holding tank. It seems more than a coincidence, I'm sure you will agree, that the timing of this incident, corresponding approximately with the time of our observed increase in crack growth, provides a plausible hypothesis for the introduction of sodium hydroxide into Number 2 LP turbine, less than a year before the disc failure."

Silence.

Henry was the first to respond. He could understand James' enthusiasm at this discovery. It could, as he had said, offer a possible explanation for caustic contamination of the steam in the case of the failed turbine disc. The coincidence of the timing of this possible error, with features on the fracture surface, was compelling. He congratulated James upon the clearly tedious task that he'd undertaken into the history of the early turbines at Winford.

Dave reminded the meeting that any hypothesis had to explain the presence of cracks in the discs on the spare rotor which had failed in the test at Runcorn. Dorinda responded to Dave's remark by pointing out that the disc from the spare rotor, which had disintegrated during the Runcorn rig test, had previously been in service at Winford for around 30,000 hours before being refurbished and held as a spare. This rotor had accrued these hours in Number 1 turbine, from commissioning right through to the beginning of 1968 and therefore had been in operation during the early period of poor water/steam chemistry control. She continued by reminding Dave that it now appeared, from Joe's recent results, that pre-existing defects could propagate during subsequent service in uncontaminated steam. This, they believed, could have been the case for vulnerable discs on the LP rotors in both Numbers 1 and 2 turbines. In the case of the failed rotor in Number 2 turbine, there was an extra suspicion of caustic contamination of the steam more recently due to a possible dosing error.

She concluded by pointing out that not only the SSA, but also other electrical utilities, would be gratified to learn that the cause of the Winford incident could, at last, be fully explained. Operators would be especially relieved to learn that the disc cracking was confined to the first two turbines at Winford and was associated with incidents of steam contamination. Therefore they could feel confident about the continued running of all other turbines.

Joe commented that on the face of it, this seemed a most plausible explanation for the West Winford incident, certainly the most plausible to date. He believed, however, that the details needed close inspection, not only by themselves within the sub-committee, but a mixture of academics and practical power station engineers, especially those with a knowledge of boiler operation. The whole hypothesis required verification and he felt that it was people such as the ones he'd mentioned, that could supply it. Dorinda said that she was pleased with the comments received and agreed completely with Joe. They had already addressed the need for wider comment and had initiated plans to hold a conference. This would take a few weeks to arrange, as they would wish to ensure that people of sufficient quality would attend and so, hopefully, arrive at an authoritative consensus. Dorinda concluded by adding that everyone realised how important it was for the whole of the power supply industry to solve this problem.

Dave travelled home in something of a daze. On the one hand, he realised that the main point of the sub-committee was to solve the problem of the Winford failure as quickly as possible and so accepting the Slough hypothesis would be good news all round. Nevertheless, he was despondent from his own point of view. Whilst he felt that he had represented SSD well and had initiated a viable work programme in a timely manner, he had barely made any contribution to the experimental programme. He had had such high hopes, secretly held, that this was his big chance to impress. He consoled himself with the thought that at least he had benefited by becoming acquainted with Professor Fletcher and the others, which wouldn't do him any harm. He could only hope for other opportunities.

16

Sue's next opportunity to continue with her research arose sooner than she had expected. Pam arrived at her door one morning to beg a cup of tea and a chat.

"I haven't spoken to an intelligent person for days," her friend complained. "Sure, old Cummings is pretty competent as far as physical pleasures are concerned but when it comes to quantum mechanics, well, he just looks at me as though I were mad."

"Oh, dear!" replied Sue, "My physics education ended with a magnet and a pile of iron filings."

"Well, in that case, we'll just have to settle for village gossip," suggested Pam with a laugh.

The two chatted pleasantly over their tea and biscuits and inevitably the subject of Sue's latest family history finds was raised. She explained that, whilst she had discovered an enjoyable and absorbing pastime, it was also a frustrating one. It was a stop – start process, dependent upon trips to London. Pam delighted Sue by revealing that one reason for her visit was to offer to take her up to town for the day later that week, as she was planning to oversee some repairs to the flat. On reflection, she thought that, if Sue fancied a girls' night out, they could go up the evening before. Sue, though tempted, declined. Her present relationship with Dave was such that she would prefer not to add to the tension, though, of course, she didn't mention that to Pam. Accordingly it was agreed that an early start on the day would suit best.

Pam's mode of driving followed its usual pattern, which Sue would probably describe, oxymoronically, as controlled recklessness. Pam certainly knew her way around London which, combined with her positive driving style, ensured that she negotiated even the central areas with remarkable adroitness. On several occasions she drew grudging admiration from 'cabbies' as she weaved between them. After dropping Sue off in Chancery Lane, Pam continued on to her flat in Judd Street. She had given Sue directions to the flat, where they would meet at five thirty.

The part of the Public Records Office which dealt with the census returns was located in a tall building in Portugal Street, which was a short walk from Chancery Lane.

The most useful censuses for family historians were those for the three years 1841, 1851 and 1861. The hundred year confidentiality rule, meant that the 1871 was not due to be released to the public for several months.

Sue found this first visit unnerving. The records were stored on rolls of microfilm which had to be read on a film reader. The indexing search system seemed complex, especially when a large town or city district was involved. Eventually, with help from others, Sue located and noted the necessary reference numbers needed to complete the request form required to order the desired roll of film.

She wished to consult the 1851 census. Her first request was for records covering the village of Woolpit, in the hope of finding her Boughton ancestors. Whilst waiting for the film, she searched the Kensington index, looking for the address given on James Loomes' birth certificate and, on finding this she ordered a second film.

Sue was nervous when the box containing the roll of film for the Woolpit area arrived. She was all fingers and thumbs, attempting to load it on to the roller and feed the film through the lens mechanism and onto the take-up spool. She had noticed a list of place names written on the side of the film box and she correctly assumed that these were other Suffolk villages in the neighbourhood of Woolpit, which were included on the same roll, presumably filmed in the order listed. With great anticipation, she wound the film through quickly as the list indicated that Woolpit was about half way through the roll. At last, she slowed and there it was, Woolpit. After a few pages, that indescribable pulse of elation. Did she make a sound? Certainly she inwardly squealed.

James Boughton – her, yes her, very own great, great grandfather, together with his wife Sarah and their family. Their son Thomas, her great grandfather, just as she'd hoped, was aged eight and born in Woolpit. James was born in a place called Pulham in Norfolk. Could that be the home of her more distant Boughton ancestors? She shakily made a careful note of everything on the page relating to this family and after rewinding, she returned the film to the desk clerk, hoping to collect the Kensington one. Alas, she was told, that it was already out being used by another researcher. What a nuisance. Couldn't be helped. Time was moving quickly and as she didn't wish to sit idly awaiting the return of that particular film, she decided to begin her search of the 1851 returns for Brighton, in an attempt to locate the two Caroline Pottens, one of whom was her great grandmother. She found the index giving the film reference number which covered Upper North Street, where one of the Caroline Pottens had been born, four or five years earlier. She put in her order and went back to check the indexes for the film number for Chichester Street, which was where the second Caroline Potten had been born.

The first Brighton film arrived and after a long search through, checking the folio numbers at the top of the filmed pages, she found Upper North Street and spooled the film slowly forward to house number forty one. Another inward squeal. Thank goodness. The Potten family were still living there. She again made notes, though she already knew the basic facts about Caroline and her parents. There were six children listed with the youngest having the unusual name of Octavia who, in 1851, was eleven months old. She also learned that Thomas, her possible great, great grandfather was forty five at the time and had been born at Sedley in Kent, which might be another of her family bases.

That was the last of her positive results, for that day at least, as the second Caroline was no longer at the Chichester Street address. So it looked as though she would have to systematically search through all the many rolls of film covering the Brighton area, which could take several hours. She rechecked at the information desk and found that the Kensington film had still not been returned, so she considered how best to use the remaining time. She was in a cheerful mood as she decided to make a start on the trawl through some of the Brighton census. She managed to complete a couple of spools of film. Even though the result was negative, it meant that she would have less to do in future.

Time to make her way to Pam's flat. Just one tube stop from Chancery Lane to Holborn and one on the Piccadilly Line to Russell Square. Following Pam's directions, Sue found herself outside the tall red-brick, art deco building in Judd Street. She went up to the sixth floor. The corridor onto which she alighted was warm and richly carpeted. The flat was small but comfortable. They had a light tea, as Pam had suggested that they stop on their way home, at a pub she knew near Hungerford and have something more substantial. After phoning Dave to check that all was well, Sue agreed.

*

Though Dave had agreed to hold the fort, he was far from pleased. He was still feeling disappointed with the recent developments within the sub-committee. Tony had been sympathetic, when Dave updated him on progress, but felt that if the evidence from the Slough labs was sound, it was likely to satisfy the SSA management. They would consider this especially timely as, should the Tories win the forthcoming election, they would almost certainly be scrutinising the performance of the SSA very closely. They would be reassured to learn that the turbine failure was the result of a one-off incident, rather than being a widespread problem. Controlling steam chemistry was the key factor, but that had always been appreciated. Tony added that the Central Laboratory staff themselves must be confident of their hypothesis, having set up a conference to publicise it. Dave had to agree, although he was inclined to the view that the main purpose of the conference had more to do with ensuring that they would get the credit for providing the answer to the widely reported West Winford Turbine Incident. His objection to this, he would claim, arose on account of the many engineers and scientists who had worked so tirelessly through the previous winter. It was their work that had provided the Slough people with most of the evidence and in return they would probably not even rate a mention. His own personal annoyance at being side-lined didn't help.

So Sue's absence from home did little to ease his feeling of disappointment. It was becoming increasingly apparent to him just how this obsession of his wife's was assuming ever greater importance. He felt that he was now relegated in her eyes, to little more than the breadwinner and useful child-minder. An additional irritation, though he was loath to admit it, was her relationship with this Peter.

When Sue finally arrived, her buoyant mood was quickly quenched by Dave's evident ill humour. Although not venturing to criticise her and risk an argument, his restraint did not go unnoticed. After all these years he could not conceal such feelings from her. She knew well enough when an atmosphere was just waiting in the wings. On this occasion, she decided to avoid confrontation, though this resulted in prolonging the uneasy, cool, manner that existed between them. In retrospect, a row might have been preferable.

The following morning Dave was surprised to receive a phone call from Henry Fletcher.

"I'm calling to let you know that the Slough people have set the date for the conference. It is to be held on the 26th of June in London. In view of this, I have decided not to hold our usual monthly sub-committee meeting. We shall all be at the conference and should anything urgent arise, we can have a get-together there. Miss Sage is advising the others, but I wanted to speak to you on a separate matter." Henry went on to say that he'd received an approach from the British Standards Institution, who were in the process of considering the situation regarding commonly used corrosion test methods. They wanted advice from experts on the desirability of standardising the variety of routine corrosion test methods, used throughout British industry.

He'd been asked to set up a meeting of leading corrosion scientists and engineers to consider the question. He was intending to hold this meeting in London on the day before the conference, as several of the experts he had decided to invite, including Dave, would be in London for the conference. Dave was delighted.

"I look forward to receiving the details, Henry, many thanks."

With almost indecent haste, Dave phoned Pauline. He would be in London on the evening of the 25th of June and would be staying over for the conference. He wondered if she would like to redeem her voucher for an Italian meal. After a quick diary check, this was arranged.

The main feature of the BSI meeting, from Dave's perspective, was the pleasure of being in such august company. He was the only unknown. He was relieved to find that, despite this, he was warmly welcomed into their midst. As for the meeting, it was agreed, after lengthy consideration, that there was indeed a need to standardise the most commonly used test procedures and a committee should be set up to undertake this work. Henry was pleased with the outcome and would report to the BSI secretary. Understandably, Dave's mind was in something of a turmoil, as he travelled the short distance from Green Street to The Bonnington Hotel. He was nervous as he took a shower and prepared himself for his date. This was unfamiliar ground for him. He correctly assumed that things would be very different now from what they had been at the time of his last date, almost twenty years earlier. He met Pauline in the downstairs bar and they made the short walk to the restaurant. The meal was excellent and the house red (Pauline was quite happy with that, she assured him) was very palatable. They chatted unselfconsciously and Dave was surprised that it was only a little after eight o'clock when they left. He was in a strangely expansive mood and insisted that he would escort her home, adding that he was allowed out until after dark these days. It was an easy trip to Shepherd's Bush from Holborn, Central Line all the way, so after a short time, Pauline let Dave into her flat, just off The Green.

Although he hadn't known what to expect, his imagination had conjured up a vague idea of Pauline's private life – he could hardly have been more mistaken. Immediately his vision of Pauline, together with one or two fellow professionals, occupying well-appointed flats in a spacious Victorian house, was shattered when he found himself in what could best be described as a cramped girls' squat. The cheap furniture in the sitting room was bestrewn with skirts, tights, bras and other assorted underwear. Unwashed cups and plates decorated many of the level surfaces around the fireplace. He found a seat on a sofa, as Pauline went off to change. Almost immediately, the two 'fellow professionals' burst into the room, one of whom was almost fully dressed, the other almost fully undressed. They giggled and asked if he was Lena's Dave. He supposed that he was. He was embarrassed. These girls were barely older than Jo, who in no time might be living in a place like this. He was genuinely amazed. He was familiar with the notion of the generation gap but until now he'd not fully appreciated it – a completely different world.

This initial impression, in itself, was sufficient to convince him that he was out of his depth in this unfamiliar environment, but the transformation in Pauline on her return compounded his confusion. It was not merely a question of the casual costume, beguiling though her new ensemble was, but an astonishing change of her whole personality as she exchanged banter with her flat mates. Surely this wasn't the Miss Pauline Sage, secretary to the West Winford Corrosion Sub-Committee?

"Coming down The Grapes, Lene?" asked Tina – the undressed one. Pauline said maybe later as she seated herself beside Dave, after consigning a half empty crisp packet to the floor. Eventually they were alone.

"Now we can have a drink, if those two madams haven't found it."

They obviously hadn't, as Pauline returned with half a bottle of gin and a couple of glasses. Dave, though not a gin drinker, was pleased to top up his alcohol level as he was still feeling uncertain as they sat side by side. As he put down his empty glass, Pauline, aka Lena, turned and kissed him enthusiastically, pushing him backwards against the arm of the sofa. He could feel her urgent breasts pressing into his chest and realised only a thin T-shirt covered her. He slid his hands beneath and she sighed as he caressed her – she felt warm, smooth and moist. She pulled away and began to remove his shirt. He began clumsily, trying to help. His tie tangled around his ears. They needed to stand, fumbling, and then staggered towards her room. Lena lay on the bed and wriggled out of her mini-skirt, whilst Dave attempted the difficult task of removing socks, trousers and pants, whilst trying to look cool. They lay naked and entwined. He was urgent and insistent and moved on top of her quickly. He was keen to establish himself as in control, credible, but it was a clumsy attempt. They coupled and Dave was firm, insistent, as he moved. Lena relaxed, still, seeming to submit. It was a ploy. As he moved with increasing urgency she did not succumb. Dave was almost at the height of his passion but he sensed a change and he paused. She moved gently, slowly turning whilst maintaining their contact. Gradually she moved on top. He was stilled. She moved, swaying gently, then firmer – releasing – firmer again – relaxing – harder still, as they moved together. He submitted, following her lead. The rhythm gradually increasing. Dave was now at the point when satisfaction beckoned, his breathing increased. It was amazing. Then, as he approached the height of his desire, she slowed, relaxed, lowering Dave's passion gently. He moaned. The passion built again. How many times he couldn't say. Then finally, at last, the craved-for ecstasy. He was taken at her insistent command.

Breathing deeply, satisfied, they lay together. The door burst open.

"Oooh! Sorry. Just letting you know Jake's got a party going upstairs. See you later."

Dave dressed quickly. He declined the party invitation and after making his farewells, left to catch his late tube back to normality, his head buzzing. Unsurprisingly, the whole episode led to a sleepless night, not entirely due to an excessive consumption of alcohol.

★

The conference on the Environmental Aspects of the Failure of Number 2 Turbine at West Winford Power Station took place at the Institute of Mechanical Engineers' Headquarters in Birdcage Walk. It was well attended. Dave was still struggling to get back onto an even keel. The combination of alcohol, lack of sleep and a feeling of disorientation, were taking their toll. He did his best to disguise his discomfort, as he joined Tony and the other representatives from the Scientific Services Department, including Sweety and Bunsen, who had travelled up from Wiltshire that morning. They took their seats near the front of the conference hall. Dave's head throbbed. In addition to those involved with the power industry, there were many other scientists from the chemistry and corrosion fraternity.

Dave recognised two eminent university professors, both of whom had been at the BSI meeting, seated behind him. Slowly, he recovered his composure and began to take more notice of his surroundings. Despite his prejudice, he had to admit that the whole meeting was conducted with great aplomb. All the presentations, detailing station design, operation, steam chemistry, failure analysis and so on, were excellently delivered with high quality slides.

There followed an open debate on what had been presented and on the validity of the Slough hypothesis. Some discussion arose suggesting that this significant conclusion, having major practical and safety implications, was being grounded upon, what was after all, relatively circumstantial evidence. As Dorinda McCann began to respond to this point, with some vigour, Dave was surprised to hear one of the eminent men behind him commenting that he couldn't understand what all the fuss was about, as this was as clear a case of caustic cracking that he'd ever seen. Even allowing for the circumstantial nature of the evidence, it was generally agreed that this was the most likely explanation – after all what were the alternatives? The conference came to an end and the Chairman, the Chief Scientist of the National Laboratories, made his closing remarks, which included the intention to publish the results widely, in the leading international scientific journals. To Dave's dismay, he went on to announce that the Technical Investigation Committee and its sub-committees would be disbanded at the end of the year. This would allow all those involved to bring their ongoing investigations to an orderly conclusion.

Dave's shock and disappointment was understandable. He felt that he had missed out upon his own advancement within SSD by becoming involved with this investigation, instead of being focussed upon his project studying marine corrosion. His technical assessment, although only a few months away, would almost certainly have yielded a positive result if he had been able to obtain even some preliminary results from his Thornton trials.

His initial reaction was to terminate the Winford work quickly and move onto his Thornton project. Hardly had he settled upon this course of action, when his stubborn nature intervened. No, he wouldn't just give up like that. He wasn't convinced about the Slough theory. He had the rest of the year to run down the investigation, but what would the sub-committee members and more importantly, his own managers have to say?

"Come on David, you're invited too." His thoughts were interrupted by Sweety, who was clearly making the most of being associated with top managers from the SSA, who had been attending the conference. Indeed, there was something of a party atmosphere developing amongst these, as the other delegates left. A light buffet had been set up in an adjoining room for participants and invited guests and this was being supervised by staff from the SSA press office. Henry appeared to be slightly abashed as he was engulfed amongst a group of senior executives, who were paying him homage. It seemed that the national press, who had been in attendance, had gone off to file their reports on the satisfactory conclusion to the investigation of the West Winford incident. The cause, they had learned, was the result of contamination of the turbine steam due to the carry-over of sodium hydroxide from the boiler water during the early commissioning of the power station in 1965. Only turbines Number 1 and 2 had been in operation at the time and these, together with Number 3 turbine had been taken out of service, pending refurbishment of their LP rotors. No further action was deemed necessary.

As Dave travelled home, the lunch-time drink having settled his stomach, he couldn't help feeling surprised and disappointed to find how easily people seemed to accept what he considered, at best, to be only circumstantial evidence. In the case of the suspected dosing error on Number 2 turbine, for example, Bunsen had recently chatted to one of his chemistry pals from Winford and had learned that it was very unlikely that the dosing mistake had in fact taken place. However, the Station Chemist, being a scrupulous man, had insisted that the possibility, however remote, ought to be included in the station operational log.

Despite his own reservations, Dave was, it appeared, in a minority, as the others were clearly pleased with the outcome. The most important point in his view, which had been neglected, was the crack initiation phase. If steam contamination had not occurred and the discs did not contain any original defects then just how could cracking occur? This was an aspect which required urgent attention. Having decided that this would be his next task, he settled into his seat and allowed himself the luxury of recalling the previous evening.

He marvelled at the difference in Pauline. He had seen films in which the rather dreary secretary was suddenly transformed into a beauty, as she discarded her horn-rimmed spectacles and roughly tumbled her hair out of its restraining pins, but this was quite different. In addition to her appearance, Pauline's whole personality had changed. As Pauline, she appeared to be a smartly dressed woman, late twenties, privately educated, who fulfilled her role as a secretary with remarkable efficiency and charm – ideal for her position in the civil service. Lena, on the other hand, appeared to be an irresponsible teenager, making the most of her first year away from home at some city college, majoring in sex and drink – given a favourable interview she might be lucky to get a job in the corner shop.

It had all been so different with the girls in Dave's own era. In the early 1950s you generally had to show a clear intention to marry a girl before you got so much as a feel and even then it was confined to the outside of her sweater. He supposed it was the pill that was mainly responsible for the change. His next thought was when he could realistically contrive to see Pauline, or rather Lena, again.

17

Sue laid her book aside. The words were blurring through her tears and not for the first time during the past month. She sensed that things were getting out of control. Certainly her life had improved with her interest in family history, her friendship with Pam and Peter, as well as the greater freedom that the car had brought. However, she viewed these as oases in the desert of her married life. They occupied a few hours amongst the weeks of isolation. Long days and even longer nights of loneliness. She had had nothing positive from her job search and she doubted that the response to her latest application would be any more successful.

Over the past few months the relationship between herself and Dave had gradually deteriorated. The reasons seemed clear enough, but the remedy more elusive. They were both doing their best to avoid open hostility, whilst channelling their energies into their respective passions. Although anxious to do everything necessary to keep their marriage stable, if only for the girls' sake, neither was prepared to retreat into the traditional roles accepted by previous generations. They were living in the second half of the twentieth century and things were changing. Women were not prepared to settle for the duties of wife and mother to the exclusion of everything else. One of the consequences resulting from these changes in attitude, was the threat it posed to the traditional concept of family life, a home tending to become a collection of individuals having their own aspirations foremost in their minds, rather than

the collective cause. But did it have to be that way? It seemed clear
to her that the reluctance of couples to adjust to changed
circumstances, was a major factor in the increasing incidence of
marriage breakdown. Would the concept of marriage survive into
the twenty first century?

Sue realised that in their own case the situation was aggravated
by a combination of unfortunate timing. She was approaching forty
and the girls were becoming increasingly independent, which was
the point in her life in which she would have anticipated greater
personal freedom. This had coincided with the move and the
consequential exciting changes in Dave's life. Quite understandably,
he could see a real opportunity for his long held ambitions to be
realised, but only if he applied himself. He had made it abundantly
clear that this was certainly no time to be thinking of increasing
family commitments. A nine-to-five mentality would get him
nowhere. So back to square one? Surely there was some room for
compromise? Something was nagging in the background.
Something missing within the present situation – it was love!

She understood Dave's increasing involvement with his work,
driven by his ambition, but the intensity was becoming
unreasonable. He barely showed any interest in family matters. He
just seemed to calculate the minimum involvement necessary to
maintain peace. Their sex life had gradually diminished and, now
become non-existent. She couldn't remember the last time it had
been anything other than a routine chore. Surely she was still
reasonably attractive? Whilst Dave patronised her, Peter showed a
genuine interest and not just because he was committed to family
history. He was interested in her as a person, an individual. Dave
might argue that he was like that when they first met, but that was
no reason for her to accept the present situation. She wanted a life
for herself, but also a shared life, shared experiences. It dismayed
her to imagine what things would be like after the girls had left and
Dave was a success. What then for her? Just someone to accompany

him? Would he accept it if the situation was reversed? Her feelings of frustration brought more tears. She had to do something, but she was reluctant to bring things to a head. In order to avoid that she decided to look for an opportunity to bring the spark back. The trip to Lynton, almost a year ago, had been so successful. If she could arrange something along similar lines, perhaps that would give them an opportunity for reflection.

★

As Dave reflected upon recent events, he became more philosophical. He had come to terms with the latest Winford developments. He still believed that, thanks to his involvement in the investigation, he was well on his way to bigger things. His professional life was moving to a new level. Membership of the Corrosion Sub-Committee had been a great experience. This had led to his invitation to participate in the BSI discussions and he was confident that this would prove to be a springboard to other opportunities.

Then there was Lena. No responsibility, no commitment, just pure selfish enjoyment. Lena, he felt sure, was just living for the moment. She was young, modern. There was plenty of time to settle down – so much more of life to experience first. Dave envied her generation. So different to when he'd left school. The importance of settling down in a job with a future was instilled in all of them. Marrying early had been part of it. He accepted that there were some benefits. Sue was a good wife and the girls were all that anyone could ask for, but it was all so restrictive somehow. He worked all the week, after which he had to accommodate Sue's wishes and spend time with Jo and Katy. Even his time away from work had to be spent in a rather proscribed way, with little spontaneity. What would things be like after the girls had left home? He and Sue together most of the time – a rerun of their parents' predictable, uneventful, lives. Just a few hours with Pauline had shown him there was so much more, at least whilst he was still active. It was clear that she lingered in his thoughts.

★

Circumstances were about to arise which, one might have thought, would have been conducive to promoting closer harmony between man and wife, but this did not turn out to be the case. It began when Dave made his next trip to Winford Power Station to attend to his test rig. He drove into the car park on a beautiful July morning. Climbing out of his car, he stretched himself comfortably. In spite of his lingering disappointment about the forthcoming closure of the investigation, he could not be too depressed on such a day. The sun was already providing a pleasant warmth as he looked across the bay. A wonderful day indeed. Were those lapwings amongst the grassy tussocks leading to the beach, he wondered? He thought that he would try to fit in a run across Winford Heath before lunch. He had to admit, even with the recent setbacks, his move from Fisher's Tubes had been for the best. The run-down of the Winford investigation, he thought, may give him sufficient time, before the next staff appraisals, to get some worthwhile results from his Thornton Power Station experiments.

As he made his way into the turbine hall, he was conscious that this might be his last visit, at least in connection with this dying project. After opening the test vessel, he removed the specimens and wrapped each separately for the journey back to the lab. The test had been running for 3,000 hours, which was about one tenth of the time the failed LP disc had been operating, before the incident.

He had plenty of time for a run. This was a wonderful area to run across, mainly heathland with few restrictions to the public. After a shower and a sandwich, he drove back to the lab and delivered his specimens to the non-destructive testing engineers, for them to make their first inspection. He stressed the importance of avoiding contamination of the surfaces of the test pieces. They confirmed that this would be no problem with the pre-cracked specimens which they would x-ray, but they could not effectively check the plain specimens loaded in the test frame. The best that they could promise, as far as an in-situ test was concerned, was the careful use of dye-penetrant solution on a couple of the specimens on the outer edge of the group. Although this would contaminate the tested surfaces, they could protect the other specimens. Dave settled for this as he could discard these two specimens if he decided to return the others for further exposure at Winford.

★

Sue received a surprising phone call. She had just made a start on her new book, Mrs Dalloway. The man's voice clearly betrayed a Midlands background. Having confirmed that it was Sue Harrison, formerly Turner, with whom he was speaking, he explained that he was her cousin Eric, Auntie Clara's son. He went on to say that his mother had passed on to him some family papers before her death and, having heard from their Uncle Stan, about her research into their family's history, he was interested in learning how she was progressing. He lived in Fordingbridge, which wasn't far and he wondered if they could meet. He realised that it was short notice but he would be passing through Chippenham the following day, on his way to visit an old RAF pal, and wondered if she might be free for an hour, late morning. Although a little wary, Sue welcomed any opportunity of talking to anyone who had an interest in, better still might be in a position to make a contribution to, her research. She agreed and suggested the local pub.

The Marden Arms was quiet when Sue arrived, having enjoyed the walk through the Highwood Estate. She would have no trouble spotting Eric. She had a recollection of seeing him at a family wedding when she was about ten and he would have been in his early twenties. When Eric arrived Sue waved rather unnecessarily, considering there was only Sam and his local wag in the bar. He joined her and placed a carrier bag on the floor by the table, before collecting drinks.

After a trip down memory lane, Eric steered Sue into her well-practised spiel. Eric expressed surprise with the progress she had made. He was able to add some colour to her recent findings with a few anecdotes. She was amused, as he related a variety of incidents relating to the Turner side of the family. Being about ten years older, he could recall some events unknown to Sue. On several occasions she had cause to laugh out loud as Eric dug deeper into his store of gossip. She found him a joy.

"Anyway, enough of these preliminaries." Eric reached down into his carrier bag and brought out a tattered bible. "Thought you might like this. As I'm on my own now, it's likely to be of more use to you than to me." Sue was delighted though embarrassed and suggested that she would be happy just to borrow it. Eric insisted. He was content for it to have a good home. He handed it to Sue, who carefully opened it.

"Oh my goodness! How absolutely wonderful," she cried, when she saw that inside the front cover was a list of hand written notes with names and dates of various family occasions. At the top there was the name 'Caroline Potten, Brighton 1863' in copperplate. This was the great grandmother whom she was attempting to identify from the two candidates. At Eric's prompting, Sue found more entries on the back sheets.

"I can't believe it," laughed Sue, her enthusiasm drawing attention from Sam behind the bar. Eric explained that his mother, Sue's Auntie Clara, had been keen to keep family business private. He would have contacted her earlier had he realised its significance. He allowed Sue to buy him another half of bitter before leaving.

★

"We've been trying to contact you," said the voice on the phone. "George here, Non Destructive Testing. We've been having a look at your specimens and you may be surprised to know that we've detected significant cracking. Thought you'd want to know straight away."

Dave said that he'd be over shortly. He didn't think that it was surprising that crack growth had occurred in the pre-cracked specimens. After all, he had noted the suggestion of crack growth during his earlier inspection at Winford. The tests had been running for some weeks since then and the use of x-ray techniques was much more sensitive. This result would not be a surprise to the other sub-committee members, as Joe had already reported crack growth in his laboratory steam rig. It would, however, be interesting to compare the rates of growth between the two tests.

George, after lighting his pipe, took Dave through the results. All the pre-cracked specimens showed an increase in crack length, in other words the pre-existing crack had penetrated more deeply during exposure to the Winford turbine steam. "Well, that's great. Thanks George. Everyone should now be convinced that a defect in a disc could extend in normal service in an LP turbine without any contamination present and so, all similar turbines are at a slight risk. It may be just good luck or good pre-assembly inspection, that has prevented other failures. I suppose it might be argued that only defects that are sharp and 'crack like' in shape could cause this growth and the presence of these is unlikely. I'll go and knock out a brief report for the sub-committee."

"Aren't you interested in the others, that are loaded into that test frame?" asked George, indicating the assembly on the opposite bench with the stem of his pipe. Dave confirmed that he was, if only for the record. He was wondering whether it might be worth putting those back in the test vessel for further exposure. He might as well use the Winford rig until the end of the year when the job finally closed. "I thought that you'd like to know that they're already cracked, at least the two that we checked are," said George. Dave was shocked, he couldn't believe it. Surely there was some mistake? Of course, the confined space within the test frame would make it difficult to examine the specimens in any detail, so it was probably a misinterpretation. George assured him that, although it had been tricky, they had been able to do the job. There was no doubt that the samples checked were cracked and well cracked at that.

Dave was shaking as he carried the test frame back to his own lab. Gritty caught Dave's mood as soon as he heard the news. He took the frame to the do-it-yourself workshop and cautiously slackened off the load from the two specimens tested and carefully removed them. Dave examined the length of both of the specimens under a high-powered bench microscope. Some discolouration in the black surface film was evident. What did Gritty think? He was not sure.

"Bugger it, let's sacrifice one of them," declared Dave decisively.

They assembled one of the specimens into a tensile testing machine, which was normally used for stretching specimens to failure to assess tensile strength and other mechanical properties. They gently applied an increasing load, which gradually stretched the Winford test piece. As they began and before any appreciable load had been applied, they were amazed to see small cracks opening up along the surface. Normal steel test pieces, loaded in this way, would gradually distort and not show surface cracking until very near their failure load.

"Bloody hell, it's cracked to buggery, I can't believe it." Gritty and Dave almost danced around the lab. They decided to continue loading this specimen to failure, upon which it was clear to see, on the otherwise bright fracture surfaces, a crescent shaped area of discolouration. This was the area of the stress corrosion crack and was almost identical to the appearance of the fracture surface on the failed Winford disc. The procedure was repeated on the second specimen with a similar result. Following this, Dave asked Gritty to carefully remove one of the other specimens, which had not been exposed to the NDT dye-penetrant fluid. He was delighted to find this also cracked. The other specimens were left undisturbed so that they could be used for demonstration purposes for anyone doubting their claims.

Dave was shaking as he took in the serious implications of this discovery. He was delighted, as he believed that he had produced the most unexpected result in the field of stress corrosion for years. Stress corrosion cracking in high purity steam! No one would believe it, but he had the proof. He had his specimens and he had Bunsen's steam analysis. The steam quality had remained high throughout. He didn't know what to do. He called Mike Pearson and Bunsen, both of whom had been so helpful to him. Ian had already arrived having been attracted by the noise of the two of them.

A couple of hours later Dave was still in a daze of pleasure. He was brought back to earth quite suddenly, as he realised that his personal joy at the findings would not be shared by the Authority or other utilities operating turbines of the Winford type. These results would send shock waves through many organisations. All turbines of this type were at risk of sudden catastrophic failure. Many had been in operation for much longer than Number 2 turbine at Winford. It was only the fact that the Winford discs had been unusually brittle that caused failure with such small cracks present. Other LP turbine discs still in service would, almost certainly, contain cracks and possibly some deep ones. There had already been one fatality resulting from the Winford failure. Next time, things could be much worse. Though there were usually few people around turbines under normal operation, more were present when measurements were being taken, or during turbine run ups, shut downs and overspeed testing.

Time was getting on and Dave was anxious to make a start on writing his report. He had the odd irrational fear that if he didn't claim the credit for this unexpected discovery, someone else would beat him to it – probably tomorrow. There was no point phoning Sue to tell her the news and say that he might be late home, as he knew that, as it was Friday, she would be at her blessed Peter's group indexing.

He settled to his work. Ian helped initially by taking a selection of photographs of the specimens and their cracks. They had photographs of the specimens before testing and the Station Chemist at Winford had taken a nice shot of the test rig in operation. Gritty cut a couple of sections through one of the specimens and prepared them for examination under an optical microscope. These showed other cracks, typical of stress corrosion, which he photographed. Soon Dave had all the illustrations that he needed and his colleagues went off on their weekend.

He stayed on and wrote his draft report, outlining the object of the experiment, and the on-site equipment details, together with the specimen design and purpose. He added the steam analysis record, quoting maximum and minimum values for impurities, which were miniscule. Then, finally, the results and a brief discussion, with such great pleasure, followed by his conclusions and recommendations. It was just past midnight. He spent the weekend putting the final polish to his report, which he would get typed first thing on Monday.

18

Sue was delighted with the Potten family bible which, via the Loomes family, came down to the Turners. It was heirlooms such as this that family historians loved to possess – a tangible link with their past. It had been her great grandmother Caroline's, whichever one of the two candidates she turned out to be. Caroline would have been seventeen years old when she wrote her name inside the cover in 1863. Amongst other things, she had listed the name of her husband and their children. The bible had been passed down to Sue's grandmother, Caroline Jane, who had carried on the tradition, recording her marriage and children's birth, including Sue's father. This was wonderful. She could now add more detail on her Turner 'family tree'.

Sue was overcome by her great grandmother's foresight and she determined, despite her difficulty with the Potten line, that this was one ancestor whom she felt an obligation to pursue, and she would. That being accepted, Sue decided that she should narrow down her research, for the present, to two families – the Boughtons and the Pottens – as these appeared to be the most fruitful.

Her thoughts turned to the forthcoming summer holidays. She knew that Barry and Velma were planning to go to Hunstanton. She wondered if they would mind having Jo and Katy along for part of their stay. There was no doubt that the cousins would welcome their company. This would give her and Dave the chance to spend time together. Impulsively she phoned Velma and found that she was happy to help out, positively enthusiastic about the whole idea. Velma and Sue's sister had intuited, from their weekly phone calls, that relations between Sue and Dave were shaky at present. So Velma's enthusiasm was, in part, a kindness to her sister-in-law as much as a favour for the girls.

Dave's euphoric mood lasted for days and he gladly endorsed Sue's suggestion. He thought that he could take a few days off work, following the forthcoming sub-committee meeting. This would allow time for all his colleagues to digest his fantastic results, especially those smoothies at the Slough labs, he thought with relish.

"These are great results David."

Tony had already scanned Dave's report on the on-site rig experiments. He was pleased as this would be a feather in the Department's cap. He would discuss it with Sweety. They considered the wider implications of the results. Tony was thinking of how best to present them to the general scientific community.

"Is this the first time that stress corrosion cracking of steel has been observed in high-purity water or steam?"

Dave replied that from his own knowledge, plus an extensive literature search, it was the first time in the case of medium strength, mild or low alloy steels. Tony, after pausing for a moment, demonstrated to Dave one of the qualities of a good section head.

"If your results are correct, how do you explain the pattern of cracking found in other turbine discs on the failed rotor? I understood from the conference, the Slough people were arguing that the most severe cracking occurred in the inlet region of the LP turbine, where there was the greatest concentration of steam impurities and it was this contamination which caused the cracking." Dave was taken aback, not by the question itself but rather that Tony had been astute enough to ask it. Clearly he had been keeping up with all the developments and understood the detail of the investigation. Dave replied that the observed pattern of cracking could still be explained if no contamination had been present, by virtue of the temperature variation along the LP rotor. The main requirement was that moisture was present, which it was, albeit cycling between wet and dry, near the inlet. The operating temperature of the various discs depended upon their position on the rotor, the hottest being near the steam inlet. This was where the worst cracking would be predicted. As the steam cooled the extent of cracking would be less severe, with little or no cracking near the steam exit. So the pattern of cracking was as expected, even without steam contamination. Tony thought about what Dave had said and after a moment, he suggested that Dave should begin preparing a scientific paper as, he believed, it would take some time to get into print. He should contact the editor of, say, *Corrosion Review* to obtain their instructions to authors.

"This is just the kind of thing that the Strategic Supplies Authority needs to fend off their critics. Let's get our own trumpet blown as soon as possible. Well done David."

Dave reverted to the train for the next sub-committee meeting. He had been unable to arrange another overnight stay. His work had begun to build up again and he had agreed with Sue to take at least a week's break, whilst the girls were away.

In addition to producing a draft paper, he had begun laboratory tests in an attempt to resolve the most difficult problem of all – just how cracks could initiate in high purity steam. He envisaged that a crack-like surface defect was a necessary precursor to the process. Resolving this was an essential part of his hypothesis. He hoped that Pauline would understand.

On his arrival at the meeting room, Joe congratulated Dave upon his draft report, which he had received the previous day. He was pleased to see that their separate results of crack growth rates, were in good agreement. Dave was full of pride as the others arrived. Henry thanked him for the report and was as charming as usual. Dorinda and James avoided the subject and their conversation centred on the positive feedback they had received from the conference. True to form, Henry had kind words for them too. They took their places around the table. Pauline arrived on cue. She smiled pleasantly around the group without any obvious distinction to any member. Dave marvelled at her. He still could not believe it. Pauline was back to her civil service best. If only the others knew. He immediately dismissed this thought as Henry opened the meeting.

James expanded upon the comments that the Central Research Labs had received following their conference. Amongst them were several from noted authorities on the subject of stress corrosion, who agreed with the conclusion that sodium hydroxide contamination was the cause of the cracking and that mechanical carryover of this from the boiler water during commissioning, probably at times of high boiler water levels, was responsible.

Henry then asked an impatient Dave to introduce his draft report. Dave, bolstered by his pleasure at all the excitement within his own department over the last few days, made a competent presentation of his outstanding results. He concluded by asking the committee to agree to his report being submitted to the main Technical Committee's press office, for approval and permission to publish. He sat back and rather childishly hoped that, in addition to impressing his colleagues, Pauline had also been pleased.

"May I?" asked Dorinda, glancing towards Henry. Having received the slightest of nods, she expressed her grave doubts about the results obtained from the Winford test rig. In her view there were several potential flaws in the experiment, including the possible contamination of the specimens. This could have arisen in workshops, at the power station itself or during inspections. There was also the question of steam quality. She accepted that the bulk turbine inlet steam had been monitored throughout the trials and no contamination had been found. However, she and her colleagues felt that Dave did not fully appreciate all the aspects of their hypothesis, which had been presented at the conference. Their ideas on sodium hydroxide build up, she reminded them, were based upon the introduction of miniscule amounts of sodium hydroxide. Such amounts would not cause any concern to Dave's chemistry colleague, but, by an alternate wetting and drying mechanism, this would gradually build up to significant levels and initiate a small crack. This process would be repeated as evidenced by the pattern of staining clearly found on the fracture surface. As Dave listened to Dorinda, his initial feeling of shock gradually gave way to anger, which he did his best to hide. He replied that he had confidence in the continuous steam quality measurements. He reminded the others that the technique used was much more sensitive than the normal methods used on modern power stations. If these were being questioned, what were the value of any measurements elsewhere?

James, continuing Dorinda's theme, pointed out that these improved techniques were not being used when the suspected period of contamination took place. Dave, determined not to give ground, countered by reminding his fellow members that he felt his confidence in the rig results was supported by the fact that his growth rates were very similar to those obtained by Joe in his laboratory rig, where contamination was unlikely. James accepted this, but it was the question of crack initiation that was the issue, not its growth. The vital step in the whole Winford failure came down to this: just how did the cracks start in high purity steam? He pressed Dave on this point. Could he explain how cracks initiated in disc steel operating in high purity wet steam? Dave had to admit that he hadn't really got very far with his ideas on that aspect, but he still believed that his results were as valid as their own hypothesis. He became angrier and ended his argument by suggesting that Dorinda and James were biased towards their own tenuous theory. They didn't want his results to be circulated as this would cast doubts upon theirs. Joe, who, together with Henry, had been a spectator during these exchanges, found it amusing to observe the two rival centres within the same organisation clashing publicly in this way. Henry was more preoccupied with the likelihood of having to make a decision of how to resolve the difficulties.

To give Dorinda her due, she did not appear to take offence at Dave's personal outburst. She merely reiterated that there was the possibility of contamination in Dave's test and this should be addressed before proceeding. She continued by noting that their own hypothesis did not have the problem of explaining how cracks initiated, as everyone knew that sodium hydroxide would do this. All they had to suggest was a viable method of how it got there and this, she contended, they had done. Dorinda concluded by reminding Dave what he was asking the sub-committee to do. The frightening implication of his results was that many operating turbines around the world, were in imminent danger of blowing up, during normal operation. If the sub-committee agreed to circulate his report, they would be seen to be endorsing this possibility and therefore she felt that her colleagues were not being unreasonable in asking Dave to obtain some confirmatory evidence, to support his initial findings.

Henry politely called a halt at that point, suggesting that further discussion could be continued outside the meeting and a decision with regard to publication could be made. He assumed that it would take Dave a while to prepare his report in publishable form. Despite Dave's annoyance, he had little option but to go along with Henry's suggestion. The ramifications of this debate occupied Dave's thoughts for the remainder of the meeting, to the extent that his intention to try to have a quiet, private word with Pauline was forgotten. On his trip home he became calmer and gave some thought to the new situation and how he should proceed.

Could his specimens have been contaminated, as had been suggested? He didn't think so. After machining, the specimens had been carefully degreased and kept in a desiccator until the loading process and this had also been done under laboratory conditions.

Following exposure, he had handed them to the NDT people making a point of requesting that only the two specimens selected for examination be subject to the dye-penetrant solution, the others would be protected. So that left the steam itself. According to Bunsen, no measurable contamination had occurred and Dave respected his opinion. No, he was confident, the results were valid. However, the difficulty was in convincing others of that. He could repeat the experiment, but that may not be enough. He really needed a different approach. Such an alternative course of action occurred to him and he began to plan his next move. He would have to work quickly.

Firstly, assuming that the test rig results were valid and low strength steel could indeed succumb to stress corrosion cracking in high purity wet steam, there was no reason why it would not suffer the same fate in high purity hot water. It would be easy to carry out a standard laboratory stress corrosion test. He could use very high purity, laboratory grade, deoxygenated water, which would be free from contamination, and if the specimens were fully immersed, there would be no chance of concentration by evaporation occurring. That would be his next job.

Secondly, he would put extra resources into the work he'd just begun, looking into possible ways that a crack might be formed in turbine disc steel in high purity hot water.

*

"So we're at the bottom of your list of priorities as usual," complained Sue when Dave announced that he wouldn't, after all, be able to take any time off. She had spent part of the day making the final arrangements. "Well sod you, the rest of us are bloody well going." Sue was shaking with anger.

Dave, still smarting from his earlier setback, found it difficult not to enter into a full scale row and clear the air once and for all, but he realised that they would quickly lose their tempers, so he left the house and sought solace at The Marden Arms. He had a pint of 6X and reviewed his position. He had been under pressure since joining the SSA, one thing leading to another, with increasing urgency. He recalled recent events, with the preparations for the Winford trial. Firstly, the rush to obtain the necessary equipment and test pieces in time for the turbine outage, followed by the difficulties of getting everything set up on site. Added to this was Sue's constant nagging. He brooded and became increasingly morose; the cheerfulness of the pub was at odds with his mood. He left abruptly.

He drove aimlessly towards Marlborough and stopped at a small village pub. The smoke-filled bar was busy, mostly agricultural workers it seemed, but, being a stranger, Dave thought that he would be left alone with his thoughts. He ordered a pint and a whisky and found a vacant table in an alcove. He drank quickly and collected another pint. This did not improve his mood and he continued to feel sorry for himself. He had been so excited. All the hard work setting up the on-site tests, followed by the elation of the unexpected and significant results. The prospect of having a paper published, which would surprise many in the corrosion fraternity and have a major impact on power plant operators worldwide, had heightened his delight. All this was now being put under threat by those smug buggers at Slough.

"Don't want their own half-baked theory ditched. Well sod the lot of you!"

He became aware that some of the locals were looking across at him. He hadn't realised that he'd spoken out loud. They turned away and resumed their conversations and Dave ordered another pint and a small cigar. Sipping and smoking, his mood mellowed.

"Mr Harrison? I thought it was you."

"Wha? Janet?"

"You're a stranger over here and on your own."

"Just felt like a change. Wife trouble actually, and after the week I've had."

Janet was sympathetic.

"Anyway, how are you settling in amongst our typing girls? Can I get you a drink?"

"A lager please." She sat down.

Dave collected Janet's drink and another for himself. He was cheering up.

"I'm really enjoying the work and meeting all you engineers and scientists. So interesting and such a change from the folk around here." She looked across to the smoke-filled, crowded bar area.

He drew his seat nearer. She was an attractive girl.

"Well, we're very pleased to have you with us. You've certainly brightened up that office."

Janet smiled. He took another swig and clumsily put his hand on her thigh. Her eyes widened, though not with alarm, but amusement. They sparkled. Dave grinned.

There was a disturbance in the bar.

"Bastard!"

Dave turned to see a figure approaching. A young, heavily built fellow. He was red-faced, sweating. Dave stood, unsteadily, and turned towards him. A final rush and a swung punch. To Dave it seemed as if in slow motion. A massive fist approaching. He stepped away, alarmed. The drink was slowing his reaction. Just half a pace and he stumbled over the chair leg and fell backwards. He was lucky. By the time he had untangled himself, a couple of locals had pulled his attacker away whilst Janet berated him. They calmed the man and suggested to Dave that he should leave. He grumbled but complied. Janet followed him out apologising. He was a former boyfriend.

Dave was shaken and realised through the beer haze that he was making a fool of himself so, after mumbling an excuse, he drove home. The experience had had a sobering effect.

★

It was an uncomfortable household as Sue and the girls began their packing, having modified the arrangements with Velma. Sue did her best to ignore Dave – she had heard him noisily arrive home last night. The female Harrisons set off early, as the journey would take the best part of the day, including breaks. This had the advantage of allowing Sue's intense annoyance to abate. For the girls' sake she pushed these thoughts into the background and willed optimistic ones in their place. She felt that she ought to include her daughters in her thoughts about the present difficulties.

"I'm sorry that things are not very smooth at home just now, but I don't want you to worry. Your Dad and I are going to set things right again very soon. Dad has been so busy lately and has had a lot to deal with at work. You remember the accident, when a man was killed, I am sure. Well this has made Dad's job so important and he's desperately trying to find the answer, so that other accidents won't happen. Shall we try to cheer him up? A good start could be for us to take back some presents for him. A few sticks of rock and a 'Kiss Me Quick' hat. What do you think?"

They arrived just before tea time and were enthusiastically greeted by Barry, Velma and their children.

The location, Sue noted, was ideal for all the girls, as it was amongst the dunes and virtually on the beach. Velma announced that the forecast was fine weather for the week, and so they had all the makings for a perfect holiday.

"Oh! Sorry, I was forgetting about Dave," she quickly added.

"He's fine. Please don't worry about him. He's more than happy for us to be out of the way, just at the moment," Sue replied.

Barry and Velma exchanged glances, realising that this was a subject upon which Sue felt very strongly. Nevertheless it did, as Velma had predicted, turn out to be most enjoyable, with everyone being pleasantly occupied in their personal pursuits. The younger girls settled happily together, as usual, spending most of the daylight hours on the beach. Jo, being the eldest, had other interests she wished to pursue. She was now reading a good deal of young adult literature and also working to develop her artistic talents. Her focus was firmly set upon going to Art College. She had brought her brushes and paints and spent several days amongst the sand dunes at her easel. However, she didn't divorce herself completely from the other girls, as she had always been happy amongst them. She joined in many of their energetic games and once absorbed into the noisy excitement, was in danger of allowing her maturity to slip.

Sue was particularly pleased as, whilst she was in Norfolk, she decided to visit Pulham, which was the site of her Boughton family roots. She found Pulham to conform to her idea of a quintessentially English village. It had all the ingredients: village green with a pub at either end, thatched cottages and church. She was taken aback when she found the door of St. Mary's locked. She checked the notice board and was relieved to find that, although the minister was absent, the keys were held by one of the church wardens, whose address was given. She found the appropriate cottage and the courteous occupier escorted her back to the church and led her into the vestry, where he unlocked the chest containing the parish documents. He asked how long she required and when Sue hesitated, he suggested that he would return in about three hours, if she had not returned the keys before then.

Sue was overjoyed at being allowed this access, also that she was not under the pressure of being supervised. Although she had seen the old parish registers at St. John's in Bremham, it was still a tremendous thrill to handle the very old parchment volumes of Pulham, with their spidery hand-written entries dating back to the sixteenth century. Having spent a few moments savouring this pleasure, she settled down to work. Her starting point was the baptism of James Boughton which, she estimated, would have been around 1805. She had decided not to look for his marriage, to Sarah

Alexander, as this may have taken place in Sarah's home parish. Sue scanned the pages carefully.

"Yes!" That now familiar jolt of pleasure – James Boughton b. 8th Feb 1813. Son of Thomas and Harriet (Thorold). Thomas was an agricultural labourer. Sue had noted that there were quite a few other Boughtons listed amongst the entries. She decided that, rather than searching out selected entries, she would copy down any mention of a Boughton as she progressed. Later, in the comfort of home, she could attempt to build up the various family relationships. She worked steadily, each turn of the page moving her ever deeper into the past, filling several pages of her note book until, with a shock, she found that she had been busy for almost four hours. Carefully replacing the volumes upon which she'd been working into the chest, she returned the key to Mr Fiske.

As the sun was still shining brightly, Sue decided to stroll around the churchyard, where she found several Boughton headstones amongst the well cropped grass. She made a note of the inscriptions and was just copying down the details of a George Boughton, when a lady, who was walking along the nearby lane, stopped and chatted. She confirmed that the Boughtons had been a well-known family around the area and added that a former resident had written a history of Pulham families. If Sue was interested and wanted to leave her address, she would make a copy of any references to Boughton and send them on. Sue was most grateful – people could be so thoughtful.

The rest of the holiday was fun for all, the two sisters-in-law laughed a lot, the cousins became reacquainted as they updated each other with all developments 'girlie', as well as exploring the beach. Jo's painting efforts were applauded by the others – she seemed to have talent, they agreed. Barry, meanwhile, took every opportunity to relax with a novel or the newspapers.

"He reads to unwind," Velma explained. Sue thought that it was a tip that Dave could well learn.

19

Dave's hangover was not as severe as he'd expected, or deserved. His lower back was sore as a result of his fall. Gritty and Ian were surprised to see him engrossed in his work when they arrived at the labs. He explained what had happened and how necessary it was for them to get some irrefutable evidence to support their hypothesis quickly. When they heard of the sub-committee's reaction to his results, they were less severe in their assessment of the Slough scientists. They could appreciate the serious implications that publishing their results would have for power station operators. If it transpired that their conclusions were faulty – well it just couldn't be thought of.

"That's as maybe," grumbled a sceptical Dave, before outlining his plan to address the criticisms made, in relation to possible contamination in his rig trials. This would entail initiating additional laboratory tests. He wanted to expose stressed samples of disc steel, at four separate load levels, to hot, deoxygenated, high purity water.

Specimens, each enclosed in a glass vessel, would be fitted into their standard test machines and hot high purity, deoxygenated, water would be circulated through the vessels. Fortunately they had all the necessary equipment and ample test pieces in stock already. They had sufficient test machines to accommodate three specimens at each load, i.e. twelve in all. Dave wanted the load on each specimen continuously monitored throughout these experiments, using a chart recorder. If cracking occurred in any specimen, it should be accompanied by a fall in load.

He asked Ian to set up these tests immediately, whilst he and Gritty continued the vital task of investigating how cracks might initiate. This was the most difficult part of the process to explain and had been seized upon by the Slough people. Specimens of disc material would be prepared to obtain a highly polished surface. Some would then be immersed in hot sodium hydroxide, as it was known that this could cause stress corrosion and others in hot, high purity water. Samples would be removed after short immersion times to detect the first signs of corrosion. They were looking for signs of localised pitting, from which a crack might initiate and propagate under stress. Gritty and Ian sensed Dave's mood and his manner impressed upon them the vital importance that he attached to these, comparatively trivial, laboratory tests – surely such things had been done before? If they had any doubts they cast them aside and responded positively to his ideas.

Dave, anxious to see Tony, phoned Brenda, not for the first time, to remind her that it was urgent. Brenda assured him that she had not forgotten but, as Dr Honey had just returned from his holiday, Dr Richards would be with him for some time in order to brief him upon developments over the past three weeks. Tony had been covering for Sweety during his absence. She would let David know as soon as Dr Richards was available. Dave was irritated. He couldn't appreciate that the vital importance which he attached to the recent developments in the disc cracking investigation, wasn't shared by everyone else. His lack of perspective led him to believe that, whilst he sat around cooling his heels, Tony and Sweety were chatting pleasantly over coffee, as they browsed through holiday snaps. His mood did not improve an hour later when Brenda called to say that Tony would not be available that day.

It was the following morning before Dave reported on the adverse reaction that his draft report had received. Tony was taken aback, more by Dave's sensitivity and perhaps over reaction to criticism, than to the fact that the Slough people had made adverse comments. However, he attempted to soothe Dave's feelings. He thought that, whatever the outcome, it was a good piece of work and he was sure that Sweety agreed.

He continued by cleverly manoeuvring the discussion, so that Dave became calmer and accepted that, given the surprising nature of his results, it was only natural that confirmatory tests were necessary before publication. Tony suggested that it would be better for Dave to look at the situation objectively and resist the urge to assume that the Central Research Lab folks were his rivals. He had confidence in the results and was sure that their corroboration would be forthcoming, at which time Dave and his colleagues would reap the reward for which they hoped.

He asked if Dave had received any indication from *Corrosion Review* regarding publication times and learned that it would take about six months from the paper submission date before it would appear in print. Dave became more agitated and he reminded his Section Head that, if his results were confirmed, there would be an urgent safety issue to be addressed. Many turbines around the world were in danger of catastrophic failure, with possibly fatal consequences. The longer it took to get his results in print, the greater this risk.

Tony remained calm and pointed out that a balance had to be struck between acting on the information in a timely way, whilst avoiding unnecessary panic. It was on this note that Tony felt that the discussion should be left. Dave rose to leave but then recalled an additional point relating to external reporting. Although publication of a full scientific paper would take several months, he had been advised that it was possible to present significant information more speedily, as a technical note summarising the main points. Certain publications offered this facility and it seemed, that *International Power Digest* was such a journal. They prided themselves upon rapid dissemination of information and it was feasible to be in print within a month. He hoped that he could count upon Tony's support to do this, as soon as confirmation of his results was obtained.

Dave returned to his office and slumped into his seat. He felt nauseous. He had been on something of an emotional roller coaster since joining the SSA. It had started with anticipation and keenness, which was natural; from the first moment he felt that this was to be a springboard for his career. Excitement had followed with his involvement in this major project, which had attracted national newspaper coverage and then, to top it all off, his surprising and significant results. Surely this was the final piece. It was this gradual increasing level of expectancy that had made the criticism that he'd received from the Central Research Labs and the caution from his own management, so upsetting and had fuelled his paranoia. He had tested the patience of many colleagues, by taking every opportunity to complain about the situation that had arisen.

Mike Pearson was more patient than many. He thought the recent general election result was a possible factor affecting the situation. It certainly would be on the minds of the senior management within the SSA. This was a critical time for the Authority which, after all, had been the brain child of the Wilson government. Obviously they would be under close scrutiny by the new administration. Difficult times indeed. Everyone in the organisation was in no doubt that they had to prove their worth and in some respects, that implied playing it safe. No one in the Authority would wish to publicise the possibility that all their turbines were in imminent danger of catastrophic failure, in addition to the simmering problems regarding energy supplies already apparent. The Authority chiefs had a very strong incentive to keep all power stations running flat out and no questions asked.

"You can see their point," Mike concluded.

"But if a failure occurs and people get killed?" retorted Dave.

"The odds on that are pretty long, you have to admit," countered Mike. "As soon as next summer's outages begin then a major refurbishment and replacement programme will get underway. In two or three years, all turbines in the SSA will have been modified to prevent failure."

"There are many other similar turbines, in this country and worldwide, so it isn't just a matter of two or three years, the risk is much greater," Dave persisted.

"All we can do about that is to publish your results as widely as possible."

"That's my whole point," Dave announced triumphantly. He added that he had virtually completed the technical note and was just awaiting approval to submit it.

There was more disappointment for Dave when, seeking consolation, he phoned Pauline. He said how much he'd enjoyed their evening and couldn't wait to see her again. Could they arrange something without having to await the next meeting of the sub-committee? Her reply saddened him. She had also enjoyed the evening, but she kindly, though firmly, declined. She gave her reasons, which, in effect, amounted to not wishing to make commitments. It was nothing personal, she was just a spur of the moment person. This disappointment added to Dave's mental turmoil, which had not been helped by his loneliness in his empty house.

The next few days were tense for the whole group, who felt that Dave's crusade was their own. Some offered their help, by taking on additional tasks, allowing Dave, Gritty and Ian to concentrate on their tests. A concerted sense of purpose enveloped them all. Dave, though in a constant state of nervous expectation, appreciated the support of his colleagues.

It was to be a brilliant period for them all. Whilst falling short of the achievements associated with the discovery of DNA, nuclear fission, or the Big Bang theory, it was for them, in its own way, pretty remarkable.

Thursday, the 6th of August. There seemed nothing particularly auspicious in the way the rising sun breathed warmth and life into the sleeping earth. Just another day. It was quiet, but not unusually so considering it was the holiday season. Sue had phoned to say that the girls were extending their stay, so she would be arriving home alone on Sunday.

Dave was at work early as he had promised to comment on a report for Mike Pearson. Barely had he made a start, when Ian burst into the room clearly excited. He urged Dave to drop everything and come to the lab. Ian led the way at a trot.

"Take a look at specimen number 11."

This was one of the three highest stressed specimens. Immediately Dave could see why Ian was so animated; the chart recorder showed that the line being traced for that specimen was curving to the left. The load was dropping from its set value. Only very slightly, but it was definite. Ian's eyes gleamed, "It's beginning to crack."

Dave agreed that it could be due to the formation of cracks acting to relieve the load, though he couldn't really believe it. Hadn't dared to hope. He perversely sought to argue against it.

"Let's just hang on for a while Ian. It could be that this specimen is slipping in the grips of the machine. That would have the same effect."

Dave checked the traces for the other specimens, but could not detect any deviation from the vertical. Although he knew that he was being foolish, he sat staring at the trace for number 11 for several minutes, mesmerised, willing it to move more quickly in response to a rapidly falling load that would be the precursor to failure of the specimen. He felt that the load recorder mocked him as the chart just inched forward, unaware of and unmoved by, his personal wishes.

The following morning Dave headed straight for the lab. He hadn't slept well. As soon as he opened the door he realised that something special was happening. Ian and Gritty were gathered around the test machines. It was a scene that Dave would remember for some time. Their attitude typified the collective response from all his colleagues to what they regarded as the challenge from the Slough laboratories. They were not prepared to give in without a struggle. The whole subject had become a crusade for them, they had identified themselves with Dave's efforts – they felt part of it. So it was no surprise to find them taking a keen interest, gathered around the chart recorder. Dave found that, not only had specimen number 11 continued to reduce load but, the other most highly stressed specimens, numbers 10 and 12, were also clearly showing the same behaviour. There was no doubt. Great news.

Dave found it impossible to concentrate on his paperwork, ever conscious of what was unfolding just a few yards away in the lab. His impatience was not rewarded that day. When he visited the lab on Sunday morning he was elated when he found a specimen from the next load level, specimen number 7, showing a loss in load, indicating that it too had begun to crack. The others would surely follow. He sat in front of the bank of tests and lost all track of time. It was late afternoon before he returned home. All that time had passed unnoticed and so Dave hadn't been at home to welcome Sue back from her Norfolk trip.

★

Sue was travelling home alone to a place that she often felt alone. She became more pessimistic as she approached Wiltshire, fearing that her husband would still be caught up in his work and likely to be too absorbed to take advantage of their unexpected freedom. It seemed so long since their Lynton trip. She could see no alternative than having a serious talk with Dave. She would pick her moment.

Her plans were put on hold when she arrived home and found an invitation to attend a job interview amongst her post. She hadn't mentioned her job search to Dave, but no doubt the company logo on the envelope would have intrigued him. She would phone the company tomorrow. She was disappointed, though perhaps not surprised, to find that Dave was not home. Following a shower she unpacked.

It was a strange reunion, with Sue, so pleased with the holiday and her Pulham trip and now this job interview and Dave so energised by the combination of his unfolding results and the search for the final piece of the jigsaw. They were almost paralysed by their situation. Without discussion, they simultaneously observed a truce, without ever having declared open warfare. It was an effort for Sue, as although Dave appeared to be taking an interest in her reports of the holiday and the girls, she could sense that, in spite of himself, his mind was elsewhere. He was looking at her across the table, but not really seeing her. His intense, almost worrying, preoccupation with his work was further demonstrated when it became clear that he had not even noticed her unusual letter.

Inevitably, Dave left for work early the next day as this was when he estimated the first of his specimens would fail. He could hardly contain himself, the anticipation was almost unbearable. Although the outcome was now beyond doubt, the tension that had been growing for the past few days had still not reached its climax but continued to stretch his nerves to the limit until mid-morning. At last. Euphoria. All the tension released. It had been worth it; had made it the more pleasurable. Now he'd show them.

Following this first specimen, the two others from the same batch were destined to fail later that week and the three specimens from the next highest stress group would lose significant load with one failing a few days later. Dave was elated, as he could now complete his submission to *International Power Digest*.

★

Sue's morning was far more mundane. She had plenty of housework and washing to catch up on, and the vigour with which she attacked these chores reflected her impatience to have them completed. Her ancestors were awaiting her pleasure. After lunch she, with a clearer conscience, began working diligently through her notes on her Pulham ancestors. Some of the recording clerks of ages past had been especially helpful. They had appended the mother's maiden name alongside the birth entries which aided her in solving some of the family puzzles. Impulsively she called Peter and enthusiastically related details about her trip and its usefulness in taking her Boughtons back into the eighteenth century. She also mentioned her fortuitous meeting with the lady who had promised to supply more details. Hopefully, if she could sort the various families out from the notes that she had made, together with this additional information, she might be able to go back even further. Peter offered to help if required and she agreed to let him know when they met up on Friday as usual.

"It could be earlier if you are free on Wednesday. I realise that it's short notice, but I am intending to spend the day in London and you are welcome to join me if you are able."

Sue was taken aback. She hadn't really settled in yet. Her initial reaction was to refuse the offer, as she still had plenty to catch up on. However, it was very tempting. It was clear that Dave wouldn't object, wouldn't even notice, he had been so self-absorbed, more so than before her trip, and the girls were not due back until Friday.

"I'll quite understand if it's difficult," said Peter, sensing her hesitation.

"No, that would be lovely," declared Sue decisively. It would be a hectic week, but so what?

20

Another early start. Sue was surprised to find that Peter was alone. It was rather a last minute decision, he explained, and the others were not able to get away. They chatted pleasantly as Peter tackled the A4. He asked Sue to look in the glove compartment as he had something that might interest her. She found a sheet of paper with, what appeared to be a poem copied out.

"I thought that it was rather appropriate, given your recent luck with the family bible," he explained.

Sue read the lines:

'While one within his scrip contains
A shattered Bible's thumbd remains
On whose blank leaf wi' pious care
A host of names is scribbld there
Names by whom 'twas once possest
Or those in kindred bonds carresst
Children for generations back
That doubtful memory should not lack
Their dates – tis there wi' care applyd
When they were born and when they dyd
From sire to son link after link
All scribbld wi' unsparing ink… '

"Well, as you say, it's most appropriate but who wrote it?"

"John Clare. It's part of a much longer poem."

Peter went on to say that he was not on a genealogy mission this trip but visiting a friend in Highgate. He learned that Sue was returning to Portugal Street, to continue her search for the other Caroline Potten in the Brighton census. They agreed that he would drop her off at Ealing Broadway tube station.

On arrival, Sue settled in for what might prove to be a long day. This looked the likely outcome after almost three hours with no success. She struggled to maintain her concentration. Her eyes were tired. Then, the little jolt. Yes! Thomas Potten, her possible great, great grandfather, aged thirty six, with his wife Elizabeth and five children, including four year old Caroline, living in Vine Place. Thomas had been born in Mayfield, Sussex. She noted down the details. Though tired, she was relieved as she could have been searching all day. She was particularly pleased as she wanted to progress with her dear Caroline's family.

Sue met Peter back in Ealing. He had had an excellent day and, learning of her success, he suggested they celebrate with a drink. Sue enthusiastically agreed. Her luck with her census search, together with all the other pleasing developments, certainly ought to be marked in some way. A few months earlier she would have been unlikely to have agreed, as she would have felt that she should get home to her husband, but he had clearly demonstrated his indifference over recent weeks.

As they approached the Devizes—Avebury crossroad on the A4, Peter turned into the Waggon and Horses car park. They entered the dark interior of the ancient, thatch-roofed pub and found a quiet corner. Sue selected a long upholstered seat and sat with her back to the mullioned window. When Peter arrived with their drinks he slid alongside, rather than opposite her.

"Well, here's to mark a successful day." He raised his glass. After taking a sip, Peter replaced his glass thoughtfully on the table. He settled back into his seat and looked across at Sue with an expression which both puzzled and, in some way, unnerved her. Without any preamble, he asked her if she fully appreciated how well her research had progressed in just a few months. He knew of many people who had encountered difficulty with their research, even at an early stage. Sue wasn't sure how to take this remark as, although it was true that she had progressed well, she still felt that she had done quite a lot of tedious searching through books and microfilm along the way. Even today, just one item had involved several hours of searching. She recalled how tired she'd been after wrestling with the large births and marriages indexes at Somerset House. Peter, as though sensing her indignation, continued by saying that it wasn't that she hadn't been working hard through the usual records to which he was referring, but rather the good fortune of her uncle's information, her cousin's bible and now the promise of a history of Pulham families.

"Oh! Yes. I agree with you, Peter, those have been surprises, and very welcome ones that I couldn't have hoped for."

"Hmm. Quite so, but there may only be so much good fortune, you know, and you may have had all yours early."

Sue replied that she realised that this might be true.

"Well," said Peter, "maybe not quite." He took a small note book from his pocket and handed it to her. Replacing her glass on the table she opened it at the marked place where she saw a drawing, a single branch diagram of a family 'tree'. It depicted a married couple with five children. Sue caught her breath as she read the father's name – Henry Potten. His birth and death dates were given, together with his wife, Felicity Groves. The five children had their years of birth included. Then the shock of pleasure made her eyes widen. Thomas Potten 1806. As she had determined to trace Caroline's family as a matter of importance, of honour even, she had all the relevant information so far acquired, fixed firmly in her mind. She knew that 1806 was the year of birth of one of 'her' Carolines' fathers, the other being about ten years younger. She was delighted. But how? Peter explained that it was a stroke of luck. He and his Highgate friend had spent the morning looking around art galleries in the area. One of these, a small place on Archway, had an exhibition of, lesser known, British landscape painters. One of the rooms was devoted to a Henry Potten, of whom Peter confessed he'd never heard. Apparently he was better known in the middle of the nineteenth century. Along with his works, were odd bits of memorabilia, including a copy of Henry's family tree.

"I made a note of where the original can be found on the following page," Peter continued. Sue saw that this was at County Hall, Maidstone in Kent. She was overjoyed and impetuously leaned across to kiss him. He turned towards her just at that moment and so her intended peck on the cheek became a full kiss, and it lasted. She felt his hand on her breast and resisted the temptation to retreat suddenly, but just gradually moved away from him to resume her position. Her colour was high and she felt breathless. Before she could apologise for her forwardness, Peter stammered his apology, clearly contrite. Despite her confusion, Sue showed remarkable control and made it clear that she was responsible. In a simultaneous nervous gesture they both leaned forwards and picked up their glasses, their hands shaking. After a deep swallow, Peter shook his head.

"To continue," he began, and Sue was impressed by his attempt at lightness, "before being so violently attacked, I was going to add that this 'tree' extended backwards into the seventeenth century, but I only had time to copy down what you see. Should it turn out to be what you are looking for, then you could contact Maidstone for the complete information."

"This is so exciting, Peter, Henry Potten a well-known – to some at least – artist. If I can prove that his son Thomas is my ancestor, then I have so much information. Oh thank you, thank you," enthused Sue and she unselfconsciously, squeezed Peter's arm.

"You're not about to attack me again, are you?" joked Peter, moving away. "I did just scan the wall chart briefly before we left and although Henry lived in London, his major paintings depicted scenes of Kent. I noticed also that many of the earlier ancestors also had Kentish connections."

Sue moved on to mention her Pulham ancestors and Peter agreed that the information from the Pulham registers should enable her to build up a picture of the various Boughton families living in the village around the eighteenth and nineteenth centuries, and this should be reinforced by the extra information that she was expecting. Naturally, this would take some time, as much had to be unscrambled, but this was a good way of advancing her new hobby at home, rather than in the rough and tumble of the various record repositories. Sue confessed that she had found the periods of waiting between trips to London frustrating and so having work which she could do at home, was welcome.

When Thursday arrived Sue, with understandable nervousness, prepared for her interview. Although the job was in the finance department and she had several years' experience in that field, she was under no illusions that huge changes would have occurred since she last processed invoices, all those years ago.

Surprisingly, the whole thing passed in a blur and was over before she knew it. As she drove home she reflected that it didn't go as badly as she had feared. True, systems had changed, but she was pleased to find that the present incumbent would be staying on for a month and so her replacement would have the benefit of working herself into the job. So there was a chance. They would let her know within a few days. Before that however, she had some mothering to do.

★

Sue was pleased to find Dave in a much more positive frame of mind than recently and when the girls returned home, he greeted them enthusiastically. He seemed almost hyperactive as he gleefully accepted their gifts of sticks of rock. He immediately donned his 'Kiss Me Quick' hat with a laugh and acted the clown to their amusement. He listened with interest to Katy's report of all her adventures during the holiday. Jo showed him the paintings she had done and he was genuinely amazed.

"Wow Jo, these are brilliant."

They were beach scenes. Dave, though not knowledgeable, could appreciate the attention to detail in some areas.

"The detail on these rocks is super and look at that piece of driftwood, it's so realistic you feel that you could pick it out of the picture. I expect you're pleased?"

"Yes I am. I concentrated on the rocks and driftwood, because I thought that the sand and sea was pretty boring. I'm thinking of making these two part of my school project."

Sue was delighted the following morning when she received a bulky letter which came from a Miss Fox of Pulham. It contained a transcription of notes, by an old Pulham resident, who had written of his research into the families of Pulham. This included some Boughtons, one being 'Barber' Boughton who, in addition to working in the glove trade, also acted as village barber. These snapshots from the past were fascinating and allowed Sue to put her ancestors into historical context and imagine them going about their daily lives in Pulham all those years ago. The details copied from gravestones, sited in the old churchyard, and the information which Sue had collected herself, appeared to offer the possibility of her being able to work backwards and follow the Boughtons to the beginning of the eighteenth century. It would take some time to sort through but the prospect gave her immense pleasure.

★

Dave had arranged a meeting with Tony to report upon his recent results. He felt confident that they could not now refuse to publicise his work. He realised that it would be some time before he saw his full results in print in a scientific journal, which was his main aim. He had completed his modified internal report and this would form the basis of his paper, with perhaps an extra section upon the crack initiation process when he had resolved it. He had slogged away examining sections taken through the samples after exposure, but nothing of significance had been revealed. Days had passed. All he could do was to expose more specimens and take more sections, in the hope of finding some clue to the initiation process. There were just so many specimens to sort through.

Thankfully, his technical note containing his major findings was complete and he hoped that it might be in time for the September issue of *International Power Digest*. Once this was done and he had highlighted his concerns regarding the safety of other operating units, he would feel easier in his mind – his duty done.

So he could now be completely focussed upon his crack initiation studies. He worked frantically and although his colleagues admired his dedication, there were times when they were alarmed by his single-minded zeal. Recent developments appeared to have affected his approach to his work.

Tony received him. If Dave had intended to keep the smugness out of his voice, he did not succeed. Tony agreed that the results from his second series of experiments certainly overcame the criticisms about possible contamination. The fact that several test pieces had failed gave added credence to his hypothesis. Tony thought that Dave's investigations into how cracks initiated would, if successful, be a neat addition to the whole thing and would certainly add to the quality of the proposed external paper. He was enthusiastic about it, this was an absolutely wonderful piece of work and just the sort of thing that was hoped for, when the department was set up. Dave reminded his Section Head that his full paper had no chance of being published for some months, but there was a clear need to alert other turbine operators quickly. Fortunately, his report to the sub-committee, together with a technical note for *International Power Digest,* could be circulated quickly and in his view, this was essential. He hoped that he had Tony's support to submit it without delay. He was given this assurance, but of course they would require Sweety's approval.

Later that day, Dave received a call from Mrs Murray requesting his presence in Dr Honey's office. As he waited in the outer office, Dave eagerly anticipated Sweety's acclaim. He sensed that this was the sort of development his department head would welcome in his efforts to get SSD on the map. The whole concept of the Strategic Supplies Authority, although primarily to ensure the integrity of essential services, also required a credible and effective technical back up service. Sweety was all smiles and invited Dave to take a seat. Tony was already settled.

First the sugar coating.

"This is a fine piece of work, David. Just the sort of thing that we want here in SSD, a well-run investigation, leading to unprecedented results of high scientific value," beamed Sweety. "Very well done indeed." He went on to say that they had been impressed with Dave's work from the start and, in particular, the way that he had handled the running of the Materials Section during the Winford site investigations. They realised, he continued, that this had had an adverse effect upon his ability to produce any meaningful research results from his own project, in time for his technical appraisal, which would mean that he would miss out on, what Sweety was sure would have been, an upgrading.

"Well, you've no cause to worry on that score," he added. "Although I had intended to let you know nearer the end of the year, I can reveal now that, on my recommendation, the national grading assessors are intending to sanction that upgrading with effect from the first of January." Dave was delighted that his efforts had been rewarded.

Then the bitter pill.

"So I hope that you feel that you are appreciated. However, as far as your recent results, relating to the Winford situation, are concerned, we want you to hang on to your data just for the present. It would not be a good time to publish just yet."

Dave was flabbergasted. "But this is a most significant development and if it isn't publicised now it will lose its impact," urged Dave.

Sweety went on to explain that he had been in discussion with, not only Tony, but also the Head of Research in the SSA and that was what had been agreed. Accordingly, both Professor Fletcher and the press office had been directed to withhold publication. It had been decided that the Slough hypothesis should stand and that the Corrosion Sub-Committee would, for the present at least, be suspended. David would surely agree that it would bring the credibility of the Authority into question if, after sponsoring a conference explaining the conclusions of the Winford disc failure enquiry, they were to come up with a different explanation only a month later. Dave was tempted to say that he had questioned the Slough hypothesis from the start and now he was being punished, however, what he did point out was there was an important safety issue involved, as well as the risk of further failures.

"David," soothed Sweety, "you can take it from me that our decision to halt all overspeed testing and our introduction of a rolling turbine disc refurbishment programme, will reduce any slight risk to an acceptable level. In fact, if we did publish your results, it would not make any difference. It just wouldn't be practical. We certainly couldn't close down all our turbines with the winter approaching, I'm sure that you can appreciate that."

"But what about the other utilities, they have similar turbines running, in addition to many overseas. My results have international implications. If just one other turbine fails someone else could be killed."

"I'm sorry. The decision has been made, there is nothing I can do, even at my level, to alter it. There would be nothing gained by causing panic. We shall be advising the other utilities in due course."

"I'm afraid that I cannot accept that." Dave was shaking with emotion. "Don't forget that the national press have already been involved."

"I shall ignore that remark," said Sweety firmly. "There's nothing more to be said." Dave looked across at his Section Head and, to give him his due, Tony had been uncomfortable throughout these exchanges.

Dave had, by this time, worked himself up into a state which didn't entertain any thoughts of calm reflection and he voiced his feelings, suggesting that resignation might be his only option. Sweety did not appear to react in the way that Dave had anticipated. He was still reasonable.

"Come, come, David, do take time to think things over. Give it a couple of days. Resigning wouldn't achieve anything, as you would still be bound by the Official Secrets Act."

Dave was confused and angry. He realised that he was not thinking clearly. He was so damned mad and Sweety was sitting there so smugly. He needed time to think properly. He stood up abruptly and left. Back in his office he couldn't face his colleagues so, grabbing his jacket, he hurried to his car and drove off the site.

He was pale and still shaking an hour later as he sat in his car in a lay-by on the A4 just below the White Horse at Cherhill. His reaction to the situation was intensified by the past weeks of gradually increasing tension, leading up to this crisis. He got out and walked briskly up the chalk path to the monument. He hadn't realised how quickly he had been walking, but when he reached the summit he was breathing heavily. He sat down on the steps of the monument and gazed across the patchwork Wiltshire countryside spreading to the north. There was a stiff breeze blowing, which was often the case at this spot, but Dave didn't notice. He contemplated the situation more calmly. He believed that resigning was his only option, but there was still the problem of the Official Secrets Act. What would he achieve? These thoughts annoyed him; made him feel impotent.

He acknowledged that he had handled things badly. There was no doubt in his mind, however, that Sweety and his paymasters were completely out of order. No matter how blandly they put their argument, they still could not justify risking people's lives. Turbine operators and other operating staff should be warned of the risk. If the unions or the newspapers found out, there would be hell to pay and where would he stand? As he attempted to put these thoughts in order, his annoyance at the way he'd mishandled the interview galled him. He had achieved nothing. If he did nothing he would be as culpable as the rest, should the worst occur.

If he acted immediately, he felt confident that a technical note could be in print in the next edition of *The Digest*, which was September. This would serve as a warning to other utilities at home and, as it was an international publication, it would also attract worldwide attention. This would cost him his job and possibly lead to prosecution. Was he prepared to accept this?

He drove home to an empty house. Sue was out with Pam. At any other time this may have annoyed him, but he hardly noticed and was surprised when Sue and the girls came chatteringly in. Sue, together with Pam and the girls, had spent the day in Bath.

Later, Dave related the day's events with increasing animation to Sue, who showed her concern which, genuinely, was for her husband's feelings, rather than the more general risk to the family's stability. In view of these developments, she decided not to reveal that she had received a phone call from the Chief Accountant of Henderson Engineering that morning, notifying her that her job application had been successful. It was this news that had prompted her to invite Pam out. Had she been aware of the appalling treatment her husband had received and his understandable reaction, she would have cancelled her day out and gone to look for him. She would have been alarmed, as she had been concerned about his mental state recently. As it was, Sue took the opportunity, whilst Dave was rummaging through his work papers upstairs, to call Tony to get a better idea of the situation.

Tony expressed his regret, but impressed on Sue that there was nothing he or Dave could do to alter the situation nor, for that matter, could Sweety. The decision had come from a much higher quarter, and so they might as well just accept it and move on. Certainly, the threat of her husband resigning would have no impact at all on the levels of management from which the decision had been handed down.

21

Sue awoke with a start and found herself alone. Donning her dressing gown, she went down to the sitting room where, to her relief, she found Dave. He was sitting staring out through the French windows, clearly distressed. He had been weeping. She was amazed to think that in just a few months her husband could have changed so much. At the beginning of the year he had been so different. He was a conscientious worker, always had been, but he had a great personality and enjoyed family life with her and the girls. They weren't a burden in those days. The change was alarming. He had joined the SSA and had worked hard, which was quite natural when beginning a new job. Then, a more noticeable change in his behaviour, as he took on a leading role in the Winford investigation. He had sensed that this was his big chance. Such opportunities didn't come along often, especially for someone with his background. He had been determined to grasp it. From that moment he had been completely driven by ambition. Sue felt herself to be responsible, although she had had no way of knowing how things would turn out. She determined to redouble her efforts to get their relationship back to how they were. The timing was unfortunate, but she would have to turn down her job offer. She consoled herself in the belief that there would be others. Her first priority was to support her husband. To begin with she needed to establish the situation from his point of view, which required calm discussion.

She cuddled up beside him and began by asking whether he had come to any conclusion yet, adding that he could count upon her support whatever his decision. She just wanted him to be sure in his own mind before doing anything dramatic. The easiest course would be to accept the situation and get on with his research project at Thornton Power Station. This would also be the best from the family's point of view, but she understood that for him, there was a matter of principle to be considered. She shared his sense of injustice and it made her angry. Dave was calmer and he explained that, in some ways, he was pleased that the decision to suppress his results had come from the highest level within the Authority and that it wasn't Sweety who had made it. It felt less of a betrayal somehow.

He admitted, a major reason for his outrage was that he was being prevented from claiming credit for his work, but he hoped that his concern about the risk of someone else actually losing their life unnecessarily, was overriding. The thought of someone's son, husband or father being killed would be on his conscience and he just couldn't imagine how he'd feel, should the worst happen. Worldwide, he guessed that there were several hundred turbines of similar design to those at Winford. The primary reason for the violent failure at Winford, was that the disc steel was unusually brittle and thus it was less likely that others would fail, until deeper cracks were formed. However, as most of the other turbines had been in service for longer than those at Winford, there was still a distinct risk.

He was appalled at the SSA management, whose motives were blatantly political. They realised that if his results became public they would have no option but to close down at least Winford and Thornton power stations immediately, and what red faces there would be within the senior ranks of an organisation set up to ensure integrity of supplies.

As the sun rose and cast its early light into the sitting room, via the French windows, Dave came to a decision, of sorts. He would take a step back and consider the whole question as unemotionally as possible. He decided to take off for the day with a packed lunch. Seeing Sue's reaction, he assured her that he wasn't planning anything dramatic, but felt that a day's trek along the Ridgeway, which he had intended to do sometime, would be a good way of thinking the whole thing through.

There were several cars already parked at Overton Hill beside the Ridgeway path early that morning, but no sign of their occupants. The usual stiff breeze was blowing in from his left, the rough grass moving in waves up the hillside, as he set off northwards. The flinty track became more rutted as he climbed the first slope.

Gradually, he became less conscious of his surroundings, as he began mentally to rewind the past months of the Winford investigation, through his mind. He recounted the important developments. Despite his success with the on-site exposure specimens and the laboratory stress corrosion tests, his investigation was not complete and it could be argued that it was the most important part that remained to be discovered. Just how could cracks initiate in what, to all intents and purposes, was pure water? It was the answer to this question that was required before he could write his definitive paper and so, for the present, that was not an issue. He had to be patient. Realistically, it could be the best part of a year before he could expect to see his detailed hypothesis in print.

His immediate dilemma really came down to the question of the technical note, which did not require such a rigorous treatment. This note would serve two distinct purposes. It was an opportunity to announce his amazing results quickly but, more importantly, it would alert all power plant operators (and this particular publication was directed towards such people) to the serious risk in operating turbines of the Winford type.

He blushed at the thought that he, an ordinary Birmingham lad, would have his name linked with this important advance in corrosion science. However, he had no illusions that his note alone would be sufficient to cause all turbine operators around the world to suddenly remove vulnerable turbines from service, as that would be impractical. His, more realistic, hope was that his recommendation, to cancel all routine overspeed tests, would be accepted, which could prove to be the difference between life and death. This information could be made available quickly and with luck, might be in time for the forthcoming issue of *International Power Digest*, though it would be touch and go. Having written it, he wondered if he would have the nerve to submit it for publication, in defiance of the wishes of his superiors and, more seriously, accepting the risk of prosecution. He found this to be a persistent, nagging worry that would not go away and the more he considered it, the more convinced he became that he had no option. It was a terrifying prospect. The possibility of major disruption to family life. Another move? This was so disheartening, after they had all finally settled so well, but how could this be compared with someone losing their life? A bleak prospect indeed.

What? He was surprised to have reached the Marlborough to Swindon road at Southend already. He checked his watch. He had been walking for two hours. He hadn't noticed his surroundings; had walked unconsciously through the hill-fort at Barbury Castle.

Although the future looked uncertain, he felt more at ease with himself having at least analysed the situation. There was little else that he could do. There may be further developments by the time he returned to work. He could only wait.

He set off on his return journey and at the hill-fort, he settled down on the grass ramparts to eat his lunch.

Having clarified his thoughts, he was able to take in the marvellous scenery which he'd missed on his way north. As he began the final descent, he noticed a ridge running away to the left forming a shallow valley across Fyfield Down. Here, sheep were grazing contently amongst the scattered stones on the lower slopes.

On the horizon to his right, the monument which he had climbed up to the previous day was shining whitely in the sunshine.

So he would return to work and continue with the crack initiation studies and get his full paper developed, which he was determined to get published, as soon as this final element was completed, whatever the consequences.

One thing he did not resolve, did not even consider, was the deterioration in his family relationships. Even though severely chastened by recent setbacks, his focus had not been disturbed, his obsession with his work clearly undiminished. In contrast, this crisis had triggered more radical thoughts for his wife.

★

Sue, although having some nagging doubts, was relieved that her husband had not taken precipitous action on his return to work, but seemed to have settled into a comparatively normal working regime. He was, however, more introverted and engrossed in his own thoughts for much of the time. She realised that this was a critical time in their lives. Despite all her recent feelings for her own situation and her relationship with Peter, she knew that now, faced with this crisis, family interests came first. This might be viewed as a betrayal of all her own aspirations as a woman, but she had no doubt that this was a price she was willing to pay. Making this radical reappraisal of her priorities did not mean giving up her interests, but rather adjusting where necessary to minimise conflict within the family, at this difficult time for Dave. The first thing was, with great reluctance, to notify Henderson's that she would not be accepting their job offer. She was consoled by the thought that it had served to restore her confidence and that she was not incapable of obtaining employment, which would be a help when the time was right.

★

Dave was working at home. The urgency of solving his crack initiation problem was driving him. He was scanning through his preliminary results.

"Those are nice. What are they?" asked Jo.

"These photographs do you mean?"

"Yes. Nice design."

"They're pictures of metal samples under an optical microscope. They're steel specimens that have been immersed in various solutions for a short time, to check for early signs of corrosion."

"What are all these bits?"

"The main part, this light coloured background is, more or less, iron. The dark grey, needle shaped structure is made up of carbon rich areas and the light grey particles are impurities of manganese sulphide. The whole structure is normal for this type of steel, which is making it difficult for me to solve an urgent problem."

"What about that blob there?"

"I just told you, they're manganese sulphide."

"But that one's different."

Dave looked more closely.

"I don't see any difference."

"Well, it's got a fine black border around it. None of the others have. Can't you see? It's time you got some glasses. Can I have a copy of that photograph? It's really neat."

"Yes, but let me keep this one for now, as I'll need it to recheck the sample."

That was his first job the following morning. He found the sample from which the photograph had been taken and re-examined it. It was difficult to be sure of the exact area Jo had seen but, after a lengthy search, he thought he recognised the features from the pattern of the grains surrounding it. He increased the magnification and he could now see the outlined particle Jo had mentioned. Comparing this with the other manganese sulphide areas, he could see a clear difference. Having decided that the electron microscope would provide more information, he went in search of John Bolton. It was a good decision. The three dimensional image took his breath away. Whilst virtually all of the manganese sulphide particles were in intimate contact with the surrounding matrix of iron, the one picked out by Jo was separated by a narrow, but deep, crevice. It appeared to be the result of localised corrosion, between the particle and the surrounding metal. So this 'active' particle was different from the rest and had produced a corrosion crevice which, in time, would result in the formation of a pit as the attack developed. He was elated. This certainly fitted the requirement as a crack initiator, for which he had been searching. This was a credible reason for the presence of cracking in his plain specimens, in high purity water and, more importantly, in the Winford LP turbine discs. It was likely that the 'active' particle had a slightly different composition from the majority of the other sulphides. He reviewed many of his earlier samples and found that many contained such 'active' particles. Some of these were elliptical in shape and so, as corrosion developed, the resultant pit was noticeably crack-like.

That evening Dave, still in a state of euphoria, told Jo that he had re-examined the specimen which she had pointed out.

"You really are a superstar, Jo. This is the final piece of the jigsaw for which I've been searching. You should really be doing science, you know."

"Not likely. You must know that I get the same kick out of art as you do science. Even so, it's nice to know that we arty-types can still sort out your science problems."

"It is a shame that science and art folk do seem to keep aloof."

"More's the pity, I say. I mean that chap, Einstein, did OK I suppose, but how much more successful might he have been if he'd embraced art and got himself a decent hair-stylist."

★

As things turned out, Sue was pleasantly surprised to find that she was able to work her other interests around the family, without much adjustment. Her indexing work had started again, following a summer break, plus Pam was back and so they resumed their regular excursions. Of course, she spent time poring over her Boughton notes, attempting to sort out the Pulham families, as well as considering how she could live up to her silent promise to her Caroline Potten and unravel her family history. So the time passed pleasantly. As the late autumn was staying so fine, she and Pam had made it a regular habit to walk for an hour or so around the Highwood Estate, or as Pam put it, "Hey old girl, fancy a stroll in my garden?" Keeping her eyes open in case the 'Mellors' look-a-like appeared, added more interest to these occasions.

★

"Fancy a trip?" Dave looked at his Section Head with interest. Just what he could do with, a change of scene.

He had intended to let Tony know that his latest crack initiation studies had finally provided the evidence for which he had been searching. It was clear that the most critical part of the disc cracking process was the initiation of a sharp pit. He had finally, thanks to Jo, found evidence that such defects could arise in high purity hot water. This had revealed that localised attack of the steel surface often began at certain 'active' sulphide particles, which were always present in commercial steels. Relatively deep pits could be produced, even in high purity water, as the local chemistry at the bottom of such pits was known to become acidic as corrosion progressed, the defects could deepen as this aggressive solution developed. Although the reason why not all particles were subject to this attack was unclear, he felt that would be best left for the Slough scientists to investigate.

Despite his earlier resolution, Dave had delayed submitting his technical note for a few days, convincing himself that awaiting the results of these latest experiments was a valid reason. Had this just been an excuse? He had almost certainly missed the September deadline as a result. The next opportunity for publication would be October. This thought brought the whole question back into doubt again. What would be the outcome if he did publish then? Would he be prosecuted? Could he find another job locally? The family were all so nicely settled – just so many reasons for not acting. He knew that this was just an excuse for his cowardice. He had been so close to submitting the note earlier in the week. He had had it typed and actually sealed in an envelope, but he had baulked at the final moment as his heart pounded outside the post office. He had walked away, ashamed. He found little consolation in the fact that no further failures had occurred, as far as he knew.

"Wouldn't mind, where to?" Dave answered.

"Soviet Union."

Dave was surprised. Tony went on to say that the British Electrical Consortium were putting together a delegation to visit Moscow on an exchange visit with the USSR Electrical Union. It was planned to be a wide ranging exchange covering most aspects of power generation and distribution. Dave's name had been put forward by the SSA to the Consortium. In fact, it was concern for Dave's mental state at present which had prompted Sweety to put his name forward. He and Tony felt that he needed a diversion just now, which in all likelihood would serve to defuse the present situation and result in a less extreme reaction to the Winford business. It was to be a ten day stay in Moscow.

*

Dave had been surprised a few days earlier to receive a phone call from Pauline as, to all intents and purposes, the sub-committee had become defunct since the summer. She wanted to meet up with him away from work. His first thought was that perhaps she had reconsidered his proposition of another social evening, but her manner suggested that this was not the case. It was something important that she wished to discuss. Dave thought that it might prove difficult as he had no reason to visit London at present. He would have to call her back.

Now, out of the blue, this opportunity had arisen in the form of his forthcoming USSR trip. He could certainly make a case for being in London on the evening before his Heathrow flight, when he could arrange to meet Pauline.

The days leading up to the planned trip were eventful for Dave. He decided to amend his note to *International Power Digest*, to include the latest crucial part of his hypothesis. He was on edge for the whole of Thursday and was not completely calm when the typed final version arrived on his desk on Friday morning. He felt like a character from a Le Carré novel as he slipped it into his briefcase ready to post. But would he? And if so, when?

He checked in at the hotel. He was still procrastinating about posting the letter, which was burning a hole in his pocket. Maybe at the airport. It would still make the October edition easily enough. He was in the bar before seven o'clock and predictably, Pauline was on time. He had forgotten in just a couple of months, how attractive she was. His mind moved on towards a shared meal, followed by the possibility of Lena revealing herself later. He ordered her a drink. It soon became clear that Pauline was not her usual self, she was plainly unsettled as she explained her reason for wanting to meet.

"I can't stay long, but I've something I want you to see. It came as quite a shock to me and following the acrimonious discussions of our last meeting, I thought that you ought to read this." As she spoke she pulled a large envelope from her briefcase. "Before you do I have to have your word that you will not reveal how you found out about this. I've taken quite a risk. I've done it partly because I felt that you were being badly treated, but also because I believe it is scandalous that such a thing should be allowed to happen."

After receiving Dave's assurance, Pauline passed over the envelope, which contained a letter which he read with a mixture of disbelief and anger. The letter, dated the 17th of August 1970, was classified as 'SECRET' and was from the Chief Executive of the Strategic Supplies Authority to the Head of Research at Slough, with a copy to the Head of Public Relations, and read as follows:

SUBJECT – *Examination of a Low Pressure Turbine Rotor after 30 years, service at the Mid-Newport Electric Works of the Welsh Petroleum Corporation.*

I enclose a copy of a report prepared by our non-destructive testing people regarding the examination of the two low pressure rotors from the No1 turbine at the above mentioned location and the discovery of stress corrosion cracking in the keyways of several of the discs. It is not only the widespread nature of the cracking, but also the depth of penetration (over one inch in two of the discs) which is alarming. This development has been discussed at executive level and it has been agreed to withhold the circulation of this report for the present.

As the Electric Works have now been decommissioned, there are no implications for the Petroleum Corporation itself and, as No2 turbine is still to be examined, this provides an opportunity for delaying reporting until this has been done, which will be at least eighteen months from now. Mr Pritchard, Chairman of the Welsh Petroleum Corporation, informs me that none of the other operating units in their organisation have the shrink-fit keyway design.

We are, of course, in a much more difficult position at present, with the turbines at both West Winford and Thornton being vulnerable. As disc cracking at Newport cannot be associated with a known contamination incident, we have to assume that our explanation for the West Winford failure (sodium hydroxide contamination) is, at best, suspect. This being the case we have to regard all turbines at West Winford and Thornton Power Stations to be at serious risk and therefore we need to modify our refurbishment programme to include all machines. The Engineering Director informs me that in eighteen months this work will be sufficiently advanced that the reporting of the Newport examinations at that time would not cause too much embarrassment.

Dave was amazed at what he'd read. The first thing that struck him was that Pauline had appreciated the significance of this letter. Furthermore, she had taken this risk. He then considered the implications. If cracking was over an inch deep after thirty years' operation at this power plant, the rate of cracking was about the same as that found at Winford. Clearly, as the letter acknowledged, the Slough hypothesis of a particular operational incident on Number 2 turbine (the contamination of the steam) could not be sustained.

"Well, Pauline, I'm so pleased that you thought of letting me see this, but how did you get hold of it? Won't you get into trouble?"

"Yes, if anyone finds out. I came across it whilst I was standing in for the woman who handles the work for the secretariat of the main Technical Committees. No one knows I made this copy."

"But is there anything that we can do about it, without implicating you?" asked Dave.

"I'm not sure. I was just so angry that I thought of alerting the national press directly. Surely if other failures occurred people could get killed, couldn't they?"

"There is a real risk, but it may not happen and it's this uncertainty that the SSA is banking on. They are in a real dilemma now that the new government is looking hard into the whole SSA concept. If they acted as they should, both Winford and Thornton power stations should be removed from service immediately and all operators of similar turbines would be advised of the danger, but that's unthinkable for them, as they approach the winter and peak demand. The programme of turbine refurbishment and the introduction of improved non-destructive examination is in hand and this should eliminate the risk when it is complete, but that won't be for at least two years. Their best hope of avoiding failures in the meantime, is the suspension of routine overspeed testing, as it is this that really does increase the risk of a repeat of Winford."

"Yes, but that is only within the SSA," countered Pauline. "By sticking to the Slough explanation they can't alert other utilities, here or abroad, to the danger. Surely there are hundreds of turbines at risk worldwide?"

Dave was surprised by Pauline's passion. She had finished her drink almost without noticing. He explained that he would be away for about ten days, which would give him plenty of time to think the whole thing through. He could give her a call at the beginning of October. Although she seemed to accept this, he could see that she was clearly agitated.

"Anyway, let's get some food," suggested Dave, but Pauline refused. She explained that she was going away on Sunday to Italy to visit her aunt. Dave was sorry. He would have welcomed her company.

He was unsettled by what he'd heard and he didn't feel up to the Italian restaurant so, after a quick snack at the hotel, he had an early night. It was to be a disturbed night as he slept fitfully. The following morning he handed in his keys at the reception desk, together with a letter to be posted. He was only sorry now that he'd missed the September deadline.

During the flight, Dave's anger subsided, but he had no misgivings about his reckless action and as he approached his destination his thoughts turned, with keen anticipation to the immediate prospects of this adventure. The British Airways jet touched down at Sheremetyevo on time. As the plane taxied along towards its designated stand, Dave noted the armed guards stationed on the tarmac around the terminal building, a collection of clones, just young lads really but their uniforms, severe haircuts and impassive expressions seemed so at odds with their years. Thank goodness we don't have the need for anything like that at home, he thought. The idea of armed soldiers or police around the streets or at the airports of Britain was so foreign.

There was more evidence of the cultural divide at passport control. Dave's passport and visa card were taken in through the booth window and glanced at by another youthful clone – a very long, embarrassing wait. Dave finally assumed he could proceed, though the wordless automaton refused to blink.

Exiting into the public area, he was amongst the waiting group of fur-clad men, women and children, together with the usual jostle of people holding up cards, hand written for the most part, with company's names, family names, and so on, displayed to catch the attention of their unknown visitor. Then he saw 'Mr Harrison' displayed by a young man whom, Dave approached. He smiled and introduced himself as Ivan Razumov from the Electrical Institute of Moscow. A car was waiting and they were driven smoothly along wide, well-paved, roads into the city centre. Dr Razumov led Dave into the spacious reception area of the Rossia Hotel. It was a huge building. His host said that he would return later. Dave registered and was taken up to the fifth floor. He wandered along a corridor, looking at the room numbers. He was challenged by a middle-aged woman, sitting at a table at the corner of the corridor.

"*Gdye vash klyooch?*" she said, and Dave could see that she was leaning forward over her table, looking sideways at his left hand, in which he was holding his key. He offered it up with a questioning look. "*Da, prava,*" she said, indicating a door on his right hand side and as he moved towards it hesitantly, "*Da, da.*" This woman, he learned, was the appointed '*dezhurnaya*' (woman on duty) who, though apparently doing nothing, acted as the lynch-pin for that particular floor. She looked after the keys of residents, answered the phone and also supervised a samovar for guests. In most westerners' eyes however, the role as a spy was thought to be her main duty.

The hotel comprised four sections, built around the periphery of a large courtyard, and Dave was delighted to find that his room had an excellent view over Red Square. As he unpacked, he idly wondered where the microphones would be hidden, or was that just in spy novels?

At seven o'clock he met Ivan and they went up to a restaurant on the twenty first floor. The service was slow. Eventually an impressive menu arrived. Dave mentioned how comprehensive the menu was and Ivan smiled. "Pardon me," he said, "I am not making fun but I should perhaps explain. You see the very long list of food and wine on offer here?" Dave nodded. Ivan continued, "You will now note how many items have their prices listed. Take the wine, for example." Again Dave nodded. There were probably over twenty wines mentioned, though only two had prices included. "So," explained Ivan with a smile, "only two wines are really on the menu. If they only listed the available items, the menu would be only one page long, not ten."

Even with this limitation, Dave was hoping that Ivan would suggest something and order for them both, which he did when, eventually, their order was taken. Of the two wines, red or white, the latter had been selected by Ivan and Dave attempted to read the label *'Tsinandali'* with only partial success. Ivan gave the accepted pronunciation and went on to say that it was a medium-dry wine, from the Georgian Republic. It was very good, as was the main meal. It was a pleasant evening and Dave learned a little of the arrangements for the week's visit. His colleagues had arrived earlier and were being escorted by an Intourist guide. Dave was pleased to be in a one to one situation, as he enjoyed Ivan's company and was interested in his information and anecdotes about life in the 'sinister' Soviet Union.

Monday morning arrived and Dave glanced out through his window. At eye level were the many domes of St. Basil's Cathedral – so foreign. It was still dark. A more familiar scene down at ground level, as clusters of dark silhouettes shuffled along the pavements to their workplaces, heads bowed, a template for a modern day Lowry. A lukewarm shower and down to the breakfast room, where he met his British colleagues.

Ivan escorted them to the meeting place. This entailed a minibus ride passing alongside the imposing Kremlin wall on their right and down Leninski Prospeck. After about half a mile, they stopped and were greeted by an assorted bunch of men and women, no doubt including the statuary KGB 'minders', and hustled into the entrance hall of a tall office block. Dave and his colleagues were organised together to be taken up to the committee room. There were two ancient lifts, brass grill fronted, one of which was waiting at ground floor level. Dave and his party were squeezed into this together with the obligatory attendant – the USSR boasts full employment! The latter pushed the button but the lift refused to move. Repeating this with increasing violence did nothing to persuade it to budge. There followed a somewhat comical scene of confusion as a woman administrator, with an unnecessary theatrical display of arm waving and herding, corralled her charges into the second lift. Off they went, leaving the former liftman rattling his cage to little avail.

After the formal introductions, each member from the host delegation gave a brief resume of their background and their area of expertise and the visitors were asked to do likewise. Amongst Dave's colleagues were a variety of specialists in areas such as high voltage systems, instrumentation equipment and reactor operation. Dave was the sole turbine materials representative. The plan outlined by the hosts was to spend the day together in a general exchange of information on electricity production matters and for the rest of the week, they would get down to detail within smaller groups. Visits had also been arranged to suit the various interests.

Dave and his colleagues quickly adapted to the routine and although they were a friendly group, Dave enjoyed being alone with Ivan in the evenings, as this experience was so different to his normal life. He was pleased to learn that Ivan had been appointed to be his guide on a visit to a power station, a little to the north west of Moscow, towards the end of his stay. Not only was Ivan good company but, being a qualified metallurgist, his area of interest was very similar to Dave's.

22

The Norvokosky Power Station was similar in design to West Winford, therefore Dave could follow the explanation of the various functions given by the turbine hall engineer – once translated. There was a major difference in the staffing levels, compared with the UK, which perhaps had much to do with the USSR's full employment policy.

The scene within the turbine hall was one of surprising activity, certainly when compared to its western equivalent. Men and women were busying themselves around all six of the steaming giants. Insulation was being patched here and there, bearings were being oiled and an army of cleaners were working, half-heartedly mopping the tiled floor, between each turbine. So many people, in addition to the normal operators. Dave shuddered inwardly at the sight. Each machine hummed, the floor throbbed and steam escaped from various pipes and joints. Tons of hot whirling metal and it would only take a tiny crack to cause a repeat of Winford, but with this level of staffing, the thought was particularly frightening.

The senior turbine operator was introduced to Dave and Ivan and he, Alexander Borisovich Denisov, provided the information on the operational detail. He also joined them for lunch. Dave instantly took to this charming and friendly man. Dave informed Alexander that, as a consequence of an LP turbine disc failure which they had suffered during an overspeed test, his organisation had suspended such tests for safety reasons. Alexander had heard of the incident and understood that it had been caused by contaminated steam. He was glad to say that Norvokosky steam was as pure as gold, as was all steam in the USSR, he added and, as if to emphasise his point, he laughed, displaying several gold teeth.

"He says it's better than holy water," translated Ivan.

"*Da, da, kharashiya voda,*" grinned Alexander.

Dave was tempted to express his view that contamination was not the reason for failure, but he was a little intimidated by the circumstances, which compelled him to support the official line.

During lunch, being free of any 'minders', they talked pleasantly about their respective lives away from work. Alexander shared Dave's interest in running and he had a regular training routine similar to Dave's, except for the addition of an icy plunge into the nearby river at the end of his route. They reminisced about some of the great runners of the past, notably Zatopek and Chatterway. Ivan was not to be left out and he brought the conversation around to football, which proved to be just as animated, as many of the famous players such as Lev Yashin and Gordon Banks were discussed. Following lunch, Alexander returned to his duties, after expressing the hope that Dave would enjoy the rest of his stay. Ivan and Dave rejoined the other visitors for a presentation by the station manager. The party then returned to the Rossia.

Before leaving the hotel Ivan suggested to Dave that they try a less touristy restaurant later, to which he readily assented. Ivan's plan was to meet outside the Bolshoi Theatre which was nearby, being just across Red Square. Dave was delighted, and even more so when Ivan introduced him to the Moscow subway system. Absolutely unbelievable! The stations were works of art, vast cavernous spaces with ornate columns and intricate carvings, all illuminated with chandeliers.

The meal was excellent and beer was the favoured drink. It was late into the evening when Ivan abruptly introduced a solemn note into the conversation. He requested that Dave would not mention that they had been alone together away from work and the 'designated' hotel, as this might cause him problems. This came as a sharp reminder to Dave, who had been in danger of forgetting, amongst all the conviviality, that this was, after all, a totalitarian state. He nodded his agreement.

"*Kharasho* – that is good," smiled Ivan, "as I have another request to put to you." Dave winced. He would be happy to take slight risks as he disliked this oppressive state, but what if Ivan's proposal was something serious? In spite of his qualms he again nodded.

"Actually we have an invitation to a social gathering, but it is absolutely unofficial, are you willing to take a chance?"

Christ! Thought Dave, this was like something out of the bloody films. He could see himself in the Lubyanka by this time tomorrow. What should he say?

"It's our friend Alexander, Alexander Borisovitch Denisov, the turbine engineer from Norvokovsky," he added seeing Dave's puzzled stare. "We're invited to a family dinner tomorrow night. Apparently he enjoyed your company so much, he was insistent that you should have a taste of real Russian hospitality. I can arrange a car if you are willing."

Dave was relieved, as there seemed to be a world of difference between attending a family dinner and conspiring with a crowd of anarchists, or the like. He agreed to be at the Bolshoi the following evening.

What a great decision it turned out to be. It was one of the most pleasant evenings he could remember. This view was, of course, coloured by the unusual, slightly dangerous, circumstances, he would admit. Nevertheless, it was a great experience and one he would not forget.

Sasha, as Alexander wished to be called, was blessed with a beautiful wife and two daughters. It was not Elena's physical beauty, though indeed she was lovely, but rather her inner beauty that was clearly evident almost as soon as she greeted Ivan and Dave. She had the most deep, soulful eyes, which lit up as she received the two of them warmly and welcomed them into her humble home. Humble it was indeed, though no more so, Ivan told Dave later, than the thousands of similar, standard state, flats with their prescribed floor area.

The two girls, Natasha, eleven and Tanya, nine were delightful. They looked very smart in their dresses and their hair had clearly received special attention. Healthy, lively children indeed, which inevitably brought Jo and Katy into Dave's thoughts. Following brief introductions, they moved across to the table and sat as formally as the tight squeeze would allow.

Sasha was the perfect host – the life and soul of the party. He produced a bottle of red wine which was a great compliment to the meal. They were treated to beetroot soup followed by a sort of schnitzel and noodles in gravy and finally, some pancakes. Dave was enchanted. He gazed around the table as he ate and when he caught young Tanya's eye, who was often staring at him, she hurriedly lowered her gaze and concentrated on her food. Natasha was also shy, but concealed it better than her sister. They were all swept up, however, by Sasha as he launched into a series of stories, the political leaders of the USSR being the butt of his humour. Elena occasionally attempted to restrain the more extreme excesses of her husband, but she found it difficult not to laugh as she feigned displeasure. At Sasha's prompting, the girls attempted some English remarks and Dave applauded their efforts, which made them blush. Sasha and Elena were clearly very proud of their daughters, with good reason in Dave's opinion. Emboldened by their success, Natasha and Tanya went to their room to prepare themselves for a short entertainment, which they had planned for their guests. Sasha sought out a bottle of vodka.

The girls returned and Ivan and Dave were treated to a poetry reading (in English), a song (in Russian) and a dance (Georgian style), the latter accompanied by enthusiastic rhythmic applause, led by a beaming Sasha. Both girls made their bows seriously but then burst into giggles. How like Jo and Katy, thought Dave. Parallel family lives separated by an ideology.

The end of a perfect evening and genuine tears were shed, as Ivan and Dave made their farewells. Dave felt unusually emotional and wondered how enmity could arise between nations when, at the individual level, such harmony was possible.

Swept up by the emotion of the occasion, Dave made a decision. Bugger the SSA – he had burned his boats anyway. He asked Ivan to pass on a few serious words to Sasha. Ivan was puzzled but agreed. Dave looked earnestly at Sasha as he spoke. He stressed the importance of what he wished to say in relation to the Winford failure and went on to summarise his recent results, from which it was clear that steam impurities were not responsible. Consequently all turbines of similar design, including those at Norvokosky, were at serious risk of failure. He realised that it was unlikely that any real action would be taken, but he implored Sasha, to at least endeavour to get routine overspeed testing suspended, as that was when the stresses on the discs were highest and therefore the risk of failure, greatest. Sasha understood and thanked him, adding that he would report Dave's comments to his superior, as he was not senior enough to be able to make such a decision himself. He was pessimistic, however, that he would be able to convince his superiors, as they had received a report saying that steam contamination was to blame for the British failure. It would, he thought, require a revised report in print to have any influence. Dave understood and told Sasha that it would be published shortly. He felt that could do no more.

How strange, he later thought, that he had hugged Elena and Sasha before leaving, which was so out of character for him, and yet it had seemed so appropriate – was this all due to the vodka?

Next day, the official visit concluded with a small reception. Soon Dave was seated, gazing through the window of his British

Airways plane, upon the bustling scene that traditionally surrounds the carcass of a loading aircraft. He felt so fortunate to have been selected for such a trip. Almost ready, he thought; the fuel tankers, luggage buggies and stairways had scuttled away. Just the chap wearing earmuffs remaining, waiting to give the pilot the thumbs-up. A roar down the runway and through the window all the things that go to make up a modern international airport, shrank to model proportions. Then into the clouds.

On the journey, Dave found himself inexplicably emotional as the miles passed. It had only needed a few days away from home to make him appreciate just how much he valued his family and the routine of his life. This had been brought into even sharper focus following the visit to Sasha's.

How precious these things were and yet how quickly he had pushed them into the background over the past months, in pursuit of his personal ambitions. He vowed to urgently redress the situation. He would continue to pursue his work conscientiously, but not to the detriment of his family. He thought about his evening with Pauline and how elated it had made him feel to be, albeit briefly, taken back to the tangled emotions and excitement of his youth. But at what cost? The stupidity of it. Sue and the girls meant the world to him and yet he'd jeopardised everything on a thoughtless, selfish, whim. Thank goodness Pauline had declined to take things further. He'd been a bloody fool. Well, from now on, the family came first. This had, indeed, been a timely reminder.

Back on the A4 these thoughts suddenly crystallised, he was jolted into the immediate. His technical note would be being prepared for publication. Christ! His heart began thumping, almost bursting through his chest. God! What had he done? In less than three weeks' time, the shit would hit the fan and no mistake. He willed himself to forget it until then and worked hard to take in pleasant thoughts as he passed the White Horse. What a lot had happened since he'd last walked up to the summit.

It was an emotional return as all three 'girls' rushed eagerly to greet him and he settled down to a real cup of tea. Jo and Katy bustled around and were close at hand when their father reached into his holdall and, in the best conjurors' tradition, plucked out two brightly coloured parcels. Both girls were in a cooperative mood and so synchronised their unwrapping to be sure not to spoil their sister's surprise. Maybe not such a surprise when they found, carefully wrapped within the box, a set of brightly painted, lime-wood, *Matryoshka* dolls, for which Russia is famous. The girls were delighted and, after kissing their father, they went to their rooms to decide where to place all six dolls to best advantage.

Dave asked after Sue's progress with her family history, on this occasion with genuine interest. She said that, although whilst he was away she had had to stay near home, she had been able to settle down with all her information and make plans as to how best to solve some of the problems. Dave gave Sue a potted history of his trip and she could tell that it had been more than just a technical exchange. It was clear that he had been touched, at a much deeper level, than could be explained by purely technical matters.

Dave decided on an early night as, although not jet-lagged, his biological clock seemed a little disturbed. Sue said that she would follow him up. Dave lay on the bed and the tears flowed freely, which for the life of him he couldn't explain. Was it just the reunion with Sue and the girls or something more complex? Perhaps something to do with Sasha's family? He thought back to the evening shared with Sasha, Elena and their girls such a loving home and clearly so happy despite the hardships of daily life in the Soviet Union. An example to many western families, who enjoy a comfortable lifestyle and yet still did not find the contentment of the Denisov family. Certainly, he felt that they had been instrumental in reminding him of the importance of the family unit.

★

With some trepidation, Dave returned to work. He felt guilty about his secret, which he felt would be obvious to his colleagues. Would someone have found out whilst he had been away? Maybe the typist had made some unguarded remark. However, he need not have worried, as his return to work was characterised by an eagerness on the part of his colleagues, to bring him up to date with significant developments. They passed quickly over the routine work. Eagerly they vied with each other to pass on the big news. Something, it seemed, had revived the interest of the national press in the West Winford incident. They had returned to the subject with a vengeance and had, in no uncertain terms, accused the Authority of suppressing results and orchestrating an elaborate cover up. Though the headlines were not identical, they all carried the same message – 'SSA Cover-up – Widespread Threat to Power Supplies' being the theme. Gritty went on to say that this was not the biggest surprise. On reading the articles they had learned that the revelations were nothing to do with West Winford, but concerned the discovery of extensive cracking of turbine discs at a Welsh industrial power plant. The defects had apparently been found during NDT inspection. The newspaper reports claimed that the results had been suppressed by senior figures within the SSA and an inquiry had been ordered.

"I reckon that you should be clear to publish the rig results now," he concluded, "now that the whole thing is out in the public domain."

Dave's mind was scrambled. The colour drained from his face and he felt that he was visibly shaking. If Ian and Gritty noticed, they didn't comment. He showed genuine surprise at learning this, which of course he was, though he suspected that he knew the source of the leak to the press. He tried to speak calmly and said that he would take it up with Tony. He greeted the prospect of having his own actions becoming public a great deal more calmly than would have been the case two weeks earlier. The whole place seemed to have gone mad.

He met Tony soon afterwards and was told officially of the press disclosure. This had resulted in actions being taken at a senior level, the most decisive of which was to shut down Winford immediately. Thornton was still operating for the moment. This was necessary to bridge the gap, while some of the mothballed older power stations were being re-commissioned, by the various utilities to take up the shortfall in supply, which the loss of Thornton would create. The Strategic Supplies Authority were naturally under the spotlight and an investigation was underway to discover the source of the leak.

"It has been agreed, in view of the changed circumstances, that you should get your technical note out as soon as possible," said Tony. "The official line is that we might as well get some benefit and show that we've nothing to hide."

Later, after checking through his mail and dealing with the most immediate demands, Dave settled down to write a letter of thanks to Ivan at the Electrical Institute of Moscow. He mentioned some of the things that had most impressed him on the technical side, as well as their pleasant social outings together. He also wrote a brief personal note to Sasha and his family, which he asked Ivan to be kind enough to translate and forward on to him. He enclosed a copy of his technical note, but wondered if any action would result

A phone call brought more welcome news.

"Mr Harrison? It's Bernard Cracknel here from the *Digest*. I've been trying to contact you regarding your submission. Bad news, I'm afraid. We are not going to be able to publish your technical note in our forthcoming issue. Simply lack of space. Personally, I believe that it should go in as it is a most significant piece of work. However, we've received more submissions than usual this time and my editor had already given his personal promise to another author that it would definitely be October for him. So that's it. Sorry. I can assure you that you're guaranteed November. It's particularly annoying as you only missed the September deadline by a couple of days, when we had space to spare."

Dave assured Mr Cracknel that he understood. He felt euphoric. He had got away with it and he had taken the difficult and honourable decision, despite the risk of serious consequences. His conscience was clear as his hesitancy had only resulted in two months' delay, which hopefully, would not prove to be significant. As soon as the information became public, surely anyone running similar plant would take immediate action such as halting overspeed testing. Dave thought that by the end of the year no utility worldwide would have any excuse not to protect their workers.

Over the next few days, Dave did say more to Sue about his trip and the strange feelings stirred. He said that he wasn't sure that it was due to a single cause, but rather the result of a combination of things, not least, the stresses of the past few months. During his visit he'd been struck by the contrast between this experience of Moscow and the people he'd met, and his earlier preconceived ideas. Before the trip his knowledge of the Soviet Union and its peoples had been fashioned by the, generally negative, propaganda reported in the west. Even though he had been sceptical of some of this, believing that most ordinary people everywhere were mainly concerned with the everyday problems of daily life rather than political matters, he had been influenced by what he'd read. So it had come as a pleasant surprise to find that the situation was different to that which he had anticipated. True, he couldn't deny that, at the official level, there seemed to be an undercurrent of menace, but that had not been the case in his personal dealings. For the most part the people that he'd met had been helpful, friendly and well, normal. He mentioned Ivan and how they had both been fortunate to be invited to visit an ordinary Moscow family for an evening and what a pleasure it had been. Although the whole experience had been heightened by the foreign setting, the genuine welcome from this charming family was undeniable. The closeness and love within this modest home and the warmth of their welcome was something he would never forget and was an example to all.

A few weeks later, the whole Harrison family were delighted to receive a small package from Sasha and Elena containing an unusual Christmas card and a photograph of Natasha and Tanya. There was a message written in very competent English, presumably from one of the girls, wishing Jo and Katy a peaceful Christmas and enclosing their address with the hope that they might become pen friends. The girls were thoroughly excited. They went straight off to compose a letter to Natasha and Tanya. Their school friends would be really jealous. They were enthusiastic as, unlike many of the duty letter writings they were normally obliged to do, in this case there was just so much to write about their lives in England and about English things in general.

★

Sue had a map of Norfolk spread out before her. She located Pulham Market, which was south of Norwich and just off the A140 on the Ipswich road. This now seemed to be an early base for her Boughton ancestors. There appeared to be four basic Boughton families, with many of the men being thatchers, though her own great, great, great grandfather, Thomas, was a wheelwright. She could imagine them in that lovely village setting, going about their daily work, little realising that over a hundred and fifty years later, they would be arousing such interest in an equally lovely village in Wiltshire.

She next turned her attention to her Potten family. She had obtained a large scale 'Explorer' map of the Kent/East Sussex area. It seemed, from Peter's information, that this family's base was possibly in Kent, indeed from her own census information, one Thomas she had found, who could be her ancestor, had been born in Kent, at Sedley, whilst the other had been born in Mayfield, Sussex. Her map indicated that it was only about twelve miles between the villages, so either Thomas was still possible – but which one? She casually looked around the two areas and her eyes almost popped from her head when she saw a small dot marked Potten's Mill. This was near Hawkhurst, not far from Sedley, just within the Kent border. Immediately she knew that this must be the next place that she had to visit, in her quest to locate her Caroline Potten.

23

This was their first formal visit and when the Harrison family arrived at the main entrance to the grand house, they found the large area in front of the building full of cars, so Dave had to join the line of those that had begun to park on the grass verge alongside the drive. They made their way to the source of music and noise around the right hand side of the house and joined the crowded scene. Fortunately, the weather was good and so it had been decided to serve drinks and snacks from long tables set outside on the Eastern patio.

Dave and Sue had been surprised to receive the gold-edged, embossed card requesting the pleasure of their company below the colourful Marden family crest. Scribbled below in hasty biro was written:

'Sorry about the old man's formality – just remember coats and wellies and we hope to be able to dig out a dry crust or two for you to munch on – Pam'

Quite a few villagers were there, including Gritty and Mary. Jo and Katy went off to gather with their school chums whilst, after collecting drinks, the adults settled at a vacant table. Shortly afterwards they were greeted by His Lordship, who was touring the various groups, welcoming his guests. Sue recognised him from photographs she had seen in the local press. Although he was dressed informally on Pam's insistence, he hadn't gone so far as to relinquish his cravat. He paid especial attention to Sue and expressed the hope that his wife hadn't been leading her into mischief – with a glance at Dave.

Later Sue and Dave mingled amongst other guests, exchanging a brief word here and there. They hadn't seen a great deal of Pam, who had waved to them earlier but had clearly been busy inside the house. Sue had been surprised to catch a glimpse of Charles through one of the hall windows, whom she had recognised even though in silhouette. She still wondered about his relationship with Pam. They seemed so often together and usually when her husband was not around. Well, she supposed that it was none of her business, but even so…

Her thoughts were interrupted when she saw Peter coming from the house with Charles. They began helping themselves to food and drink. Peter, looking around, caught sight of Dave and Sue and made his way over to them. They learned from him that the main reason for the 'do' was to celebrate the completion of the work on the East Wing of the house, which had been under renovation for over two years. It had been decided to mark this with a bonfire-night gathering. Peter thought that the renovation was a great achievement considering what the place had been like before Pam arrived. She, of course, had been the driving force behind the project and her decision to bring in Charles to oversee the interior design had been a great move. So, Sue's mystery was solved. This commercial reason for the relationship between Charles and Pam hadn't occurred to her. In a way she was a little disappointed that the less innocent reason she had ascribed hadn't been correct, as it had a touch of glamour about it.

"I'm not sure whether I ought to raise this matter with you now," continued Peter mysteriously addressing Sue. "It's thinking about all this work that's been going on, has reminded me."

"Goodness this does sound ominous. Please do tell."

"Well, I'm in need of help and it's quite urgent," Peter explained. "My local history work has been quite constant for the past four or five years. A steady stream of investigations on behalf of clients, mostly from abroad. However, in the last few months, the inquiries have about trebled, for which I believe the increase in popularity of personal genealogy is probably responsible. In short, I need an assistant and it needs to be someone who has an interest in the subject. You know how tedious some of the work can be. It could be part time, though it would require at least three days a week, but the hours could, to some extent, be flexible." Dave glanced across and was pleased to see Sue's evident delight at the prospect that seemed to be presenting itself.

"You would be ideal, Sue, if you felt able to undertake it. You have a car, which is essential. I envisage that the work would be largely confined to the Wiltshire archives, encompassing places such as the County Record Office at Trowbridge, Salisbury Diocesan Record Office, in addition to parish churches around the county. Do have a think about it, but if you could let me know within a week or two. I need to find someone by the New Year."

Sue did her best to contain her immediate reaction, which was excitement at the prospect. She would relish the challenge which the job offered. It was with a considerable effort of will that she resisted enthusiastic acceptance there and then. She needed to discuss it with Dave in private. She thanked Peter and assured him that she would let him know within a few days.

"Fine. Oh! Another thing is this programme from my trip to the Archway art gallery, which I mentioned. On looking through it, after I got home, I saw it contained a brief piece about your possible ancestral artist, Henry Potten. I knew you would be interested, especially as an example of one of his paintings was included."

"How marvellous. Thank you so much."

Pam arrived and asked Sue and Dave to stay on afterwards, which they did and as the other guests drifted away, Pam and

Charles took them around the newly completed rooms, proudly displaying their achievements. It seems that modesty had prevented Peter from explaining his role in the project, as advisor upon the numerous paintings hung in the various rooms and hallways. Yet another of the talents of this unusual man.

★

Moscow – Norvokosky Power Station.

November. Peak demand. The usual noise and bustle of activity in the turbine hall. Six machines operating at full load. The floor vibrating in tune with the mechanical workhorses shimmering in the steamy heat haze – powering the socialist revolution.

In addition to the mechanics and turbine operators busy with their statuary duties, there was the inevitable army of cleaners and supernumeraries around all six turbines, applying themselves haphazardly, so it appeared, to a variety of trivial tasks with little direction or enthusiasm.

The operator of Number 3 turbine sat before the instrument control panel smoking his pipe contentedly.

"Dimitrov!"

He was startled by the voice raised above the background noise. It was the Deputy Station Manager.

"Why hasn't the overspeed test on Number 3 turbine been carried out?"

"Sasha asked us to wait. He's gone to check with the Senior Operations Engineer to see if these tests should be suspended. He has information that it was overspeed stresses alone that were responsible for the British turbine failure last year."

"Damn him. Alexander Borisovitch has no right. Get the test started this instant." The operator and two junior assistants did as they were ordered.

★

Leaving the Senior Operations Engineer to consult with the Station Manager, Sasha returned to find the turbine test already underway. The rev counter was up to 3,200 and rising. He was annoyed that the operator hadn't waited, it would have only been a short delay… then the noise… the tell-tale change in pitch… out of balance…

"*Bozhi Moy!* The bloody steam leaks are worse than ever."

Immediately Sasha realised that the operator hadn't cleared the area around the turbine as he'd instructed. He could just make out a group of cleaners in the mist. Were they mad or just plain stupid?… The turbine was vibrating… increasing violence… his warning shouts were futile.

His men stood transfixed, helpless, as Sasha raced along the side of the turbine towards the LP cylinder – shouting… screaming… until lost in the fog of steam.

★

"Hi! Gritty?"

"That you Ian? I thought you'd be trekking along Hadrian's Wall by now."

"I'm just off, but I wanted a word with Dave before he left work."

"He's off for a few days – back after the holiday. What's the problem?"

"I forgot to let him have last week's batch of journal references. There was one in particular he would want to see. They're on my bench. Would you let him have them?"

"Sure, I'll see to it. Have a good Christmas."

"Thanks Gritty. Same to you."

Gritty went into the corrosion lab to make his final checks on the experiments that were to be kept running over the holiday.

Amongst them were Dave's stress corrosion tests on some newer turbine disc alloys.

"Hey, get your arse in gear, beers are waiting to be drunk," Geoff called from the doorway.

"Be with you in a tick," said Gritty. He went to Ian's bench and scooped up the reference cards. Ian had developed an efficient system for Dave, which allowed him to check relevant references to corrosion related matters, from selected journals. Gritty took the cards with him and left them in the centre of Dave's desk. As he slipped on his jacket, he read from the top card:

USA Power Nov 1970
New Heat Exchanger Tube Material for Sea Water Cooled Power Stations.
High Purity Titanium Installed in Condenser at
Corpus Christi Power Plant Texas.

Gritty could see that Dave would be interested in that item, in connection with his Thornton seawater trials. He joined his colleagues for their Christmas booze-up. On almost any other day Gritty would have looked through all the reference cards out of interest. Although only a scientific assistant, he was keen to keep on top of things and during his time at SSD, had proved himself a valuable member of the team. Had it been any other day, he would have noted and taken in the particular significance of the next card reference:

EDF Review Dec 1970
LP Turbine Disc Failure – Second in November.
The sudden failure of a turbine disc at Xanlu Power Station in China,
with serious casualties, has been reported. No details are available. This
news is of some concern following so soon after the unconfirmed reports of a
similar catastrophic break up of an LP turbine disc in the USSR earlier
this month. It is only just over a year ago that the first failure of this kind

occurred at the West Winford Power Station in the UK.
Full details of these recent failures are awaited.

Certainly Dave would have wished to have seen this earlier.

★

Earlier in the month, Dave's pulse had quickened when he received a phone call from Pauline. He asked how the bad news had been received at HQ. She maintained a business-like manner – perhaps there were other people in the office – and replied that, as he could imagine, an internal investigation was underway to find the source of the press leak. The reason for her call was to let Dave know that it had been considered necessary to have a final wind-up meeting of the Corrosion Sub-Committee before the year's end. This was required by precedent, as an established committee could not be allowed to be disbanded without an orderly closure, even in the present circumstances.

Accordingly, a week before Christmas, Dave had to make a trip to London for this final meeting. He suggested that Sue and the girls should join him and have a shopping trip and overnight stay. The evening of this announcement saw the female Harrisons busy with their final preparations. As they were spending the holiday in Birmingham in a few days' time, they were aware that time was short. The girls were making Christmas present lists for their cousins and school friends. Sue was going through the information on her Potten family history, and the discovery of Potten's Mill had intriguing possibilities.

"Which of you two is mine?" she pleaded looking at the two birth certificates for the umpteenth time. She really hoped that it was the granddaughter of the famous artist, Henry, and was encouraged, when she had looked through his details in the pamphlet Peter had given her. It included one of his pictures which, although reduced in size, clearly showed that he had a great eye for fine detail which, she thought, Jo's Hunstanton holiday efforts resembled. Sue felt that her Caroline had been a thoughtful, intelligent lady, who, of course, had helped so much with her dedicated recording of her family. She thought that her foresight should be rewarded and this would, in a small way, be appropriate. If her Caroline Potten was the granddaughter of Henry, it would provide her with details of her own ancestors back into the seventeenth century, which would be an added bonus.

She had a road atlas, showing the south east, open in order to roughly place the area of Potten's Mill (too small to be marked at this scale) in relation to London. Hmm! She mused. It was not exactly conveniently placed, but Dave had been so much more his old self since his returning from his USSR trip, so:

"Do you think that we would have time to make a small detour on our trip? It's only just in Kent," Sue asked, with an encouraging smile. It has to be said that Dave's agreement owed as much to his hazy knowledge of geography, as it did to Sue's persuasive manner. Sue's plan was to visit Potten's Mill and possibly the surrounding area, during their London trip.

They started early, as Dave was due to be at Walton House by eleven o'clock. He had been delighted that Sue had arranged for them to park their car at Pam's London address. This was convenient for The Bonnington as well as Walton House. The journey was enlivened, with a pleasant bubble of chatter, as plans were finalised.

After parking, it was off to St. Paul's for Dave, with his female accomplices, rather predictably, heading for Oxford Street. Before taking leave of them, he gave directions to The Bonnington. He would join them there, after collecting their overnight bags from the car, en route.

★

This final sub-committee meeting, which consisted mainly of a review of recent developments, was less formal than hitherto. Even so, Pauline was her usual efficient self and showed no especial reaction towards Dave. Joe reported that the cracks in his laboratory specimens were continuing to grow in a linear fashion. The others all accepted that the discovery of severe cracking at the Welsh Petroleum Corporation's Newport site, plus Dave's crack initiation results, had overshadowed everything. They were happy to support Dave's request to publish. He was grateful, but sorry that this was the worst possible outcome for the Authority or, indeed, the whole of the electrical supply industry.

As far as Dave's results were concerned, he was interested to learn that the senior managers within the SSA had readily latched onto these, in an attempt to refute any suggestion of a cover up, citing the fact that a summary of the results of their investigations was already with the publishers. They were also keen to point out that their refurbishment programme was well underway and they would be shortly in a position to provide cover for the other UK utilities, when they began their more extensive refurbishments. This surely was the very ethos of the SSA and vindicated its existence.

Dave gave more details regarding his crack initiation studies, aided by his daughter, which highlighted the importance of certain 'active' sulphide inclusions, always present within the structure of commercial steel. These appeared to be the likely sites of crack initiation. He considered that this provided the complete explanation for the cracking of these LP turbine steels in high purity hot water. He flushed, as he added that his detailed paper was now ready to submit to *Corrosion Review*.

Appropriately, it was Henry who concluded the business of the sub-committee. He said that the occasion could not be allowed to pass without formally acknowledging the admirable contributions made by its participants. He believed that the successful outcome was due to their enthusiastic efforts and the teamwork displayed. He went on to summarise the particular contributions from each technical member and concluded by drawing attention to Pauline's role. He was full of admiration for the manner in which, in her own quiet way, she 'had run the whole show'. Although this comment formally wound up the business of the West Winford Corrosion Sub-Committee, it was Dorinda who had the final word as, on behalf of them all, she thanked Henry for his calm guidance, especially through the odd patches of heavy weather. They all enjoyed themselves as they chatted amiably over a festive lunch.

Dave took the opportunity to have a word with Pauline. She surprised him with her news, that she had given in her notice and would be leaving the SSA at the end of the year. She brushed away Dave's regret that she thought this necessary, by explaining that it had been planned for some time. She was looking forward to her new challenge, which was to run the administrative side of her aunt's business, in Italy. Dave wished her well.

James Collingwood caught up with Dave in the Gents on his way out, and surprised him by saying that he had a message for him.

"It's from a chap called Razumov."

Dave was surprised and asked how James had come across him.

"Last week we had a USSR delegation visit, about a dozen, including their 'minders'. Razumov was one of the delegates. He asked if I would pass on his best regards. You met him on your Moscow trip, I understand?"

"Yes, very nice chap. Is he well?"

"Fine as far as I could tell. It was a bit odd though. He mentioned a fellow called Sasha, any idea?"

"Yes, he worked at the power station we visited," replied Dave rather noncommittally. "What did he have to say?"

"Well that was the odd thing really, he became very serious and he asked me to pass on a message to you, but before he could say more, one of the 'minders' closed in on us and he clammed up. What a bloody country, eh?"

As he had been speaking, James had been changing into tatty jeans, sweat shirt and trainers, which he had removed from a

232

rucksack. The transformation was amazing, the bespectacled, swotty looking, scientist metamorphosing into a hillbilly hobo in less than a couple of minutes.

"Well, you obviously have the rest of the day off. Doing anything interesting?" asked Dave.

"Sure am. Pauline and I have plans." He swung his bag onto his shoulder and turned back, as he reached the door. "There's a whole lot more to that young lady than you could ever imagine," he added and with a wink, was gone.

Dave smiled to himself, somewhat ruefully – modern girls, eh?

He wondered what message Ivan had wished to pass on regarding Sasha. Perhaps he would learn something when Jo and Katy next heard from their new Russian pen friends.

He left Walton House in a buoyant mood, despite regretting that their work had finished. It really did appear that he'd done the right thing as far as alerting people to the dangers of stress corrosion in these vulnerable turbines. Very soon, he felt that this warning would be acted upon by even the most backward operators.

He arrived at the hotel to find that the others had just returned. Sue explained that they had decided upon a trip to a cinema in Shaftesbury Avenue, to see 'The Railway Children', which they had enjoyed.

"So you've started without me," bemoaned Dave. "Well, no matter, we've another treat shortly."

"What Daddy? What Daddy? Tell us, go on," came the girls' chorus. But this only elicited a response of "Wait and see."

The evening surprise was a meal at the Italian restaurant. It was a fun evening, Jo and Katy deriving great pleasure from competing to see which of them could suck up the longest piece of spaghetti. Sue and Dave shared a litre of house wine and so their spirits were high in every sense. Fortunately, the hotel was not far and all four of them rather drifted away from the posse of waiters who waved them off.

Sue and Dave took the opportunity of some practice in anticipation of a third honeymoon in the near future.

24

Dave left the girls to gather up their belongings whilst he collected the car. It was an early start from Bloomsbury over Tower Bridge and on to Greenwich. They stopped briefly to stretch their legs in the park, which was lovely in the weak winter sunshine. Sue was anxious to get over to Sedley, in time to have a good look around before dark. Accordingly, they didn't stop for lunch, but bought sandwiches to eat on their journey.

From Greenwich they drove to Bromley and southwards down the A21 towards Hastings. Just over the Kent border, they arrived at the picturesque village of Sedley. Sue had a copy of the diagram she had made, which located Potten's Mill. She matched it, as best she could, with their freshly purchased OS map. Surprisingly quickly, they found the small junction with a lane leading to the mill, but it was unsuitable for cars. "So it's trekking time," said Dave. Jo and Katy pleaded tiredness and stayed in the car whilst their parents, wrapped up in their coats, set off on foot. They found the small stream and in amongst the tangled undergrowth was a ruin that presumably had been the mill. Three partial walls remained, the fourth having tumbled completely. There seemed nothing of interest inside the walled area but, as they were leaving, Dave drew Sue's attention to the top of the archway which he assumed had been the main entrance to the building. The keystone was still in place at the top of the arch and it had an inscription. Although not clear, it seemed to be initials, beneath which was a date. It looked like HP with the date 1775.

"It could be P for Potten," suggested Sue hopefully.

"Quite possible, given the mill's name."

"It would be wonderful if I could prove it was my ancestor," Sue added with enthusiasm.

"Well, we best get going, if you want to check the churchyard out. I don't like the look of those grey clouds coming in from the west."

Back in the car, Sue reported their discovery and she was surprised at her daughters' keen attention and eager offer to help her look at gravestones – a spooky adventure. St. Anne's church was not far, being in the centre of the village. Sue had been so optimistic that this would be the burial place for many of her Potten ancestors. Consequently, it was an anti-climax, when a thorough search of the churchyard failed to reveal any. She tried to hide her natural disappointment, as it had been such a lovely family trip.

"Only just finished in time. I reckon there's snow in the offing and it's getting pretty dark," warned Dave, looking upwards at the encroaching black clouds.

They drove away and, almost immediately, came to another village which, Sue was surprised to find, was called Sedley St. Peter. Another Sedley! She thought quickly. Would the 1851 census enumerator have been specific in recording which Sedley after all? Sedley St. Anne or Sedley St. Peter? Indeed, it appeared that this was the larger village. She just had to know. They had come all this way. The others could understand the situation and agreed that they should at least stop for a quick check through the churchyard here. Their natural instincts would have been to get home quickly, but the feeling of togetherness, of family harmony, seemed to have affected them all. If they all helped they might just beat the worst of the weather. The snow had started to fall, but only lightly.

"Oh, Dear! There are more here, we shall have to hurry as this snow is getting heavier. It will be covering the inscriptions soon. Let's spread out."

Dave moved to the left and worked his way along the side of the church. Sue searched along the boundary wall, with Jo and Katy attempting to fill in between their parents as best they could. Whilst Katy's enthusiasm was evident, Jo's was a little less so, but she was doing her bit. Nothing. They moved to the other side of the church and repeated their slow, patterned, search. Occasionally there was a half cry of joy, from one of the girls, followed by an apologetic 'sorry'. Whilst some of the headstones were in good condition and the inscription clear, many were not, and the combination of lichen growth and erosion made identification impossible. At least the undergrowth was not rampant at this season, but the snow was not helping. Sue was becoming despondent as it looked as though the snow was winning the battle. Then triumph.

"Quick, Mummy, over here, I've found one," exclaimed an excited Katy, jumping up and down clapping her hands. "It's a Potten. Quick, come and look."

"Don't shout Katy, remember where you are."

The three of them rushed to join her as the falling snow thickened into large sticky flakes, ideal for making snowmen. It began to stick with a purpose to clothes and eyelashes, as it was swept by a strengthening wind. The headstone recorded the passing of a Neri Potten and his wife Mary.

"And another one," called Jo from a behind a yew tree. Whilst Sue attempted to write legibly, turning her back to the snow flurries, Dave went to join Jo. They read this one with some difficulty, as the snow was obscuring some of the stone – George Potten died 1835. Sue hurried over to make notes; it was difficult to get the pen to write on the damp paper.

"Over here. This is a big one," called Dave, half turning to keep the snow to his back. The others struggled over to him, the ground was very uneven. Sue bent down and saw the partly covered headstone and could just make out part of the inscription.

'In Loving Memory of Thomas Potten... Eliz... 1810 1856... Devoted Wife... Beloved Daught... Oc... 2yrs and Caroline... mes 1846... with her... '

"Oh, my goodness," she gasped, as she knelt down and hurriedly brushed away the settling snow. It was thickest at the lower part of the inscription. Finally it became fully legible:

'In Loving Memory of Thomas Potten 1806 – 1858 and Elizabeth 1810 – 1856 His Devoted Wife with Beloved Daughters Octavia aged 2yrs and Caroline Loomes 1846 – 1891 Reunited with her Family.'

"Oh, my goodness," she repeated. "Look, even young Octavia's here and Caroline. It's her. See her married name? She's mine. At last," gasped Sue. "I've searched for you for so long."

Dave, taking a scrap of paper from his pocket, suggested that he noted the top two lines and Sue the rest before they became obliterated again. Having done this, he stepped back with Katy and Jo either side of him. They stood quietly whilst Sue, rising to her feet, gazed down on the grave. "Thank you," she whispered. She straightened up and smiled sheepishly, as she brushed the snow from her face along with her tears; tears of joy. Dave, flanked by Jo and Katy, also felt emotional as they watched her. A brief pause.

"Come on then," said Dave, putting an arm protectively around the girls either side of him. "Let's get home and celebrate," and all four of them linked arms, a family united, and walked down the path and through the gate – happily through the thickening snow.

★

The snow increased, the flurries swirling in the arctic wind. The gravestones took on a greyish hue. The bitter chill cut deeply. Two girls held hands whilst their mother swept the snow from the inscription, her tears almost frozen as she gazed down with love.

Alexander Borisovitch Denisov
"Sasha"
1934 – 1970
Beloved Husband and Devoted Father
Tragically killed trying to save others.
12th November 1970
R. I. P.

★

It was two months later that Dave heard the news of Sasha's passing and it came as a dreadful blow. Although it was to be expected that his death and its cause would be distressing, added to this was a feeling of guilt. He sat in his office and found himself shaking and emotional. If he had not prevaricated over submitting his paper, it might have made all the difference. Certainly, he knew that he had passed on his concerns to Sasha and emphasised the urgent necessity to take action, which may have prevented the tragedy, but could he have done more? He would have been sad whoever the victim had been, but having met Sasha and his family added greatly to his sorrow.

The Harrison family mourned. They sent a message of condolence to Elena and the girls. Dave also wrote to Ivan requesting more information and news of the Denisov family. Several weeks later a letter arrived from Elena, translated by Natasha, which thanked them for their kind words and hoped that they would keep in touch, as they so much enjoyed hearing all the news from England.

★

Dave's technical note did, as promised, appear in the November

1970 issue of *International Power Digest*, the definitive paper being published in *Corrosion Review* in May 1971. This was well received and in the following months his correspondence contained many invitations to attend meetings and conferences worldwide. He was delighted, but was only able to accept a few due to his workload. He had become heavily involved in the British Standards Institution's Corrosion Committee, in addition to his normal work and although he still had ambition and enjoyed his work, this was now strictly balanced with his private family life.

One invitation that he did accept, was to return to Moscow to receive an award from the USSR Electrical Union. This had obviously passed through Ivan's hands as he had appended a note, informing Dave that he would have an opportunity to meet the Denisov family.

As his flight approached its destination, Dave's thoughts returned to his earlier trip. The airport bureaucracy retained its previous menace. Dave was delighted to be greeted by Ivan. They shook hands warmly and swapped news, as they were driven into the city. The hotel this time was the Intourist, overlooking Red Square, where they shared an evening meal.

The following morning Dave joined the official breakfast party, hosted by the event organisers, before travelling out to Moscow State University, a magnificent edifice, situated in the Lenin Hills. As they disembarked from their taxis, the group of guests paused to admire the panoramic views over the city, before being escorted to the main conference hall. Following a long welcoming speech, the awards ceremony began. Dave was last to be presented. He received a medal and scroll. He was embarrassed and humbled by the overstated citation highlighting his ground-breaking discovery which had led to the modification of power plant operational procedures and potentially saved many lives. He was invited to say a few words before he rejoined the audience.

Then an added item was announced and from the side of the stage, Elena, Natasha and Tanya appeared. After a brief welcome, a presentation was made. Elena, with great dignity, accepted a special posthumous award, in recognition of Alexander's brave, selfless, action, which had saved many colleagues.

A reception followed, which allowed Dave time to talk to the Denisovs. He was pleased to find that Natasha's English was so assured that he could be confident that his sympathy, good wishes and his family's sadness, could be accurately conveyed to Elena. He then presented them with gifts from the Harrison family. To Natasha and Tanya, books – *The Phantom Tollbooth* and *The Mystery of the 99 Steps* and Elena was delighted to receive one of Jo's paintings, even more so when Dave explained that it was a view of their home in Wiltshire.

Before leaving, Dave expressed his hope that changes in the political climate, might soon allow a greater freedom of movement between their countries. He knew that Jo and Katy would be so excited at the prospect of one day meeting Natasha and Tanya.

*

Sue had not been idle since the New Year. She had worked her way slowly into her collaboration with Peter. Although many of the enquires, mostly from overseas, could be dealt with using records with which she had become familiar, others required her to delve into unknown archives, such as Wills, Bishops' Transcripts and Monumental Inscriptions. She tackled all enquires with gusto, as she empathised with the 'customers', having experienced their passion. An additional spur was the experience she was gaining, which would be invaluable as she continued to pursue her own ancestors. As the months passed, her accumulating knowledge of Wills and Monumental Inscriptions increased and, gradually, her articles in magazines and contributions to family history conferences, became popular.

*

Thus life in the Harrison household settled into a comfortable, though busy, routine for Dave and Sue. They were fortunate as their respective passions were to prove to be a great help as they approached a major upheaval in their lives. This began with Jo making her final preparations to begin her art studies at Sheffield. Although she had eagerly awaited this time and was excited, she realised that it was an important moment for the family and the final goodbyes were emotional for them all. Hardly had they adjusted to this new situation, before it was time for Katy to follow. She was not staying on to take 'A' levels, as she was eager to begin a career in nursing. She had been accepted to begin her training at a Bristol teaching hospital at the age of seventeen.

Barry and Velma were in a similar position, as their girls were away from home too. The Turner family bond remained firm. At times of special significance and even sometimes on a whim, celebrations were held. The traditional format was maintained, with Barry in his customary role as MC. These occasions were always eagerly anticipated by all the family. Although the youngsters had matured, and were away with their studies, they were still keen to be part of the celebrations; the treasured family ties evident as they filled the house with gaiety.

Though Sue and Dave felt the loss of their daughters sorely, with great fortitude they had acclimatised, realising that love is proved by the letting go. Their lives moved to a new level. They became much closer, each supporting the other. They took a keen interest in each other's activities. Dave even found time to make a modest attempt to research his own family tree and was Sue's willing assistant in supporting her work.

Ah, but a woman's reach should exceed her grasp,
Or what's a heaven for?

★

AUTHOR CONTACT : jamparker @ talktalk.net

Acknowledgments

The main theme of 'The West Winford Incident' – the turbine failure – is based upon the failure of a steam turbine which occurred at Hinkley Point 'A' Power Station in 1969. Unlike the fictitious Winford incident, the management and execution of the Hinkley Point inquiry was a credit to everyone involved. The former Central Electricity Generating Board and the turbine manufacturers mounted a huge investigation and both the publication of results and adoption of remedial measures were accomplished with commendable efficiency.

I have been fortunate to receive the help and guidance of many folk through the ups and downs of this adventure. My particular thanks to Edward Fenton for his insightful assessment of the draft manuscript, Tony Baker for his encouragement to persevere, Mike Sadler for his advice on various aspects of power plant water chemistry and of course, the folk at Troubador.

The onerous task of proof reading, computer advice and general support was undertaken by, the ever willing, Mike Parker.

Finally to my wife who, in addition to encouraging and sustaining me during the hours of toil, coped admirably with the mood swings and was a tremendous help in the last vital final stages of manuscript production. Despite the help from those mentioned and others, errors and omissions will have intruded for which I accept full responsibility.

A Note to the good folk of North Wiltshire.

The portrayal, in this fictional story, of Wiltshire locals as a sad, unadventurous lot living in the past, is merely a literary device. On our arrival into the real Wiltshire, 25 years ago, we were received warmly into the community. Having retired, we were particularly pleased to find a wide variety of activities available to make life stimulating and pleasant. Thank you all.

Poem: (Chap 20) – extract from 'A Sunday with Shepherds and Herdboys' by John Clare.